# Making Ends Meet

S.L. Armstrong & K. Piet

Illustrated by Diana Callinger

## Storm Moon Press

Exceptional authors. Exceptional stories.

Storm Moon Press LLC
12814 University Club Drive, #102
Tampa, FL 33612

Publisher's Note

This is a work of fiction. Names, characters, places, and incidents either are the product of the authors' imaginations or are used fictitiously. Any resemblance to actual persons, living or dead, events or locales is entirely coincidental.

The publisher has no control over and does not assume responsibility for any third-party websites or their content. The uploading and distribution of this book via the Internet or via any other means without the permission of the publisher is illegal and punishable by law.

Cover and interior art by Diana Callinger

ISBN-13: 978-1-937058-79-1
ISBN-10:    1-937058-79-4

All my love to R. who—day in and day out—has given me nothing but his unending support.

~ S.L. Armstrong

Thanks must go to Melanie and Blaine for their feedback as *Making Ends Meet* came into being. And we want to thank our developmental editor, April, and our line editor, Amanda, who helped *Making Ends Meet* be the best it could be. We'd also like to give our thanks to Diana C. for the gorgeous artwork on both the cover and interior of the book; she captured our characters perfectly.

# Chapter One

Mae began to fuss in her car seat as Zach buckled her in. He smiled down her at toothless, tiny face and tickled her belly. "Please, Mae, no screaming today. Daddy has one *hell* of a headache."

It didn't seem Mae cared, and as Zach shut the door on his very used Corolla, she began to cry. He leaned against the door and rubbed at his face. Christ, it was hot, even for five in the evening. If he could, he'd move the hell out of Florida, but as it stood... Mae let loose a shrill shriek, and Zach pushed off the door and waved at his Mom in the house window. He braced himself, slid into the car, and began the short drive across town.

And, God help him, Mae screamed from Dale Mabry Highway all the way to 22nd Street. He should have asked his mom if she'd fed Mae. Good chance she had, but he'd been late picking her up, so maybe Mom hadn't given Mae her second bottle? As he drove by the McDonalds, he stared longingly at the glowing sign, but payday wasn't for another three days and his bank account was low. ACCESS wouldn't refill his card for another four days, and he'd run out of the WIC checks yesterday. In his head, he added up how much money he had left versus how much formula Mae still had at home, and when the light turned red, he rested his head against the steering wheel.

Dammit.

He didn't want to ask his parents for more money, but rent was due. Mae sniffled behind him, and he sighed; the light shifted to green, and he turned into his apartment complex. It wasn't the greatest or safest, but it was someplace he could afford, and that was all that mattered to Zach. His stomach twisted with hunger as he stepped out of the car and opened the door to the backseat where Mae waited, still crying. He grabbed his backpack and her diaper bag, and then hoisted her four-month-old self out of the car seat.

"Please, Mae, Daddy will feed you once we're inside, so stop crying, huh?"

This wasn't the first time he wished he had someone to help him take care of her. Bethany certainly didn't want to, and Zach could hardly blame her. They hadn't meant to get pregnant, and Bethany had college in a couple months. As Zach turned the key in the lock of his apartment, a stab of resentment rushed through him. Bethany *could* go to college, but he couldn't. No, he'd had to drop out of school at seventeen, get his GED, and go the hell to work because he'd be damned if he'd give up his own child.

Inside the cool, dim apartment, Zach dropped the two bags and leaned against the door, patting Mae's back while humming softly. No, he'd never give Mae up, and he didn't regret a minute. He'd had to give things up, sure, but Mae... Mae was his *daughter*. How could he give her up? Besides, after that one night with Bethany, Zach was absolutely sure women just weren't his thing, and this might be his only chance at having kids. Yeah, he resented Bethany for walking away from the mess they'd made, but he didn't resent being Mae's daddy.

A smile curved his lips when Mae belched loudly and finally quieted. "Oh, I see. She fed you, but no burping? Come on. Let's get you changed and fed anyway. I have a test tonight. Think you can keep quiet for three hours?"

Mae gurgled, and Zach's heart melted as she grinned at him. God, how could he love anything so much as he loved his little girl?

"Three hours is all I'm asking," he said as he went into their room. He laid out the changing blanket and set to work. "Only three, and then you can keep me up all night if you want. I actually have tomorrow off." Another bout of gurgling and kicking, and Zach laughed. "Yeah, yeah, I know. Daddy's princess does what she wants, when she wants."

In minutes, he had her changed and sucking on a bottle while he checked his email. Nothing important, except the reminder of his English Comp I test that night. He might only be taking two courses a semester—and through distance learning, no less—but, damn it, he refused to work at the Walmart for the rest of his life. Mae deserved better, and so did he. He shifted Mae to burp her, checked the time, and nodded to himself. If Mae went down easily, he'd have time to make some Easy Mac for himself before the test started.

As he stood up and talked softly to Mae, he prayed she'd go down easily for once.

But he didn't hold out much hope.

Zach's stomach grumbled as he stopped in front of the apples in the produce section. He'd taken the test hungry, but the multiple-choice questions had been a snap. He'd managed to only time out on one short answer question when Mae had made a real fuss and wouldn't be ignored for

five minutes. Once he'd held her and hummed her favorite tune while bouncing her gently, though, she'd gone quiet, and that had been worth missing the ten points that short answer was worth. He'd made up for it on the persuasive essay portion.

B+, maybe a couple extra points for those references he was able to drop in his essay, though that score would take a little longer to get than the immediate grading of the mixed choice questions. Not that anyone he passed in the grocery section knew about it, but it still made him push the cart around with his back straighter, his head held just a little higher. Mae gurgled in the seat he'd rigged to the shopping cart, and he leaned forward with a grin. "We did well, didn't we?" he asked her in a playful voice, making faces and tickling her until she squealed happily and reached up for him. Her little fingers gripped weakly at his lips and nose, and he stopped walking, afraid he would ram into something and ruin Mae's good mood. "I'm gonna need those bits back, you know. We still need to hit aisles thirteen, ten, and two."

It was kind of pathetic that he knew the aisles that well, but after stocking them himself several times, they were easier to memorize than the rest of the damn store, which sometimes changed its layout twice in a single week. He offered Mae his finger as a consolation prize when he pulled back. "No fussing, now," he told her, smiling as she suckled at his fingertip. "The last part is your favorite. The freezer section!"

Shopping for his parents was easy enough, and he was glad to do it when it meant sneaking in a couple essentials for him and Mae. Food stamps only helped with food, and after gloating to his parents about his good grades, he knew they would let him get away with adding deodorant, razor heads, shampoo, and a new toothbrush to the cart. Once they hit the freezer section, he took the opportunity to entertain Mae. She never liked the noises of the Walmart, so it was a challenge to keep her engaged enough to distract her from the bustle of things she couldn't see or understand yet. He held the door open as he put a giant bag of frozen chicken breasts into the cart. The door fogged up, and he played peek-a-boo with Mae, her little smile more than enough to chase the chill of the freezer from him.

He was just finishing writing 'Mae' backwards into the fog on the freezer door when another cart stopped next to them. The woman steering it looked to be in her late thirties, but Mae suddenly had eyes only for the other baby strapped into the cart. They stared at one another and started making the cutest noises Zach had ever heard.

"Hey," he chuckled softly to the woman, closing the freezer door and wiping his hand on his jeans. "They're a little young to start romancing one another, don't you think?"

The woman smiled at him. "Sorry. I thought I'd stop and let them say hello to one another. Could you pass a bag of chicken over?"

"Sure thing." Zach dipped into the bottom bin of the case and handed the woman one of the bags. Looked like he wasn't the only one shopping in bulk.

"Thank you. It's so nice of you to take care of your sister while you help your parents out. They're lucky to have a kid like you. I can't get my oldest away the computer for a few hours without it being like the next World War."

Zach stiffened, gripping the bar of his shopping cart a little tighter as his heart sank. It took all he had to let go of the bar and run a hand through his hair, make some kind of casual gesture instead of jumping into the freezer to hide for a good stint. "Actually..." He swallowed thickly, hating that his voice came out strained. "She's my daughter, not my sister."

The silence that followed was awkward, and he shifted on his feet, watching the woman do the same. Jeez, why did it always feel like he was making some sort of announcement to the world whenever he proclaimed himself Mae's father? It was like he was being placed under a huge microscope and found somehow lacking. The woman looked him up and down, and there was something in her eyes, some mixture of shock and disapproval that made his stomach churn with humiliation and anger all at once.

"Oh," came the eventual response, though the brightness in the woman's voice was gone. "Sorry. I just presumed..."

Zach shrugged, trying to play it cool. "It's all right. Happens all the time."

Another short silence made him want to hit something, or at least get up on a soapbox and start ranting like a lawyer in a courtroom making his case to the jury. Unfortunately, he didn't have the nerve or the bad manners for either. The woman spoke up again. "Well... I should get back to shopping. She's cute." Her attention went back to their giggling, smiling children. "Come on, Cynthia. Say bye-bye."

Both kids started fussing the instant the woman began carting Cynthia away, and he managed a quick, "Have a good one," before doing everything he could to soothe away the frown on Mae's face. He'd be un-happy, too, if his conversation were so rudely interrupted. "It's okay, Mae. You'll see plenty of other babies soon. You have all your friends over at the daycare to look forward to."

The Hillsborough Catholic Charities organization was their next stop. They helped him out with his own food, gave him rent assistance, and, best of all, watched Mae during his day shifts when his mom was too busy to look after her. He made quick work of the other frozen items his mom had on her shopping list and hurried to the one checkout line manned by some newbie worker he hadn't met yet. He didn't want to chat with coworkers right now, didn't want to fake a smile for anyone but Mae.

It wasn't just that some middle-aged woman had gone from prais-ing him to making a hasty getaway; it was that it wasn't the first time this had happened, and he could only assume it wouldn't be the last. He was seventeen with a four-month-old baby girl. He was a single father. He was gay. Was there anything else fate wanted to slap him with for people to judge? It pissed him off almost as much as it depressed the fuck out of him.

If a mother like that could judge him so harshly, how the hell was he ever supposed to find a guy? He indulged himself by actually laughing at that as he paid with his mom's debit card. He pulled the hood of Mae's seat out so she wasn't blinded by the sunlight as they made their way out to the car. He wouldn't trade his daughter for anything, but sometimes, all he wanted to worry about was what clothes to wear or who he was going to date tonight.

Once they were settled in the car, Zach looked over his list. "Bank, check. Walmart, check. Just need to stop by the church and the WIC of-fices, Mae, and then we can go to Grandma's. I hear she has an awesome casserole waiting for us."

It was his day off, but damn if it didn't feel like more work. At least he'd make a couple extra dollars for picking up his mother's groceries. He carefully pulled out of his parking place and headed out into traffic. He needed to go by the church with his power bill. It was a pain in the ass, but if he brought it with him, they'd issue a check to cover the bill so long as he mailed it from the church itself. While he was there, he could pick up some pantry goods and new clothes for Mae from their clothing donations. As he headed toward the church, he hoped they had a pretty dress or something for her. She looked sweet in lavender and ruffles.

# Chapter Two

Zach yawned for at least the eighth time. It had been one hell of a night with Mae. She was sick with a sniffle. At least, he hoped it was just a sniffle. The last thing he could afford were doctors' bills. He glanced at his watch. Only two more hours and his shift would be over. Fuck, his feet and back were killing him, and he still had to drive to Northdale to pick up Mae from his mom's. Once he did that, he'd have to go home, feed Mae, give her a bath, try to get her comfortable with the humidifier, and then he had to study for the math quiz he was going to take tomorrow. If he was lucky, Mae would sleep until he was done, and then he could feed her and they could both go to bed for the night.

He was exhausted just thinking about it, but, then again, he was always tired. It wasn't Mae's fault, and he knew that, but sometimes he just wanted to be seventeen and not someone's father. He hadn't thought that part through a year ago. If he had, there wouldn't be a Mae in his life, and that wasn't what he—

"Excuse me?"

Zach blinked and looked up from the toilet paper he'd been mindlessly running over the scanner at his checkout stall. The man in front of him was tall with blond hair and that Florida tan Zach himself hadn't sported since the beginning of junior year. Blue eyes seemed to sparkle at him. "Hmm?"

"I was saying, that isn't mine."

A flush stole over Zach's face. "Oh, God, sorry. I totally zoned out." Quickly, Zach voided the toilet paper and had the computer reissue the total. "That's $52.47."

"Long night?" The man chuckled, fishing out a card from his wallet and swiping it through the machine. "You look like you could use a break."

Zach let out a longing sigh but smiled. The guy was kind of cute, sporting that college-kid-on-summer-break glow. Not to mention, Zach rather liked it when people talked to him like he was a human being rather than a living corpse who'd sold his soul to corporate America. "I wish. Someone has to man the grindstone, though." He checked the display on his register and frowned clicking a few buttons. "Uh, your card has been declined."

That got him a flustered look from the blond that made him bite back a grin. "Shit," the man mumbled, swapping out one card for another. "Wrong card. Guess I got distracted." Blue eyes darted up at him, and Zach's eyebrows twitched. Was he...? No way. This guy was checking him out! The knowledge sent an instant zing of energy through him, and his heart pounded as he grinned like an idiot, knowing it was totally inappropriate given the situation with the card.

He tried to school his face, to not jump to conclusions, but he couldn't help but comment. "Guess we both could use a break."

"No kidding," the guy chuckled. "When do you get off work? Maybe we could grab some coffee? A danish or something?"

Zach did his best to untangle his tongue and stamp down the gut-twisting combination of desire and disappointment. "I... uh..."

"Can we move this along, please?" The next customer in line fiddled with her credit card and offered him a frown.

Zach snapped out of it and shook his head. "Look, I'd love to. I mean, *really*, would love to, but tonight's not good." God, it felt like a blow to the chest to turn down an opportunity like this, but Mae was waiting for him. He had his plans laid out, and any deviation just wouldn't work. He turned the carousel of shopping bags around so the bagged groceries were facing toward the man. "Rain check?"

When he handed the man his receipt, the man paused, reached over for a pen, and wrote down his number. "Don't lose this, now," he demanded as he passed the receipt back. "Call me."

Zach took the paper dumbly, and all he had time to read was the name at the top. "Wil." No, that wasn't a flush heating up his cheeks. It was just the heat of the Walmart in September, despite the air conditioning. It wouldn't get cool in Tampa until January, if they were lucky, and... He jolted back to reality. "Wil. I mean... I will. Call you, I mean."

Stupid. So damn stupid. But Wil just smiled at him, so that was good. "Looking forward to it," Wil said and, taking up his shopping bags, gave a little wave before heading for the sliding doors. Zach watched until the next customer raised her voice again, and he scrambled to start scanning, shoving the number into his back pocket. He mumbled an apology, even though he didn't mean it—*keep the customer happy, Zach*—and the rest of his shift went by in a pleasant haze.

"Wil?" Zach's heart was racing as he paced his small living room, the phone held tightly in his hand.

"Yeah?" Even over the phone, Wil's voice was smooth. "Who is this?"

Zach flushed. "Oh, I'm sorry. I'm Zach. You... came through my checkout line yesterday and left me your number?"

There was a pause, and then he heard a chuckle. "So your name is Zach?"

A stupid grin crossed Zach's face as he looked out over the dingy patch of grass his complex called a courtyard. "Yep. Zach. The Walmart sales associate who stole your heart."

"Stole my heart, huh?"

Zach could have kicked himself. "Well... I... got your attention, right?"

"Yeah. You busy tonight?"

"Tonight?" Zach glanced at the bedroom. "Umm... I might be. Why?"

"Have you ever had bubble tea?"

Zach wrinkled his nose. "No. What's that?"

"How about you meet me at the International Boba House? It's behind the Sweetbay on Fowler. A little joint, but you can't miss it. That way, you can try bubble tea without me giving an unappetizing description of a really amazing drink."

Another goofy smile lit up Zach's face. "How does eight sound?"

"Sounds perfect."

"I'll see you then, Wil."

"See ya."

Zach hung up the phone and gave a quiet squeal, unwilling to wake Mae up. Hopefully, his mom would be able to watch Mae for a couple hours tonight. Just a few. God, a chance to go out. Go out with a cute guy! He laughed, excitement bubbling inside him, and then Mae began to cry. He glanced at the clock. Right on time. Lunch, and then he'd call his mom.

Mae's screaming made Zach's headache all the worse. He bounced her on his shoulder, patting her back, trying to get her to calm down. He looked at the clock again, time ticking away. "Two hours, Mae," he murmured. "You've been crying for *two hours*. I've fed you, changed you, cuddled you... what more do you want, sweetheart?"

He shifted her in his arms, her little body shaking with the force of her crying. His fingers moved over her face, and he nearly wept for her. She was so hot! He'd given her the infant Tylenol the pharmacist had told him to use. Why wasn't she feeling any better? Zach rocked her, but after another fifteen minutes, he was near tears. He sat with her on the bed, wiping her small, angry face with a cool cloth. At this rate, he wasn't going to make his date with Wil. Worse, if her fever wouldn't break, he'd have to bite the bullet and take her to the walk-in clinic.

Another shriek and he was up off the bed, grabbing his keys. "All right, Mae, all right!" He snatched his wallet and slipped on his flip-flops before scooping up her diaper bag. "The clinic's open until eight," he muttered to himself. "A bit of a wait at this hour, but we don't have much of a choice." Zach rushed out, locked the door, and headed for the car. Mae never stopped crying, and as he started the car, Zach's nerves were absolutely shot. "Hang on, princess. Just a few more minutes," he said, backing out of his space. "Give Daddy just a few more minutes."

The trip from his apartment down south along Interstate 75 seemed to take an hour, every minute dragging on as Mae cried in her car seat behind him. In reality, though, it took only eighteen minutes, three red lights, and one drive around the CVS to find a parking spot. Mae was screaming so hard by the time he parked, got out, and rushed to the back door, she was trembling in her seat. "Shh, Mae, it'll be all right," he said, and he hated how his voice shook. He needed to be strong for her, keep himself together, and he slammed the door with her in his arms. "Not much longer, princess, I promise."

The CVS Minute Clinic was packed, and the waiting area was buzzing instead of being a quiet place to pick up a couple essentials. He'd made it just before the cut off for sign in, and after putting his name on the list, he sat in a corner chair, rocking Mae. She was inconsolable, though, and there was nothing he could do but wait. By the time the nurse called his name, his eyes were wet and Mae had spit up. If the night could get any worse, Zach wasn't sure how. Reluctantly, he handed Mae over to the nurse once they were in the exam room, and he swore she didn't do much at all before handing over her diagnosis.

Zach shook his head as he cradled the still-screaming Mae against his chest. "Acute otitis media? I–What does that even mean?"

The nurse smiled encouragingly at him, and he had to admit it eased the worst of his nerves. "It's a middle ear infection. They're very common in babies and kids younger than four years old."

"But, it's an infection." Those were always bad news. Zach remembered being miserable as a kid, getting sick all the time, though he can't even remember what he'd had so many years ago. Mae shrieked in his arms, and he held her just a little tighter, his heart hammering in his chest with a need to simply make it better, make it so she wouldn't cry anymore.

"Easily treatable," the nurse promised, her slightly Middle-Eastern accent oddly comforting. "I'm going to write you a prescription for an antibiotic. It's going to be in liquid form, so you just give it to her with the dropper in the bottle. It isn't an instant fix, but she'll get better in a couple days. She'll be a very unhappy baby until then, but this is nothing to worry about. Just take good care of her and use a moist cloth on her face and head to help a little with her fever."

Zach let out a slow breath, gently bouncing Mae and rubbing her back with his palm. Okay, okay, he could do this. "I have to make a couple phone calls. Can I write you guys a check for everything?"

The nurse nodded with a smile. "I'll print up the invoice and give the prescription to the pharmacy right next door. They'll have everything ready for you in fifteen minutes."

"Thank you," Zach sighed, and when Mae started another bout of crying shrieks, he did his best to keep his cool. "Shh... shh, Mae. We're going to get you medicine, and then you'll be okay. Daddy's going to make it all better." He rose from his seat, giving the nurse a watery smile as he hefted up the diaper bag and shuffled out of the little examination room.

God, he didn't have the money for this. He didn't have the money for the clinic visit or the medicine or anything, not if he was going to pay rent and his internet bill. But Mae needed it, and she came first. She came before his studies, his pride, and–shit. His date! In the rush to get Mae seen before the clinic closed, he'd forgotten to at least call Wil.

He fished out his cell phone from his pocket and checked the time. Shitshitshit! He tapped the buttons of his basic, old-school phone and found Wil's number in his recent call history before tapping again and putting the phone to his ear. A quarter 'til eight. Three rings. Four. Wil's voice came up, but he could instantly tell it was the voicemail, and he sighed as he waited for the beep.

"Wil! Uh... hi, Wil." *Don't sound like a dumbass. Don't sound like a dumbass.* He repeated the phrase over and over in his mind for a couple seconds. "I'm... I'm really sorry. I know you're probably on the way to that bubble tea place, and I should be, too, but I'm not, because my daughter is sick and..." He sighed, squeezing his eyes shut as Mae screamed again as if on cue. "I have a four-month-old daughter, and I was planning to tell you tonight, but she's come down with an ear infection, and I can't dump her on my mom so I can go out, you know? But I didn't want to stand you up, and I'll totally understand if you don't want to reschedule or be around me 'cause I'm seventeen and have a kid and all, but I hope you understand I re-ally wanted to meet up and—" The phone beeped, and an automated voice began telling him to press numbers if he wanted to re-record. He hung up the phone with a whispered but adamant, "Shit!"

He'd never get a call back. First chance to meet up with someone new, and he'd blown it big time. He hugged Mae, leaning his head against hers and preparing himself for an all-nighter filled with lots of crying. He'd get her through this, take good care of her no matter what. That was all that really mattered. He rifled through the diaper bag for his checkbook.

He could write the check, but all it would be was a promise of money he didn't have. Grinding his teeth together, he knew what he had to do. There wouldn't be any way around it. His next phone call was going to be even more unpleasant. His mom might not pick up, either.

By the time there was a knock at his door, Zach was beside himself. Mae had just cried herself into exhaustion, and Zach was starving, had a pounding headache, and desperately wanted a nap. He opened the door and could have cried. "Mom."

Mindy Grayer stepped inside and hugged Zach. It was always odd now to hug his mom. In the time since he'd moved out, he'd shot up in height, and now Mindy was a few inches shorter than him. She shut the door behind her, her plump cheeks flushed from the heat. "Where's Mae?"

Zach backed up to give her room. "In her crib. She... she just fell asleep, I think."

"What did the nurse say?" Mindy put her purse on the counter and turned to the kitchen.

"An ear infection. They... gave me amoxicillin for her. Drops I'm supposed to give her a couple times a day. She doesn't seem to like them much."

Mindy chuckled, pulling her gray-streaked brown hair back into a ponytail. "You didn't, either, when you were a baby." She bustled about his kitchen, finding what she needed to cook with, and then ducked into his fridge. "Had the worst ear trouble. I'm not surprised my granddaughter has the same issues."

Zach watched his mom make eggs, toast, and tea while turning the night over in his head. He watched her deftly flip eggs—he always broke his yolks, but she never did—and then she buttered the toast perfectly. There wasn't a single morning he could recall in his childhood that his mother hadn't buttered his toast in the morning. Her hands seemed always so sure and steady in everything she did. Insecurity gnawed at him. "Was I doing something wrong, Mom? Should I have... noticed or...?" God, he felt so stupid. Terrified he was a bad father.

"No." She smiled at him, putting the food in front of him on the bar. "She was probably a little fussy, but nothing else until it just slammed into her. You did very good taking her to the clinic."

He poked at the eggs. "About the clinic..." Zach took a deep breath. "I have to take today and tomorrow off, at the very least, to take care of Mae, and I had to write a check at CVS." He licked his lips. "I... I don't have enough to cover the check and the rent I have to pay. I..." Zach *hated* asking his parents for money. It was nothing but him admitting his failure as a fa-ther and provider. "Can I please borrow some money?"

Mindy stared at him for a moment, and Zach thought she would say no. She had every right. His parents had wanted him to stay with them, keep Mae at their house, but they would have wound up raising his kid, not him. But, then she reached into her purse and pulled out a pen and check-book. "How much do you need?"

Relief rushed through him. "Two hundred?"

She nodded. "All right. You go lay down, and I'll look after Mae for a few hours."

"Really?" Sleep? Precious sleep would be his?

"Eat. Sleep. Mom's here."

Zach laughed and stabbed a bit of egg with his fork. "I love you, you know."

"Yeah, yeah." Mindy ripped the check out of the booklet. She held the check out to Zach with a grin on her face. "I love you, too."

As always, he was thankful he had the parents he did. They may have yelled, screamed, and gnashed their teeth when they found out

Bethany was pregnant. They may have told him to let her give the baby up. But when he had decided he was going to keep his daughter, and he was going to do it on his own terms, they'd backed him up. Sometimes they let him fall. Sometimes they helped him back up. And, sometimes, like now, they threw out the safety net. He hoped with every fiber of his seventeen-year-old heart that he would be as good to Mae as his parents had been with him.

His mom began to clean up the kitchen while he ate her over-cooked eggs, and he felt safe.

# Chapter Three

Zach rolled out of bed and squinted at the clock. Eight-thirty? Oh, hell! He'd slept all damn day! He jumped up from the bed and stumbled out into his sparse living room. It took him a moment to understand what he saw. Usually, the open space was merely littered with toys, a playpen, a sofa, and a small dinette table. Not today. Dozens of Walmart bags lay scattered about the floor, and his mother was talking softly to Mae, who was in a swing... a very nice swing. And he smelled his mom's beef stew. He rubbed his face for a minute, and then headed right to his mother and daughter.

"Did some shopping?"

Mindy laughed as Mae gurgled up from her swing. "You were out of some stuff, and Mae needed some new clothes, some toys, and how could you not have a swing? It's the best thing for a fussy baby."

"Umm... because I couldn't afford it?" Zach flopped down on the couch. "You didn't have to, Mom."

"I know." She looked over at him, setting her hands on her full hips. "I wanted to. She's my first grandbaby. I also deposited the check into your account. I wanted to make sure the money was in there."

"Does Dad know you're here?"

"Your father is in Chicago for the next week. There's a convention of some sort for real estate agents." Mindy waved her hand in the air, and round her face lit up with a smile as she said, "He told me all about it, but I really didn't pay attention. You know how he likes to go on." Mae squirmed in the swing and gave a happy squeal. "So, I thought I would get you some things for Mae, the house, and yourself, and then I started some supper for us."

Zach shook his head. "You're crazy." He leaned down and began to sort through the bags. Three bags of clothing for Mae, two bags of toys, a bag of clothes for him, all sorts of household supplies and toiletries... "Mom, did you buy out the store?"

"No," she scoffed. "These are the essentials. I bought what every parent should have in their house for their child and themselves."

"Even if their house is actually a one-bedroom apartment?" That made his mom blush in a way that had her looking ten years younger. He chuckled as he stood up and went into the kitchen, giving her a hug. "Thanks, Mom. That smells fucking delicious."

"Language!" she laughed, *thwapping* him with her wooden spoon. "You have a child now. You'll have to tone down that mouth of yours. Honestly, who taught you any of that?"

"You're kidding, right?" Zach grinned. "Learned half of it from Dad when he thought I wasn't listening. Jackass clients sometimes get to him, and I... sometimes happened to hear as I was sneaking out."

"Oh," she said, waving the spoon at him. "I really don't need to be hearing this now. You keep an eye on that girl when she gets to be your age, you hear? No sneaking out!"

He leaned forward and kissed her cheek. "I'll do my best, just like you did. Trust me, much as I adore Mae, I'm... not eager for her to follow in her daddy's footsteps."

Mindy was about to say something back when his phone chimed. It wasn't one of the family or work ringtones he'd set up, so it had to be some-one else. Who would be calling him so late at night? His eyes suddenly widened, and he all but bounded over the sofa to get to his cellphone on the coffee table.

"Is that your father? I told him to give you a call, but he should still be on the tail end of his convention day."

Zach bit his lower lip for a moment as he looked at the number. "Uh... I kind of met this guy through the checkout line, and he kinda checked me out while I was, y'know, checking him out. Do you think you could...?" He gestured wildly to everywhere but where he was.

His mother's eyebrows rose up so high, they disappeared into her bangs. The phone kept ringing and vibrating in his hand. "You going to an-swer that? You should."

A nervous smile twitched up at the corners of his lips. Shit. The phone. Was that five rings or six? He scrambled to press the little green button, putting the phone to his ear. "Hello?" His voice came out as almost a high-pitched squeal. He cleared his throat and tried again. "Hello?"

"Zach? It's Wil."

Zach's heart began to race. "Hey, Wil. I'm really sorry about last night. I tried to call and tell you I couldn't make it, and I hope you got the message before you went out of your way to meet me somewhere I wasn't going to be because I'd feel so bad about that and I—"

Wil's laughter was warm and toe-curling over the phone. "It's okay. A couple of my dorm buddies were there, we had some boba, and we watched a movie they were showing. I was sorry you couldn't make it, but I understood."

Now came the part Zach hated most, when a gorgeous guy like Wil told him it just couldn't work out between them because of Mae. "I'm glad you had a good time, and, like I said, I'm really sorry."

"You have a daughter?"

"Yeah, I do. She's four months old. She's got this ear infection, and I needed to be here for her." Zach closed his eyes and took a deep breath. "I'll understand if you don't want to call me again."

Wil was quiet for a moment. "Why wouldn't I call again?"

Zach's eyes shot open. "Because... I have a kid."

"It happens. People have babies all the time. It's not a social disease."

Laughter bubbled up out of Zach, and he felt his shoulders begin to relax. "It can feel like it sometimes."

"How about you call me when your girl is well again? We can meet up then."

"It's really hard to get someone to look after her, Wil, and I work when I'm not with her or studying."

Wil made a soft, agreeable sound. "Then why don't we meet up at the boba shop next week when she's better. All three of us."

"You want to meet my daughter?"

"Yeah," Wil laughed. "I do. Call me next week?"

Zach felt an excited grin spread over his face. "Next week. Sure."

"All right. Take care of that baby. Ear infections are shitty."

Zach hung up the phone and turned around. His mom stood there with Mae, smiling. "I take it he wasn't scared off?" she asked.

"No. He... wants to meet Mae."

"It's a good start, honey." Mindy gave Mae's diapered backside a pat. "Now, you go give Mae her bath while I finish up supper. I'll help you clean up, and then I'll go home while the two of you rest."

Zach rushed over to her and hugged both his mom and daughter. "You're the best, Mom. Thanks for everything."

Mindy kissed the top of his head. "Remember that come Mother's Day. I've been after a new blender for two years."

Taking Mae from his mom, Zach headed for the small bathroom. "New set of sheets, got it!"

"Smartass!"

"Language!"

# Chapter Four

Zach killed the engine once he was lined up in his parking space behind the Sweetbay on Fowler. He'd never realized there was a strip of stores behind it, and he'd lived nearby for a while now. The 'Boba' sign above the store glowed in the fading sunlight of early evening. His butterflies returned, flitting about in his stomach as he eyed the posters and mirrors half-obscuring the store's front windows.

He pocketed his keys before stepping out of the car and going immediately to the backseat. He smiled nervously at Mae, unbuckling the harness of the car seat and smoothing down her new dress—lavender and ruffles. He wasn't sure how the hell his mom had known what he would have been looking for in the baby clothes aisle, but Mae looked adorable in the outfit.

"You ready, princess?" he murmured, taking a little headband out of his back pocket and wiggling it onto Mae's head, the little bow completing her ensemble. She merely grinned up at him, that beautiful, toothless smile melting his heart. She had gotten over that ear infection like a pro, and she seemed to be rewarding his love and care with endless smiles today. "That's what I like to see. You just be a good girl the next hour or two, okay? We want to make a good impression."

He disconnected the car seat with practiced efficiency and lifted it out, grabbing the diaper bag and locking the doors with his free hand. The door of the boba shop jingled as he entered, a little wind chime shaking on the door frame to announce his arrival. The shop was obviously a hangout spot, with chairs and sofas littering the front portion of the store. There was a small stage with a sound system, a television set up with an X-box 360 and one of those Kinect consoles, and artwork was mounted on all the walls with little price tags. The whole place had a vibe to it, welcoming, relaxing, and artsy without feeling trendy or contrived. It brought a smile to his face.

He took a couple cautious steps inside, but a voice rose over the sound of blenders and New Age music, catching his attention. "Hey, Zach! Over here!" He turned toward the voice and found Wil in the opening between the counter and a divider that separated the front of the store from the back. His heart pounded at the sight of Wil. The blond looked even more gorgeous than he remembered from their brief encounter at the Wal-mart, and he felt himself grinning like some lovestruck teen as he hefted up Mae's carrier and walked past the chairs and sofa. "Glad you could make it," Wil said with a grin as he approached.

"I never make the same mistake twice, if I can help it," Zach said, wondering if Wil could hear the excitement and nervousness in his voice. "Couldn't leave you hanging again, especially after you gave me a break. Plus, Mae's excited to meet you. She's been smiling all day." He lifted Mae's carrier up and set it on a nearby table. "Mae, this is Wil. Wil, my daughter, Mae."

Wil instantly leaned over and smiled at Mae. "Hi, Mae. Well, aren't you pretty, all dressed up for your night out?" Mae giggled and squirmed, reaching up toward Wil with the most enthusiasm Zach had ever seen from her with a stranger. Wil's eyes lit up as they glanced up at him. "She's adorable. Can I touch her?"

"Go for it," Zach chuckled. "She'll think you're snubbing her if you don't let her grip your finger. She likes to suck, though, so I hope your hands are clean."

"Spotless, actually. I'm just a little compulsive about it. Hand sani-tizer in my backpack and everything." Wil wiggled his finger against Mae's hands, and Mae instantly gripped it with both hands, a pleased gurgle es-caping her. "Sort of comes with the territory of taking so many classes about pathogens and medications."

That piqued Zach's curiosity. "You in med school or something?"

"I thought about it," Wil admitted, "but after a couple courses and some research, I found out I wanted to go into pharmacology instead. It would pay the bills, and I like knowing about all the different drugs, how they interact with one another, and how the body reacts to them."

"Still gets you one of those sexy white coats," Zach said, running his fingers over the sparse hair atop Mae's head.

"True," Wil laughed, and the sound calmed some of those butter-flies in Zach's stomach, putting him more at ease. "You want something to drink? My treat."

Zach looked over his shoulder at the menu. "I've never had any-thing like this. What do you suggest?"

"Their frozen drinks with boba are pretty awesome."

"I bet Mae would like something cold and new. Umm... just some-thing fruity?"

Wil gave him a wink and nodded. "Gotcha. Now, Miss Mae, you'll have to give me my finger back if I'm to get your daddy a drink." Mae kicked her feet and grinned up at Wil. "I know, I'm a looker to the ladies, but if you want something cold and sweet, you're going to have to deal with the heartbreak." Again, there was kicking and gurgling before Wil could ease his finger back. "Promise, sweetheart, I won't be long."

Zach could have hugged Wil for his attitude. He watched as Wil placed the order, and then he picked up Mae's car seat and diaper bag. In moments, he was settled with her on one of the sofas. It was much more comfortable than a table, and he hefted Mae out of the seat and into his lap. As they waited, he wiped her face, fixed her dress, and tickled her chin. She was squirming happily by the time Wil joined them again, sans drinks.

"It takes a little time," Wil explained as he sat down beside Zach, moving the car seat onto the floor at their feet. "They'll call my name when they're ready. Hello again, Miss Mae. I see you've forgotten about me already." Wil pressed his hand over his heart and frowned. "I'm wounded."

"Womens' affections are so fickle, aren't they?" Zach smiled, bouncing Mae gently. He leaned down to Mae, murmuring to her. "You remember Wil, don't you Mae? Don't you?" He rubbed his nose against hers like his mother used to with him when he was little—Eskimo kisses, she called them. Mae laughed in that wonderful, loud way she only did when very happy, and he pulled back with a grin, looking up at Wil. "You've got her in a great mood, you charmer. Should I be worried, with her as competition?"

"Nah. I prefer boxers and briefs to diapers," Wil said, and the way Wil looked at him then made his heart beat faster. "So, what do you do? Besides take care of this adorable kid and work at the Walmart, I mean."

"Not too much else, honestly, though I try." Zach shifted in his seat, hoping his answers wouldn't be too pathetic. "I'm taking a few courses online right now, just some of the general studies I need before I take the specific classes for my criminology degree."

"Criminology, huh?" Wil smiled. "That's one I haven't heard before. You want to be in law enforcement or doing the CSI kind of stuff?"

"More along the lines of criminal profiling. I want to help the people investigating crimes figure out what unknown criminals are like so they can be found. Once we catch them, I can help with interrogation strategies." Zach relaxed a little in his seat, smiling when Wil reached forward to give his finger back to Mae. It was easy to talk about his passions, and Wil seemed to genuinely care, not just letting the words go in one ear and out the other. "Not exactly something working at the Walmart prepares me for, which is why I'm taking as many classes online as I can in my spare time. It'll take me twice as long with Mae here, but I don't mind."

"You seem really devoted to her," Wil commented, glancing down at Mae and wiggling his finger against her chest until she giggled and squirmed. "I think that's really cool. Lots of guys would freak out at the mention of kids. That you're not letting it stop you from having goals and going after them is just... well, awesome." Wil shook his head. "I don't think half of my friends at college have that much determination."

"When the stick winds up with two pink lines, you grow up fast." Zach kissed the top of Mae's head. "It's hard sometimes, but I manage."

Wil tilted his head a bit. "Where's her mother?"

Zach couldn't help but roll his eyes a little. "Bethany's nice and all, but she's not really mothering material. At least, not yet. She wanted to give Mae up, but I couldn't do that. So, my parents got me a lawyer. Luckily, it wasn't as messy as it could have been, and me and Mae have been together ever since."

"You weren't in love with Bethany?"

Now Zach flushed, shifting again. "It... was stupid. Really stupid. Bethany was my friend, and I didn't know if I was gay or what. Not a whole lot of guys my age lining up so I could test the waters." He shrugged. "It was one night, but that's all it took. One night, some really awkward moments, and one bad condom later, I got to be the proud daddy of this little ball of sunshine," he said, giving Mae a bit of a jiggle in his lap.

A woman called out Wil's name, and Wil excused himself, coming back a moment later with two brightly colored drinks. "This is the Pikachu with pineapple jellies, and this is the Spartan with regular boba." Wil's eyes sparkled. "I figured, if you didn't mind too much, the three of us could share the two of them."

Zach eyed the strange drinks with a half smile. "Sounds good to me. What's with the tops, though? I don't quite get the whole layer of plastic sealed over it." He'd never seen a cup like that, with a thin piece of plastic film brandishing colorful Japanese anime renditions of the Zodiac. How were you supposed to drink the stuff? "Do you pull the plastic off somehow?"

Wil chuckled and held up a couple very thick straws. "That's what these are for. You poke the pointy straws through the plastic and suck up the boba pearls and jellies along with the icy part." With the odd look from Zach, Wil grinned. "Boba are the little beads at the bottom. Tapioca pearls. A little sweet. A bit tasteless. Lots of fun with texture."

"Okay," Zach said, eyeing the cups. "Tasteless, texturally-interesting beads."

"Exactly," Wil pronounced. "We'll slit the tops open so you can use a spoon for Mae, though." Wil demonstrated with one straw and let him follow suit with the other cup. He had no idea what to expect as he took a swig of the red icy drink, but a strange combination of flavors practically exploded over his tongue. Amidst the thick liquid were the boba pearls, and he chuckled as he chewed them for a few seconds before swallowing. "Okay, this is really weird, but I think I like it."

"Want to try the Pikachu with the jellies?"

"Definitely." He took a sip of the bright yellow smoothie and hummed. It was completely different, a mixture of citrus and bright flavors that seemed to tickle his tongue. The jellies pulled the same response from him as the boba. It was so strange to chew a drink, but the flavors and texture weren't bad at all, and he unwrapped the little plastic spoon that Wil offered him before slitting open the plastic with his finger and feeding a little of the Pikachu smoothie—without the choking hazards—to Mae. "What do you think, Mae? Do you like the citrus?" Mae's answer came in the form of leaning forward when he had reloaded the spoon, and he chuckled as he gave her a little more before setting the spoon down and reaching for the diaper bag. He pulled out her burping towel, bib, and some wet naps, and before long, she was drooling some of each smoothie down the front of her bib.

"Good girl, Mae! She eats without much fuss," Wil commented.

"It's been a very good day. There are times I worry that I don't get enough into her, but then there are other days when she eats enough for a kid twice her size. I only just started her on actual baby food. She likes everything except pea puree so far." He made a childish train sound before scooping a little more icy liquid into Mae's mouth.

"I'm not a fan of peas myself." Wil sipped the dark red drink and chewed on the brown pearls the straw brought up. "Mom made peas almost twice a week when I was growing up."

Zach shook his head. "My mom's thing was green beans. I can't stand them." He glanced up at Wil again. "So... you said you're going to school to become a pharmacist? Do you go to USF?"

Wil nodded. "Yep. Third year. I could be finished, I think, if I'd just do what my dad wants and take the summer session classes, but summer's my time off."

"That makes you... twenty?"

"Twenty-one last April." Wil chuckled. "Like older men, Zach?"

A flush stole hotly across his face. "I—well—I mean—"

"It's all right." Wil bumped Zach's knee with his own. "I'm only teasing."

Zach wiped Mae's little bow-like lips with a napkin, and then swapped drinks with Wil. "I don't date much. Mae makes it a little difficult. Work, school, and being there for her doesn't leave much time to go out."

"I understand. But, do you *want* to date someone?"

"Fuck, yeah, I want to." Zach laughed, and then hid his face behind his hand for a moment. "I mean, yes, I would."

Wil smiled. "How does your Wednesday evening look?"

"Work. I'm off Thursday night and Monday morning, though." Zach heart pounded in his ears. Wil knew he had a kid, but he was going to ask him out anyway? God, what did he do right lately to land this chance?

"I work Monday morning, but if you want to get together Thursday night, I'm game." Wil leaned forward and tickled Mae's knee. "And if you can't find a babysitter, we can tailor our night to what Miss Mae might enjoy."

Zach grinned like an idiot. "Really?"

"Really. School starts in a couple of weeks, so now's the best time to chase after you."

"Chase after me, huh?"

"You're not an easy man to corner." Wil took a long drink of the yellow slush, but the silence was comfortable. "We could go to MOSI. I haven't been in a couple of years."

"The Museum of Science and Industry?" Zach chuckled. "Haven't been there since my junior high field trip. That actually sounds like fun. I had a great time way back when, though I can't actually remember too many details. Junior high wasn't the best time of my life, y'know?"

Wil hummed, a wistful smile curving his lips. "I think that's true for just about everyone. Sounds like we have a date, then."

The broad grin Wil flashed him made him blush again. "A date. Next Thursday." It was really going to happen. This hot guy was planning on taking him out. It would take him a while to process it, to get past the initial shock, but it felt so good to be out in a new place with a new person, especially when that new person knew about Mae and still wanted to be involved with him. That was the best part.

"So, does this mean I can steal a kiss?"

Zach blinked, jolting out of his thoughts and back to reality. "I—what?"

"Kiss," Wil chuckled, and the glint in his blue eyes sent a tingle directly to Zach's groin. "You know... my lips against yours for a few seconds? Or does that have to wait until we're on the first official date?"

Mae gurgled, and Zach clung to her as if she were a security blanket that would give him strength and confidence... or at least hide the way his cock was starting to stiffen in his jeans. His eyes darted around. "You mean right now? In public?" He wasn't sure if this was a good place for that. God knew he didn't need any trouble being openly gay when he was sitting there with Mae. While he knew she might catch some flack later on for her daddy being gay, he really didn't want to expose her to all that *now*.

"It's all right," Wil said. "The people here are cool, and there's really no pressure. I'll wait if I have to, 'cause I'm sure it's going to be worth it."

Zach fought not to shiver, but failed to keep from shifting in his seat a little. "Maybe I don't want you to wait," he breathed, his lips twitching up into a smile.

"That's what I like to hear," Wil murmured, his voice pitched at that spine-tingling level that made Zach's heart pound even before Wil leaned over. Wil reached out to cup his face. His hand was cold from holding the boba drink so long, and it made Zach's breath catch right as Wil's lips brushed over his. He held his breath, caught in that moment for what seemed like an eternity, and then he craned his neck forward and kissed back.

It was simple, almost innocent, but the heat the kiss sent through him, the reaction his body had to it, was anything but innocent. He choked back a moan as he felt himself grow hard. It had been too long since he'd kissed someone, since he'd even touched someone with intimacy in mind, but his body remembered. What experience he did have was limited to the mother of his child, and so he had a lot of pent-up lust. He could have been turned on by rearranging matches, much less a great kiss. And it was; Wil was an amazing kisser, lingering at his lips but never making him feel like he had to pull away. The kiss drew to a slow close, and Zach shivered. "Wow."

Wil grinned as he sat back, looking really damn satisfied with himself as Zach just struggled to breathe properly. "There's more where that came from," he chuckled. "You'll get another one when I see you Thursday. I guarantee it."

"I look forward to it," Zach laughed, and the sound must have pleased Mae, because she giggled in his lap right along with him. It seemed Wil had earned Mae's stamp of infant approval. Zach couldn't help but agree with her taste.

# Chapter Five

"You have a *date*?"

Zach squinted up at the hot sun, and then laughed when Mae splashed him with pool water. The only things that made the Florida heat bearable were air conditioning and the YMCA pool. Beyond the pavement and fencing separating the kiddie pool from the family pool, he sat with Mae in the shallows of the large play area. Parents lounged in the shade while the toddlers splashed in the spraying fountain or slid down one of the slides that ended in the water. It was a child's delight, and Mae's eyes darted about with all the movement in front of her. She splashed in Zach's lap, and Zach turned to look at Samantha. "Yeah, I do. He's a pharmacy major at USF, and he wants to take me to MOSI."

Samantha gave him an odd look. "MOSI? Are you twelve?"

Ever since meeting Samantha at the free daycare service the local Catholic church offered to those in need, Zach had become used to her sarcasm. She was rife with it. "Well, he suggested it in case I couldn't con Mom into looking after Mae. Mae would like a place like that."

Samantha's little girl, Sophia, twirled around in the fountain spray, waving her floatie-bedecked arms at them. "We could watch her," Samantha said, splashing a little at Sophia as a little boy ran by screaming with a skinned knee.

"You want a four-month-old and two-year-old under the same roof, alone, for a whole night?"

"It's not that bad." Samantha nudged him. "Mae's a good girl, and Sophia keeps asking for a sister. As if that's going to happen."

Zach wet Mae's suit down again as the sun baked them. "Josh not around anymore?"

"Nah, he headed out the door the minute Sophia called him 'daddy'. I tried to explain she just didn't understand, but..." Samantha shrugged. "Gary was such a jerk. He won't even send child support anymore."

"He can't *stop* paying it, Sam. He's legally required. He's her *father*."

Samantha smiled at him. "Just like Bethany's Mae's mother, but something about it doesn't stick with them. Which is why you wind up raising Mae on your own, and I wound up on my own with Sophia at nine-teen."

Zach ducked, kissing Mae's fuzzy head. "I'd have wound up either watching Bethany raise her, or raising her on my own. I'm gay. That doesn't lead to the mother-father sort of set up."

"I guess not. Though..." Samantha hesitated for a moment. "You had sex with Bethany, so doesn't that make you bisexual? Kind of?"

Zach shook his head with a lopsided smile. "Oh, no, I'm gay. I'm surprised I even got through the once with Bethany. I was experimenting, trying to go against that gut feeling that I was gay, and that just cemented it all. I mean, I get that it's not that way for a lot of people. I know a few guys like Jared—you remember Jared from that group brunch—could totally go either way with guys or girls. Might have worked out better for someone like him, but me?" He chuckled and tickled Mae until she squealed and started another series of splashes. "I'm gay. And Mae loves me anyway, don't you, Mae?" He picked her up for a moment so her feet walked on the water's surface, and then he blew raspberries against her skin until she was stuck in a fit of laughter that made him grin.

Samantha just laughed, her attention drawn a short distance away to where Sophia demanded she watch before twirling around in the most adorably clumsy way Zach had ever seen. Samantha just yelled an encour-agement to her and leaned in close to murmur, "They are going to sleep *so* well tonight!"

Zach hummed, dropping his head back longingly. "God, I hope so. I need as close to a full night as I can get."

"Still worn thin? You sure do work a lot."

Zach shrugged. "I have to pay the bills and find a way to cover all her food as she makes that jump to baby food. I'm still kind of recovering from her being sick. I couldn't have gotten through that without my mom's help."

Samantha nodded, glancing over at him for a second before con-tinuing to watch Sophia in the water. "It's good to have that support. Isola-tion would be the worst thing, which is why I love these little play-dates you manage to squeeze in... and why I think it's great you'll be taking a night off to go on your date." She paused a moment, and Zach could have sworn a smirk twitched on the far side of her mouth, where he could barely see it. "Is he hot?"

He felt heat rise to his cheeks. "You do know that's not all I'm looking for in a guy, right?"

"Yeah, yeah, I know, but is he?" Now, the smirk was firmly in place.

Zach laughed and settled Mae on his lap again. "Yes, all right? He's hot. He doesn't look like he's a big sports guy, but he's trim, tall. Mae didn't start screaming the minute he touched her."

"Hair color? Eye color? Come on. Don't hold ba—Sophia, I see you. Don't you pour your sippy cup in the pool, young lady!" Samantha stood up long enough to snag the cup from Sophia and give her a doll to play with in the water. "I swear, that girl is going to kill me one day. Now, specifics, Zach! I have to live vicariously through you for the moment."

"He's blond. Blue eyes. Tanned." Zach splashed more water on Mae. "He has a really nice mouth with full lips, and his hands... his hands are big. Long fingers. Wil's just really nice to look at. The whole package." He paused a moment and looked out over the family pool, where lots of older kids were playing in the deeper water. "Makes me wonder what's lurking beneath the surface."

Samantha nodded. "Good looking, nice attitude, likes your kid. Yep, murderer in disguise."

Zach kicked her feet in the water. "Not funny," he said, though he laughed. "I worry about it. I've got Mae to look after, and I don't want to parade a bunch of shitty men through her life 'cause I was horny and lonely."

"Hey, I get you being cautious and all. Hell, you're obviously more responsible on that front than I was, right?" She waded over to him and splashed him and Mae with a grin. "But don't get too paranoid, okay? Don't let that ruin things before they even get the chance to get started. I might not have known you six months ago, but you're the type who's going to take care of Mae. If this guy is worth it, he'll have already seen that just by seeing you with your daughter. If he's willing to go all in, then be sure *you're* game, all right?"

Zach smiled at her, splashing back. "What are you, my counselor now?"

"Shut up, that was deep!" She laughed, splashing him again. She was soon joined by Sophia, who had wiggled and dog-paddled her way over to Samantha and copied her without delay. He had to shield Mae from some of the water, but Mae didn't seem to mind, giggling and kicking on his lap, even when a little water splashed the top of her head and dripped down her face.

"You bullies! Splashing a poor, defenseless child who can't fight back! When Mae's two, we're going to get you back, just wait and see!"

"By then, Sophia will be four!" Samantha picked Sophia up and spun the laughing child about a bit. "God, four! She's growing up so fast."

Zach wiped Mae grinning face. "I know what you mean. Mae has already outgrown half her wardrobe. Mom was great, though. Bought her a dozen new outfits."

Samantha put Sophia back down and came to sit with him in the shallower end of the kiddie pool. "She'll grow like a weed, just like Sophia." She looked at her daughter. "Enjoy it. I know I am. Every moment." They were both silent for a moment, watching Sophia play with her Barbie in the water, and then Samantha turned to him again. "So, I'll be taking Mae for the night on Thursday and you'll pick her up Friday morning?"

"I guess you are, and yeah, Friday morning. Nine o'clock." Zach nudged her with his shoulder. "Try not to have one of your wild parties."

"Yeah, that's me." Samantha grinned. "A wild child. Party hard. It'll be an awesome girls' night in."

Zach hugged Mae to him, those butterflies reappearing in his stomach now that he knew for sure he'd see Wil again. Without Mae. Maybe even get another kiss. God, that kiss. He'd thought of nothing but that kiss for days now. No MOSI. No baby. No one waiting up for him. Just him and Wil and those gorgeous lips. Damn it, what was he going to wear?

# Chapter Six

It didn't matter how many times Zach paced past the bathroom door. Every time he walked by and glanced at himself in the mirror, he knew he wasn't dressed appropriately. He had left a giggling, happy Mae with Samantha and Sophia only an hour ago. It wasn't the first time he'd thanked God for throwing him in Samantha's path. She was making this night out possible, and if he could simply get over his nerves, it might turn out all right in the end.

He walked by the bathroom mirror again and paused. The blue shirt was better. Blue looked good on pretty much everyone. Wil probably liked blue, with how gorgeous the color looked with Wil's eyes and all. Yes, the blue shirt, not the red one.

He'd made it as far as the closet when the doorbell startled him. Wil had called to let him know he was about ten minutes away. It couldn't have been ten minutes already! He pulled the blue t-shirt over his head and shut the door to the disaster area otherwise known as his bedroom before dashing to the door, smoothing his hair back down into place. Force of habit dictated he check the peep hole before opening the door, and just that quick glimpse of Wil set his heart pounding. His palms began to sweat as he slipped the locks and opened the door with a smile.

"Hey there, handsome," Wil said with a sweeping glance and a smile. "Are you and Princess Mae ready for a night on the town?"

Zach forgot to breathe. Wil must have noticed the shirt choice. Blue had definitely been the way to go if he was 'handsome' at first glance. He blushed and swallowed as he came back down to earth. "Actually, I managed to find a babysitter for Mae. One of the other single parents I know was willing to cover for me, so..."

"That means no MOSI, huh?" Wil chuckled warmly, a glint in his eyes. "I'd hoped it would work out that way. I know the perfect place to take you for dinner, then. Ready to go?"

"Yes!" Zach answered hastily, and then scrambled to correct himself. "I mean, let me grab my keys and turn off the lights and... I'll be right out." He made quick work of those tasks, and then followed Wil to his car. "A hybrid?" he said skeptically. "You know the manufacturing of those does more damage to the environment than you prevent by driving it, right?" Zach paused and flushed as he looked over to Wil. "Um. I mean, cool car."

Wil laughed. "I don't delude myself. If I really wanted to save the environment, I wouldn't drive at all. But my parents made me choose between this or a Volvo. The choice was obvious."

"Yeah, I can't picture you in a Volvo." Zach fastened his seatbelt, silencing the incessant ding of the car's alert system, and Wil pulled away from the curb.

Zach alternated between lame small talk and listening to the radio, mostly not paying attention to anything beyond calming his twitching nerves. Before he knew it, Wil was turning into the big shopping center where Fletcher Avenue met Dale Mabry Highway. Zach had gone to the Publix here for groceries a few times, but he rarely paid attention to the other shops. When you didn't have money to spend, it wasn't nearly as much fun to window shop. "Okay, where are we going? Picking up some supplies for a picnic?"

Wil chuckled as he parked near the Publix. "While that does sound lovely, it's hot. I'd rather be indoors."

"I was worried that maybe the sun had melted your brain." Zach got out of the car and looked around. Was there a restaurant here? He didn't remember there being one, and there wasn't one in sight.

"Come on." Wil held out his hand to Zach. "If we hurry, we should be able to nab a table."

Zach blushed a little as he slid his hand into Wil's. "A table *where*?"

Pulling Zach along, Wil laughed. "Your curiosity will be sated in just a moment."

Zach shook his head, heart racing, but he kept up with Wil. They were touching. Wil was holding his hand. Bethany had held his hand a little, but this was different. It was more like when he'd tried dating David, the guy in his high school Bio I class. Holding hands under the lab table while Mr. Griffin yammered on about cell structure and homework. But this, this was *more*. At least, Zach wanted it to be more. Did Wil? Was it normal to feel like this on a first date?

Wil opened the door to the restaurant, and a blast of cool air whispered over Zach's sweaty skin. Just walking from the car to the establishment behind the Publix, he was damp with sweat. He looked around the dimly lit reception area. "The Melting Pot?" His brow furrowed. "I didn't even know this was here."

"A lot of people don't. You have to want to find it." Wil smiled at the hostess. "Is there room for two?"

The hostess smiled at them. "Yes." She plucked two menus from behind her station, and then motioned at them. "Follow me, please."

Zach walked back into the restaurant, his hand still in Wil's. He couldn't help but peek in at some of the people already sitting and eating. One couple only had salads, but another group had what looked like raw meat that they were dipping into some kind of cooking pot. He leaned closer to Wil. "What kind of restaurant is this?"

"You've never had fondue before?" At his blank look, Wil just chuckled, "Oh, this is going to be more fun than I thought."

Zach was about to ask what Wil meant, but they were shown to their table before he got the chance. It was a small, secluded little booth for two, and the privacy of the setting sent a little tingle down his spine. He had to relinquish his hold on Wil's hand to slide into his side of the booth, but he couldn't help but smile at Wil, who looked so at home in the posh restaurant.

The hostess' introduction about their server went in one ear and out the other. Zach was far too busy admiring Wil to pay much attention. Once the hostess retreated to give them a bit of privacy, Wil looked at him. A little half-grin began creeping onto Wil's face, and Zach knew he'd been caught. "Something in my teeth?"

"No," Zach laughed, hoping he didn't sound as jittery as he suddenly felt. "Sorry. It's just... a first for me. Date night, my daughter safe so I don't have to worry, and a guy like you taking me a place I've never been. I feel like I haven't gone out just for fun in ages."

"Mae's priority one," Wil said with an understanding smile. "I know that has to be how it feels, but sometimes, you have to make *you* priority one. Relax, take a breath, and treat yourself. That's what tonight is about. You, me, and having a great time feeding each other food off sticks."

Zach took a breath and the growl his stomach made at the thought of food was positively indecent. The wonderful smells coming from a nearby table tempted him. "Definitely not something I've done before, except the occasional corn dog. I'm gonna make a mess of it, I just know it."

A glint entered Wil's gaze at that. "That's part of the fun. Making a bit of a mess... and then cleaning it up."

Zach had to take a moment to remember how to breathe as he imagined the various ways they could clean up. It made his mouth go dry.

If anything happened like the images in his head, he wasn't about to complain. In fact, he was suddenly looking forward to making a mess. "Let's get started, then. How's it work?"

"It's pretty easy, really," Wil said, grabbing a menu and opening it in the middle of the table, angling it so Zach could see. "Some people think it's stupid to pay to cook your own food, but I think it's intimate." His eyes darted up to meet Zach's. "Sexy."

Zach felt his cheeks heat again. God, was he going to spend the *entire* night blushing? "How many guys have you seduced this way?"

Wil laughed softly. "You think this is a line?"

"I think it's really weird that you're all gung-ho over a seventeen-year-old single father."

Wil sat back, the menu held loosely in his hand, and watched Zach for a moment. "You're not that much younger than me. You have a daughter, which made you mature a little faster than guys your age do. Why don't I run screaming for the hills because you're young and have a kid?" He shrugged. "I'm surrounded by kids. Nieces, nephews, younger siblings, baby cousins and second cousins. Kids don't scare me, Zach." Wil then leaned forward again, a glint in his eyes. "Besides, this is just the first date. I want to make a good impression so that, maybe by the fourth date, you'll invite me in for a nightcap."

Embarrassment rolled hotly through Zach. "Sorry. It's just... new. Weird and new."

"We'll work it out." Wil angled the menu his way again. "Now, food. We can either order individually for the main event, or we can do a four course meal. That's a cheese fondue that you dip bread and veggies into, a salad and a main course, which is meats and vegetables that you cook yourself in a flavored broth, and then a dessert plate of fruits and cakes that you dip into melted chocolate. Personally, I love the whole experience, and since it's your first time, I highly suggest we go with the four course meal."

Zach eyed the price on that meal and swallowed thickly. There really wasn't more than *one* course he could afford, and even that was stretching it. "Uh..." How did you tell someone you were flat broke, and even if you did have the money, it meant taking it away from your child? Zach felt another blush creep up on him. "Wil, look, I—"

"*I* asked *you* out, remember?" Wil flashed him a bright smile. "Four course meal. Doing it right. I want you to remember this first date."

"Oh, I'll remember it, all right," Zach laughed, shifting in his seat. Their waitress arrived, and Zach watched as Wil ordered. Drinks, each of the four courses—adding lobster to their entree—and then it was done. Wil handed the menus over, the waitress disappeared, promising to bring back their sodas, and they were alone again. "I swear, you have to do this on a regular basis to be able to choose everything so quickly."

Wil shrugged. "I've been here a few times. High school prom, graduation, and every summer, my parents drag me and my sisters with their husbands here. It's nice. Quiet. Dimly lit." He reached across the table and laced his fingers with Zach's on the tabletop. Zach's pulse fluttered as he stared into Wil's eyes, which were so very dark in the dim lights and flickering candle flame. "I think it's better for a date than family outings," he murmured.

Zach couldn't look away, and he didn't want to. A small, hesitant smile curved his lips as he squeezed Wil's hand. "Yeah," he breathed. "I think so, too."

They stared for a moment, or maybe it was a full minute. Time seemed to stand still with Wil. Things were simpler, wonderful, and so much more relaxed. He didn't feel like he had to worry about anything. He could indulge himself, give in a bit to the parts of him that got pushed to the side so he could be a responsible father. His eyes began to wander over the details of Wil's face. The lighting threw the angles into a bit of contrast, and the way Wil's skin almost glowed made it clear he'd shaved himself smooth. A little stray thought flitted into Zach's mind, whispering wicked things like what Wil's cheek might feel like against his lips, or how Wil's lips might find his if he leaned just a little closer.

Zach startled as he realized he was all but drooling and snapped his eyes down to his placemat. He carefully pulled his hand out of Wil's to comb his fingers through his hair. Words. He needed words, something to talk about other than how good Wil's lips looked in the mood lighting.

Luckily for him, it didn't seem Wil was as tongue-tied. "I guess this is the perfect opportunity to learn more about each other." Wil chuckled. "Maybe ask a few of the more intimate questions we've both thought about but stashed away for the right opportunity."

Zach wet his lips. "Intimate ones? Like what?"

Wil's lips twitched. "Well, I don't have to ask if you've ever thought about having kids down the road."

Zach couldn't help but laugh, and the release of nervous tension he'd started to feel building in his jaw and shoulders was great. "Guess not," he agreed, "and I can only assume you want a family as large as the one you've already got?" Turnabout was fair play, after all.

"Not necessarily as large, with the handful of kids my sisters have, but a family I can call my own." Wil paused for a moment to ask the waitress for drink refills, and then turned his attention back to Zach. "Just 'cause I'm gay doesn't mean I don't want that kind of thing, you know?"

Zach nodded as he thought about Mae. "I didn't plan ahead. Still, I couldn't imagine it another way now. Family's important. Mae's important."

"Glad we agree," Wil purred.

That tone teased Zach. It caressed over him, sent his body tingling, and just wasn't fair! He didn't have ammunition for this kind of battle, and every time Wil pitched his voice like that, his eyes were drawn back to those lips. He blushed and kicked Wil's leg under the table. "Stop that."

"Stop what?" Wil asked, his face far too innocent to be taken seriously.

Zach laughed again. "Distracting me! You keep doing that, and I'm going to burn myself with molten cheese or chocolate or something!"

Wil laughed. "All right. I'll behave." His eyes sparkled. "For now." Their waitress brought their new drinks, and promised to return shortly with their food. Wil's blue eyes focused on Zach once more. "You've given up a lot to have Mae. I'd like to know why."

It was a very personal question, one that made heat flush in Zach's cheeks. "How could I not? She's a part of me." He smiled stupidly at his drink as he swirled the straw about. "I'd like to think she's the best part of me. It's hard, don't get me wrong, like... *really* hard, but when I'm cuddling her or watching her sleep, it's all worth it."

"I think that's the best reason." Wil's foot nudged his under the table. "If I have any kids, I want to think that way. I want to love them more than the whole world and show them how much they mean to me. Not just say it, *show* it."

There was something odd, almost sad, in Wil's voice. Zach leaned forward and tilted his head. Wil was the rich boy, the one with his whole life ahead of him and every opportunity at his feet, but there was something missing in it all. Before he could stop himself, he asked, "Were you not shown, Wil?"

Wil looked at him for a long moment, and then gave a little shrug, a false smile—the first Zach had ever seen—making it way to his lips. "Who can say? I was the unplanned baby. I think my parents were done raising their kids when I came along. Lucky me, I had all the extra curricular activities a kid could want, and I had a massive extended family to drive me crazy."

But Wil hadn't been loved enough. Wil didn't have to say it. It was right there in that false smile. It broke Zach's heart. "Any kid will be lucky to call you Daddy," he said, holding his hand out across the table to Wil.

"You think so?" Wil slid hid his hand into Zach.

"Mmm-hmm. I know it."

The false smile morphed into that bright grin Zach preferred on Wil's face. "Aw, you sweet talker, you."

# Chapter Seven

The walk from Wil's car up to Zach's apartment door was slow. At least he lived in a gated complex. It was one of the best selling features. It wasn't the greatest neighborhood in Tampa, but it wasn't the worst, either. The gate was an extra measure of safety. It was quiet, and for the moment, the air was still. He mounted the stairs up to the second level of apartments, glancing behind him every few steps. When they paused outside Zach's door, he hesitated. A gust of wind blew humid air through the breezeway, though it didn't do a thing to cool him down.

God, he was still so full from the lavish dinner Wil had treated him to. It had been amazing. Soft conversation, long stares, and Wil had even fed him. But, Cinderella's coach turned back into a pumpkin at midnight. As they stood in the first uncomfortable silence of the night, Zach knew his dream date was over. Didn't mean he wouldn't savor the memory, though.

Zach fiddled with the hem of his t-shirt. "So..."

"So." Wil leaned against the door jam. "Have a good time?"

A grin spread over Zach's face. "A really great time, Wil. Thank you."

Wil's finger moved over to brush a bit of chestnut-colored hair back from Zach's face. "Was it a great enough time to maybe do it again?"

Zach's eyebrow rose a little. "Again?"

"Yeah." Wil smiled, and Zach couldn't stop thinking about those full lips and how soft they would be against his... and how the idea of Wil twining their tongues really turned him on and— "Zach?"

"Huh?" Zach blinked, his gaze rising to meet Wil's. "What?"

Wil chuckled, a low, sexy sound. "I said, maybe we could take Mae to the Lowry Park Zoo."

"You want to go on a second date with me and my daughter?" Was this guy for real? Because Zach had either lucked into one hell of a guy, or he was about to get the ax murderer treatment in the near future.

"Yes. You. Me. Miss Mae. At the zoo."

"In the Florida heat."

Wil brushed the hair back from Zach's damp brow again. "You're quite nice to look at all flushed and dewy."

"Shut up." Zach gave Wil's chest a light *thwap* with his hand. "When?"

"Are you working Sunday?"

Zach nodded. "Yeah."

"How about Monday?"

"Monday is good," Zach said, eyes drawn to Wil's lips.

Wil leaned a little closer. "How about I pick you and Mae up around nine? We can grab a bite to eat at the zoo."

Zach's heart fluttered with excitement, a newly familiar sensation to him. "That... sounds amazing." He licked his lips, eyes darting between Wil's lips and eyes. "It's late. I have to pick Mae up from Samantha's at nine tomorrow morning for daycare."

"I know you're not going to invite me in yet, but how do you feel about a kiss?" Wil murmured.

Zach's pulse skyrocketed. He did his best not to jump forward, not to make demands or make a fool of himself. He managed to lift his hand without it shaking, and his fingers combed through Wil's blond hair. It was slightly damp with sweat, but he didn't care. He gently pulled Wil forward, and the heat of the Florida evening seemed to double as he craned his neck and whispered against Wil's lips, "A kiss would be nice."

It was such a lame invitation to his own ears, but he saw the pleased glint in Wil's eyes and felt Wil's lips curve up into a smile as they pressed against his. They were just as soft as Zach remembered, the press of them just as sweet as the first time. Wil's lips caressed his, and each movement just sent another thread of pleasure tingling down his spine. He could feel the thud of his heartbeat along every inch of his skin, and when Wil's lips parted and he felt that first slick hint of tongue, he gasped, pulling back for a moment.

"I'm sorry," Wil said quickly, though he stayed close instead of shying away. "Moving too fast?"

Zach shook his head, though the movement was small. His cheeks flushed with embarrassment, but he smiled as he said, "No. Let's just try that last part again." When he pulled Wil's lips back to his, there was no resistance, just one of those soft, deep chuckles that traveled directly to Zach's groin. The second kiss was a little more confident on his part, and when he felt that tiny swipe of Wil's tongue again, he opened up, tilting his head a little more.

It was an invitation Wil seemed eager to take. Wil's tongue slid past his teeth and teased along his in a way that made his toes curl in his shoes. Zach couldn't stop a soft moan from escaping him, and as his head spun with the pleasure of the kiss, he had the vague sense of moving, shifting. He was so caught up that it felt like he was floating, but then Wil's hand was at the junction of his neck and shoulder, the other cupping his hip, and he felt his shoulder blades press to the metal of his apartment door.

Being pinned even that small bit as Wil kissed him made him harden instantly in his jeans, and he put one hand back against the door to catch himself as his knees nearly gave out. What was Wil doing to him? It was like he was drowning in the heat of the night and the smooth taste of chocolate fondue that lingered on Wil's lips and tongue. He might have done anything Wil wanted in that moment, but that was the instant Wil chose to gently pull back, leaving him panting and dazed and half-certain he was going to faint.

"Monday at nine?" Wil asked, his breath still teasing against Zach's damp lips.

Zach's eyes fluttered open, and he fought to put two words together as the question moved through his jumbled head. "Yeah... Nine."

Wil chuckled again, and the sound did terrible things to him as he tried to get his feet under him and stand upright. "I'll see you then. Good-night, Zach."

Wil stepped back with a smile, but his hand gave Zach's neck and jaw an affectionate little squeeze before he turned away, and Zach grinned as he watched Wil walk down the stairs. Wil was opening his car door when he finally managed to call out, "Goodnight!"

It earned him a bright smile and a wave, and then Wil was in his car, out of the parking spot, halfway down the lane of the apartment complex, as if the actions appeared in snapshots. Zach reached back for the doorknob and managed to get his key into the lock while still staring at the empty street.

The apartment was blissfully cool, and it sent a wave of goose-bumps springing up onto his arms and legs, making him aware of just how hot he was. The air conditioning unit hummed, but it was still quiet. With Mae over at Samantha's, he had the apartment to himself, and the chance to simply grin like an idiot and relive every moment of the kiss was almost as exquisite as the kiss itself had been.

He kicked off his shoes once he was in his bedroom and groaned as he peeled off his jeans. God, he was so hard. He couldn't remember the last time anyone had made him feel like this. It was as if every heartbeat brought the feeling of being kissed back to his lips, and he licked them as he threw his dirty clothes into his hamper, set his alarm clock, and flopped back onto his bed, his legs still dangling over the edge.

Zach closed his eyes as he reached up and touched his lips, remembering what Wil's had felt like just a minute before. His body was still hot, his cock still hard, and he ran his hands across his skin as he replayed the kiss yet again in his mind. Wil's lips against his. Wil's tongue curling inside his mouth. The thought pulled another moan from him even now that he was alone. Such an amazing date, such an amazing guy, and Wil had such a talented tongue. Not that he had much to compare it to, but then again, he didn't really need to. He imagined what else that tongue might be capable of, what it would feel like dipping into his belly button or trailing lower. Zach took himself in hand and stroked, moaning as he lost himself in the fantasy of Wil's tongue lapping at him, teasing him in ways Bethany never had. Wil would kiss along the length of him, lick him, maybe even— "Oh, fuck!" he gasped, spreading his legs and stroking faster as pleasure spiked through him. It was hard and fast, his body so ready. He cried out softly as he came, his mind filled with fantasies of Wil while his hips strained upward and fluids smeared his hand and abdomen.

Zach laughed breathlessly, reaching blindly for the box of tissues on his nightstand and grabbing a handful to clean himself up a bit. Happiness was bright inside him, a strange companion to the exhaustion that made his limbs feel so heavy after such a great orgasm. He was dating a guy who liked him, who liked his daughter, and who had the most amazing kissing skills. He couldn't think of a single thing that could top that. He rolled over on his bed and tugged up the covers. He flicked his bedside lamp off before cuddling against his pillow, a smile lingering on his lips even as he fell asleep.

# Chapter Eight

The fridge slammed, and Zach looked over his shoulder and into the small kitchen. "Damn it, Jamie, I told you to be *quiet.*" He shook his head. "Mae is sleeping. If I play my cards right, she'll sleep until midnight before needing a bottle."

Jamie held up his hands, a soda in one of them. "Sorry," he said before running his free hand through unruly black hair. "I was just thirsty."

Zach turned back to the small study group that met at his apartment once a week. Just the four of them, students who also worked at the Walmart with him. Devain and Jamie went to USF, and Piper attended Hillsborough Community College. Zach attended HCC, too, but he had yet to arrange his schedule enough to fit in an actual campus-held class. "Can you bring me a bottle of water? Quietly?"

"Yeah, sure." This time, Jamie was almost silent opening and closing the fridge.

"How old is she now?" Piper asked, popping a pizza bite into her bow-like mouth. She was pink from too much time in the sun lately, her elfin features fine and delicate. Zach sometimes thought that, if the brawny men Piper preferred actually preferred her, they might snap her in two.

Still, the mere thought of Mae brought a smile to his face. "She just turned five months. I swear, just yesterday, she was a tiny, squirming thing that squeaked every time I picked her up."

Jamie handed Zach the bottle of water, and then sat in his chair, which groaned under his bulk. Jamie was Piper's type, but Piper wasn't Jamie's. "And what about that guy? The one that dropped you off last week when your car was in the shop?"

Zach winced. "Don't remind me about the car. The mechanic said it's something to do with the piston ring." He sighed and flipped through his English textbook. "I don't know what it is, what it does, all I know is that to replace it, it cost me sixteen hundred bucks... plus the cost of an oil change." And he'd called his parents in a panic because he didn't *have* that kind of money, but he needed a car.

"That doesn't tell us who dropped you off." Devain grinned, teeth flashing bright white in his dark face. "Do you have a brother or something?"

A blush crept up Zach's neck and face as he fiddled with his pen. "No. Wil's... my boyfriend, I guess."

"You guess?" Piper gave him an odd look. "I would think he either is or isn't."

"Well, he hasn't actually *said* he is," Zach said. "We've gone out on a few dates, and he was a godsend when my car was in the shop. He took me to Mae's pediatrician, helped us with groceries. He's been great."

Jamie swapped out his English textbook for his math book and flipped through the pages. "Have *you* asked him if you guys are an actual item?"

"No," Zach said with a frown.

Piper nudged him with her foot. "Why not?"

Zach shrugged. "I don't know."

"Yes, you do." Piper leafed through her paper. "You're afraid."

"I've never *had* a boyfriend." Zach glared at his English assignment. "I had one awkward thing in high school, screwed around with my best female friend, and then I was a dad. I didn't really have time to play the field."

Devain snorted. "You can't play the field now?"

"No." Zach met Devain's dark eyes. "I won't do that to Mae. I want to be serious about the men I date. I don't want her to have a new uncle every week. We both deserve a lot better than that."

A smile lit up Piper's face, her gray eyes sparkling. "You are quite a catch, and Mae is absolutely adorable. Wil would be lucky to have you as a boyfriend. Just ask him. He might not have said anything because he doesn't want to scare you off."

Zach held up his hands. "All right. I have a date with him in a couple of days. I guess I can have that awkward conversation then. Right now, I have to figure out how to politely explain a twink and how they do not relate to drag queens."

Jamie choked on his soda, and Piper's pencil fell from her hand. It was Devain who asked, "This is an English assignment?"

"Classification-Division essay. I was told to pick whatever topic I wanted." Zach grinned, eyes darting from friend to friend. "I chose gay male stereotypes."

There was an odd silence for a few seconds as his friends all exchanged glances, and then Jamie burst into laughter until the other two managed to shush him. "God, I'd love to see everyone's faces if you did an in-class presentation on that. What else is on that list of stereotypes?"

Zach smirked. "Well, there's also the bears and the leather daddies."

"Saving the different flavored condoms for the Compare-Contrast essay?" Jamie asked from behind his hand, nearly on a fit of giggles.

"That's actually a great idea," Zach chuckled, making a show out of writing it down into his notebook.

"You know, I think your essays will be a breath of fresh air for your professor," Devain remarked, snatching the math textbook from Jamie and flipping it to a different page before giving it back and pointing, which got him a grunt of thanks.

"It's what keeps it interesting to me," Zach said, scribbling down the next sentence as it came to him. He just hoped he wrote the commas in the right spots, unlike in his last essay. "I have to do something I find amusing, or I think I'd end up ripping my hair out from the stress of it all. Part of me wishes I could just say 'screw college', but the rest of me knows I can't just work at Walmart for the rest of my life."

There were murmurs of agreement around the table, and everyone settled into their textbooks and notebooks again for a couple minutes. Zach took advantage of the lull and managed to finish another paragraph of his essay before pausing to address Devain, who kept looking over Jamie's shoulder at his work, more supervising and giving him pointers than doing homework himself. "So, how are things on campus lately? Anything interesting?" He couldn't help but pry. He knew campus life would just never be his reality, with Mae and work, and now Wil, taking up every spare moment of his time.

"Nothing in particular," Devain chuckled. "All the fraternities and sororities are getting ready for their fall rush. The football players are back, so there's a lot of practice going on. I see them all the time in the commons and stuff."

"Mmm, men in uniform," Piper hummed, a dreamy smile lighting up her face as she rested her cheek on her writing hand. "I should visit the USF campus more often, just to see more of the athletic scholarship types."

"Nah, football isn't the best," Jamie argued with a half-smile, not even looking up from his math problem. "It's the swimmers and tennis players that are hot."

Zach tossed a balled up piece of paper at Jamie. "Hey, I might be a taken man. I shouldn't be thinking about football players, tennis players, or swimmers!"

46

"You can look, babe," Piper said. "You just can't touch. Unless you're into that gang-bang scene?"

Oh, could Zach flush any brighter? "No!" Jamie let loose a loud cackle, and at that, Mae began to wail. "Dammit. See what you did?" He tossed another wad of paper at Jamie. "Loudmouth."

Jamie chuckled. "Dude, it's almost midnight. I think this is our cue to head out."

Piper began to collect her things, and Devain helped Jamie clean up his little mess. "Yeah," Zach said. "I have a shift at nine in the morning, which means I have to be up at seven." He headed into the kitchen to warm a bottle for Mae.

"Seven?" Devain hefted his backpack onto his shoulders. "You live five minutes from the store."

"I have to drop Mae off at my mom's, and that takes me forty-five minutes there and back." Zach put a pan of water on the stove and pulled out a can of formula. Piper, Devain, and Jamie filled the small doorway into the kitchen, watching him as he measured out six ounces of the formula, sealed the can with a lid, and put it in the fridge. The minute the water steamed a little, he shut off the burner and set the bottle inside it. He turned to them and crossed his arms as Mae shrieked in the background. "Are you three going?" he asked with a wry grin. "Or is preparing a bottle of formula *that* riveting?"

"None of us have kids," Piper pointed out. "And I'm an only child."

"Devain is the youngest, and I'm a twin," Jamie said. "Never seen it."

Zach shooed them. "Now you have. Out! I'll see you tomorrow, Piper. Maybe I'll see you, Devain, if you show up on time." In a rush of goodbyes, Zach got his friends out the door, shutting and locking it with a sigh of relief. As much as he liked study nights, he liked it being just him and Mae, too.

He snatched up the bottle, wiping it off and testing it on the inside of his forearm. Perfect. Zach rushed into the room and scooped up the red-faced Mae. "Shh. Daddy's here." He sat on the bed with her cradled in his arms and slipped the nipple of the bottle between her quivering lips. Immediately, she quieted, sucking hungrily on the bottle and staring up at him with her bright, hazel eyes. He smiled at her, rubbing her cheek with his finger. "Just you and me again, princess. Just you and me."

After a few minutes, he asked her, "What do you think of Wil?" Mae blinked, her hand flailing a little up to where his held the bottle for her. "Yeah, I think so, too. He's really a catch. Maybe it's time I ask him where we stand, hmm? Before our next zoo trip." Mae kicked a little, making a soft, wet sound as she drank down her formula. "Okay, okay. Trip to the zoo first, and *then* I'll ask if he's my boyfriend. The sacrifices I make for you," he said with an exaggerated sigh. "You're lucky I'm your daddy."

Mae squirmed again, offering him a milky smile around the nipple of the bottle. His heart leaped his chest, and he grinned down at her. "Yeah, yeah. I'm lucky you're my princess. Now, settle down and eat. You had your diva moment tonight. Bedtime once I have you changed."

Bed. Sleep. God, that's what he wanted, but for now, he savored feeding Mae, still marveling she was his. He hoped that wonder never faded.

# Chapter Nine

When Zach opened his apartment door, Wil was leaning against the railing of the breezeway, a careless smile on his lips. He looked gorgeous in his sandals, dark cargo shorts, and dark green USF Bulls t-shirt. Wil was the epitome of casual style, and Zach's tongue was suddenly stuck to the roof of his mouth. Words? What were those? All he did was stare until Wil laughed and held up his hands.

"I finally get an invite into your apartment, and all you're going to do is stand there and stare?"

Zach shook his head and opened the door wider, motioning for Wil to come inside. "If you don't want me to stare," he murmured, cheeks blazing, "don't look so jumpable."

"Oh, I'm jumpable?"

"You know you are." Zach shut the door after Wil and locked it. "I'm sure you've got your choice of eligible bachelors."

Wil leaned down and kissed him sweetly. "And I chose you."

Zach didn't think his cheeks could burn any hotter. "Yeah, you did. Hungry? My mom brought over at least six casseroles this weekend. I'm trying to work my way through the freezer."

"Sure. What's our choices?"

Zach hurried into the kitchen, flipping the oven on to 350, and then pulled open the freezer. "Lasagna, chicken pot pie, a Mexican lasagna —whatever that is, and I think these are stuffed shells."

"Stuffed shells." Wil leaned on the bar and watched him. "I love cheese and pasta. Can't get enough of it."

Putting the frozen casserole dish into the oven, Zach grinned. "I do, too. I could live off them, and I obviously do. It'll take about forty-five minutes. I've got some movies, if you want to watch one. Mae's asleep at the moment, but it's only seven, so she'll be up in the next hour or so for her next bottle."

"She's doing well, then? Daycare and outings with Samantha and Sophia treating her okay?"

"Yep. She's also taking her occasional baby food meal better and better. She loves her fruits," he chuckled. Zach loved that Wil even asked, that he showed concern for Mae and her little social life with the kids from the daycare. It made what he had to say next even more difficult to bring up. He set out plates and fiddled with the silverware for a moment before forcing himself to meet Wil's eyes. "Wil... Before we settle in for a movie or whatever, I'd really like to talk to you about something."

Wil arched an eyebrow at him. "You ask me to your place for the first time, you're making me dinner, and now you want to talk. Something wrong?"

"Yes, I mean, no, I mean... I *hope* not," Zach said quickly, tapping at the plastic of the countertop for a few seconds.

"It's all right," Wil said with a smile, though Zach could hear a note of concern in his voice. "Come over here and sit with me. If there's trouble, I want to fix it before it becomes something bigger."

Zach took a deep breath and let it out slowly, trying to calm his nerves a bit before rounding the divider separating the kitchen from the living area. When Wil held out a hand to him, he smiled and took it, leading Wil around to the worn couch. They sat down, and Zach glanced over at him. Wil's back was just a little too straight, a little too tense, and he couldn't stand keeping Wil in suspense for long. "It's not *that* bad. Really, it isn't. I was just talking with my friends a couple days ago, and it got me thinking, and I need to know." Zach wet his lips. "Are we together? Like, *really* together? The dates are amazing, and *you're* amazing, and I want to be able to tell everyone that we're actual boyfriends. I know it's kind of juvenile to have to label it, but... I need to know, 'cause I like you a lot. Mae likes you a lot. I just hope you like us both back."

Wil smiled at him, reached out, and cupped his cheek. "I like you a lot," he murmured. "And I like Mae a lot, too." He leaned in and brushed his lips against Zach's. "Yes, I'm your boyfriend."

Excitement filled Zach, and a bright smile lit up his face. "And I'm yours."

"Mmm-hmm." Wil kissed him again, a little deeper this time.

Zach lost all track of time as they kissed, inching closer to one another on the couch. Kissing Wil was so easy, and his pulse pounded through him, settled hotly between his legs. When the timer for the pasta rang, Zach was all but straddled across Wil's lap, panting against Wil's lips. "Dinner's ready," he said with a goofy, breathless grin.

As they were disentangling themselves, Mae began to wail from the bedroom. "Go get Mae," Wil said, straightening his shirt. "I'll pull dinner from the oven."

It was such a strange thing, not to have to rush to get the food out of the oven in order to run to Mae before she cried herself hoarse. Zach went into his bedroom and picked her up out of the crib. In minutes, he had her changed and dressed in a sweet mint-colored one piece, and then they headed out into the living room once more. Wil had set the battered, second-hand dinette table with Zach's cheap dishes and flatware, the stuffed shells enticingly set in the center. He smiled, hugging Mae to him, and wondered when this would all fall apart on him.

"So domestic," Zach said with a nervous chuckle.

Wil flashed him a wide grin. "Making you nervous?"

Zach wet his lips. "Yeah, it is. It's almost too good to be true." Mae squirmed and kicked in his arms. "Could you set her highchair next to my chair?" It was the newest addition to the baby furniture in the house. "I need to feed her, too."

"Careful," Wil teased. "That almost makes this a family dinner."

"Just get the damn chair," Zach laughed, waving it off when Wil tsked at him for his language. He bounced Mae in his arms as Wil crossed the room to grab the highchair. "Don't look at me like that. My *mom* gives me that look. Stop it."

"Your mother is probably a very lovely woman," Wil said as he brought the highchair over and set it up right next to Zach's seat.

"She is. Both my parents are, really. They wanted me to live with them, but I wanted to be able to raise Mae on my own. I didn't want to end up one of those teen parents who really just let their own parents take care of the kid while they mooch." Zach made a playful little buzzing sound as he flew Mae around in a circle before settling her in her new highchair, adjusting the seat so it leaned back just a little so she was comfortable. "You don't happen to know how to make a bottle of formula, do you?"

"Remember that talk we had about my cousins and second cousins?" Wil asked with a grin.

"All right, all right." Zach could take the hint. He grinned as he kissed Mae and tugged Wil back into the kitchen. "It'll go faster with two people, and then we can actually sit down and eat."

Getting Mae's bottle ready was a snap when Zach had an extra pair of hands. He didn't even have to tell Wil what to do. He barely even had to point. It was as if Wil read his mind, and he swore to himself that the other shoe had to drop soon. It was too perfect to be with a guy who wasn't scared off by Mae and liked helping him out. Wil just seemed so together.

There had to be a weakness there, a chink in Wil's armor that he hadn't caught a glimpse of yet.

They settled in their seats just as Mae was starting to fuss for her bottle. Zach set the infant spoon aside with a small jar of pureed sweet potatoes. "It's coming, princess. We have your dinner right here, see?" Zach cradled her in one arm, holding the bottle in place for her so she could suckle while Wil served up their plates. The smell of the cheesy pasta made his mouth water.

"Oh, what do you want to drink?" Wil stood, heading back into the kitchen.

"Whatever. Everything in there is something I'll drink." Zach pulled the half-consumed bottle from Mae, repositioned her, and opened the jar of sweet potatoes. "Can you bring in a washcloth, too?"

"Sure thing."

Zach thought the whole moment was surreal. Food. Baby. Help. Company. He wasn't alone. Tonight, he wasn't alone, and he had a boyfriend. He put a small bite of the potatoes into Mae's mouth and grinned at her surprised look. "Sweet potatoes. I thought you'd like them," he said with a laugh, feeding her another spoonful.

Wil set two glasses of milk on the table, and then took his seat again. "So, does this mean I'll get to spend time with you here, in the apart-ment?"

"Yes." Zach glanced at him between feeding bites of sweet potato to Mae. He'd kept Wil out of the apartment more often than not, choosing dates out rather than in. "Your wallet can rest assured not *every* date will be out now."

"It's not my wallet I was thinking about." Wil cut into a stuffed shell. "I'm moving into a shared apartment with four other guys. Friends from school, but... goodbye privacy."

Zach looked up. "You don't live on campus?"

Wil chewed and swallow. "This is good. This is... really good. Your mom is an awesome cook."

"I always thought so." Zach shifted Mae in his arms. "You don't live in a dorm?"

"No. I spent my freshman year in a dorm. Sharing an apartment is better than the dorms. Besides, my parents didn't like the cost. They thought it was better economically to share an apartment near campus with some of my friends."

Zach tilted his head. "I thought you had a scholarship."

"Partial." Wil smiled. "My parents pay the uncovered tuition, my books and lab fees, and my rent. I pay my car insurance and cell phone, buy my food, and anything else I want to have."

"That's pretty cool, I guess," Zach said, spooning another bit of sweet potato into Mae's mouth, smiling when she swallowed and gurgled up at him. "I didn't want any help from my parents."

"I noticed that," Wil murmured around another bite. "You've said that they've tried, though."

"Oh, they've tried," Zach chuckled. "I just... I feel like I need to do this, y'know? I need to do this on my own and be a good father to Mae. I don't want to feel like I can't make things work." He shifted a little. "Besides, I might have to ask them for help. I think they're going to start cutting hours at the store. I can't manage with fewer than I currently have," he murmured. The last thing he needed was *less* money coming into the household.

There was a bit of awkward silence as Zach continued to feed Mae, and he had the feeling that Wil wanted to say something, but wouldn't. He could tell it was probably something bad, maybe saying he was crazy for not letting his parents help out. He wasn't sure he would want to hear that, not after how hard he'd been working and how well he had been doing. He started worrying about the silence, but then he saw a smile slowly work its way up onto Wil's face, and Wil leaned over and cut a piece of pasta for him. When Wil offered the bite to him on the fork, he blushed and grinned. "You're going to feed me while I feed Mae?"

"Mmm. Do you have a problem with that?" Wil wiggled the fork a little, enticing him to crane his neck forward.

"I think it's silly. You're silly... but I kinda like it," Zach admitted, taking the bite and moaning softly. His mom really knew how to make pasta dishes. His parents were amazing, always giving and ready to jump to his aid if he needed anything, even though he was determined to do as much as he could on his own. He used the washcloth to wipe Mae's smiling face. "I know how I sound." Zach glanced at Wil. "You think I'm stupid for not taking their money."

"No." Wil's brow furrowed. "No, Zach, I don't. I think your heart is in the right place. You want to be the best father you can be. I respect that. I just think that... well, things might not be so difficult for you and Mae if you'd let your parents help. I mean, you let the charities and state help, why not them?"

Zach blushed. "Those choices were best for Mae."

Wil held out another bite for Zach. "And why wouldn't your parents' help not be best for Mae?"

"Because..." Zach frowned, snatching the bite off the fork. "Because."

"Do you think I'm less because my parents pay for my schooling?"

Zach shook his head. "No. Parents do that. College trust fund and all that."

Wil smiled. "Then call your dad tomorrow and ask them if they'd be willing to help *you* with school. Just like you live for Mae, I'm sure they still live for you. You're their only kid, after all."

"Stop being so logical." Zach shifted Mae from his lap into her swing, setting it on the gentlest setting. "They just gave me the money to fix my car. How can I ask them to give more?"

"Maybe, if you ask them to help with school, you'll have money for things like the car." Wil shrugged, returning to his own meal. "Just a thought." He smiled. "So, what movie were you thinking of for tonight?"

Zach felt his whole body relax at the change of topic. "How about *The Crow*?"

"Oldie, but goodie."

"And... maybe more kissing."

Wil eyes sparkled. "Maybe. If you eat all your dinner."

# Chapter Ten

Leaning against the countertop in his parents' kitchen, Zach plucked another strawberry from the full basket his mom had already hulled. He dipped it into a small dish of sugar and popped it in his mouth. "It's going well," he said.

Mindy looked up at her son, a small smile on her thin lips. "Going well? I don't think there's a week yet you haven't seen Wil. Do you intend to ever let us meet him?"

Zach wrinkled his nose. "Bring the boyfriend home to meet the parents? Nah." He grinned. "Dad would bore him to tears with all the talk about home ownership."

"Your father talks about other things." Mindy began slicing strawberries. "If we're watching Mae so you can go out on dates, you could at least let us meet the boy."

"All right. Soon. Just... not yet." Zach thought back to what Wil had encouraged him to do about his financial situation. He cleared his throat and shifted on his feet. Stalling, he reached out to bounce Mae's carrier, and when Mae smiled up at him, he couldn't help but smile back. "Mom?"

"Mmm?"

Zach glanced from Mae to his mom and back again, who was now peeling some peaches. "My summer classes are almost over, and I'm going to need to register for fall."

"Things go well? I still think you're a glutton for punishment, taking on a compressed summer schedule with a new baby." Mindy held out a large slice of peach. "Give this to Mae. She can gum at it."

"And make a massive mess." A look from his mom and Zach gave Mae the peach slice. "I can't believe she's almost six months old."

Mindy smiled sweetly at him, holding out a peach slice for him. "Time flies, honey. Now, what about school?"

Zach's heart fluttered in his chest, his nerves twisting up his stomach. "I registered back in April for the fall semester, and payment was due last month, but the financial office gave me an extension." He let out a slow breath. "It's more money than I've got at the moment. I don't... I don't think I'll be able to pay for the classes on my own." There, he'd said it. Between Mae having another ear infection and cold from daycare, his car repairs that he'd been determined to pay half of, and the fact they'd cut his hours at work, he just didn't have the money to pay for the classes, and time was running out. "Can you and Dad help?"

"How much is it?" Mindy washed her hands before going to her purse. "Is this a loan thing for you?"

A flush stole across his cheeks as tears filled his eyes. God, he felt like such a child, asking for money and practically ready to sob on his mom's shoulder. "No," he croaked. "I can't pay you back. They hired on a couple of new people at the store, and my hours were cut." Mindy paused, walked over to Zach, and took him into her arms. He'd been doing pretty well until that moment. Once his mom had her arms around him, though, he began to cry.

He was tired. Broke. Barely employed. But, he was trying! Dammit, he was trying so hard, and Wil was great, and Mae was the sweetest thing, and... and he was just *tired*. Zach clung to his mother and cried like he hadn't in years, letting his frustration and anger out with a good sob. Mindy didn't say anything, didn't belittle him or offer useless platitudes. She just held on and combed her fingers through his hair. When he was done, pulling back a little, she had a tissue ready for him and an under-standing smile on her face.

"It's not easy," she murmured. "I know. It's hard as hell, especially when it's just you. But you don't have to do it *all* on your own. Your dad and I, we're here for you."

Zach blew his nose and nodded. "That's what Wil said."

Mindy laughed. "More and more for me to like about this Wil. Now." She walked back to her purse. "How much is the fall semester?"

"Six-thirty. Two three-credit courses, plus the twenty-five dollar late fee," Zach said, reaching for a bottle of water.

"When is Spring Registration?"

Zach took a swallow of his water. "November is registration, and payment is due the first week of December."

Mindy nodded. "All right. November, I'll take you down to HCC myself, we'll make sure you're all registered for the spring and payment is made *on time*." She gave him a wink. "Honey, I am so proud that you're de-termined to do it all on your own, and I think you're a wonderful father to Mae, but sometimes being a wonderful father means reaching out for help. Understand?"

Another flush crept over Zach's face, and he nodded. "I think I'm starting to." He hugged her tightly. "I love you."

"I love you, too. While I write the check, go wipe Mae's face and hands." Mindy laughed. "She's made one hell of a mess out of that peach."

Zach wet some paper toweling and brought it over to Mae. He clucked as he wiped her clean. "Princess, you certainly do know how to make a statement." She kicked her feet and grinned up at him, shoving her fingers into her mess. "Uh-huh. Just as I thought. You're a drama queen."

Mindy held out the check. "She'll balance you out in the long run, then. Keep you on your toes."

Gratefully, Zach accepted the check, folded it, and slid it into his pocket. "Don't encourage her."

"It's a grandmother's prerogative." Mindy ticked Mae's feet. "Isn't it? Yes, it is. If I want to spoil you and send you home to your daddy, that's what I'll do."

Zach rolled his eyes. "Thanks. When's Dad coming home?"

"He should be here in about half an hour." His mom put the cut strawberries in the fridge. "You staying for dinner?"

"Can I?"

Mindy swatted his hip with her dish towel. "Of course you can."

Zach paused. "Wait. What are you making?"

That earned him a glare. "Fried chicken."

"Then I'll stay!" Zach grinned as his mother called him a brat, and then he turned his attention to Mae once more. The check in his pocket eased a lot of his worry, made some of the knots in his gut untangle. It wasn't a permanent solution in his mind, but if his parents wanted to help with school, he wouldn't fight them on it anymore. Mae was too important for him to quibble over the money. "Let's get you fed and changed," he murmured, hefting Mae out of her carrier.

It wasn't perfect, but Zach would take what he could get.

# Chapter Eleven

Zach laughed and pressed closer to Wil as they watched the antics of Robin Williams trying to teach Nathan Lane how to act like a man in *The Birdcage*. Movie night was going really well; their supper was already cleaned up, with half the leftovers packaged up in tupperware for Wil and the other half in his fridge. He loved that Wil always helped him clean up quickly after they'd eaten. He hated having a dirty kitchen, but with Mae trying all kinds of baby food, and even a few kinds of semi-solid foods now, dishes had a way of piling up. Wil was a godsend during these movie nights, trading off between dishes duty and playing with Mae until she was sleepy enough to nap through the movie.

Come to think of it, Wil had been cleaning up just about every mess in his life. Sure, there were things like the kitchen, but Wil's sugges-tion to accept help from his parents had taken the worst of his stress away. Wil still took him out on occasion, and when they brought Mae along, he had no problem helping during a quick diaper change or buying her the next size up of clothing as she started growing like a weed. It felt like every aspect of his life was just falling into place with Wil around, and it made him smile all the time.

He laughed again as Nathan Lane's character struggled to keep his pinky down while drinking a glass of water. "I love how he goes for the most outrageously flamboyant behaviors, all the little details he puts into the character."

Wil chuckled deeply next to him. "You know one of the things I like best about this movie?"

"What?" Zach asked, taking the bait without looking away from the screen.

"Shows two guys who have been together a long ass time... raised a kid together."

That got Zach's attention. He looked up at Wil, a smile slowly working its way up onto his lips. "Go on."

"Well," Wil continued, turning to face him on the sofa, "they've been through it all, you know? They've accepted one another. Armand ac-cepts that Albert is flamboyant and a drag queen and loves him for it. And then, you have Albert..." Wil trailed off as he leaned down and kissed Zach's lips sweetly.

Zach hummed at the attention. "Mmm. What about Albert?"

"He's devoted to Armand. He knew Armand had a kid with Katie, but that didn't stop him from being part of the family, helping raise Val."

Another little kiss, and Zach's cheeks were pink. He could see where Wil was taking this, drawing the parallels between the movie and his own life. He reached up and traced a finger down over the screen print of Wil's t-shirt. "And... you like that, huh? A gay man raising a kid?"

"I especially like that he has someone else around to help, someone who likes him, and who obviously grows to love the kid, too," Wil purred, kissing him again.

He forgot all about the movie, shifting forward into each kiss until he was straddling Wil, brushing his lips across Wil's smile. His heart pounded, his skin already tingling with pleasure just from the light kisses and gentle touches that seemed to come second nature to them both now. "Are you trying to tell me something?"

Wil's chuckle nearly made his toes curl in his socks. "Nothing you don't already know."

Was Wil saying what Zach thought he was? That he loved him? Loved Mae? Wanted to stick around? No, that couldn't be it. Just because he admired Albert for sticking with Armand in the movie and helping to raise Val didn't mean that's what Wil wanted to do with him and Mae. Movies weren't the same as reality. He couldn't get his hopes too high. Every day that Wil didn't run screaming from the craziness of his life with Mae was something to be thankful for. He didn't want to take it for granted. That would just make it hurt all the more when Wil decided enough was enough. And he would decide that eventually, or so Zach almost convinced himself until Wil's lips closed on his again and he lost his train of thought, moaning softly while Wil teased his mouth open into a deeper kiss.

God, it felt so good. Pressed close, the taste of Wil on his tongue, and the way Wil's hands moved on him. Wil stroked up and down his back, squeezed his hips, and pressed their groins closer together. He combed his fingers through Wil's hair—which was always so soft, like cornsilk—and he moaned into the next kiss when their bodies rubbed just right against each other. Zach was so hard that he ached, and then Wil's hands cupped his ass, squeezed.

Zach wanted to pull their clothes off, move against Wil, know what it would feel like to experience what he'd only seen in online porn. And even as Wil's hands slipped under his shirt, touched his bare skin, and their tongues slid along one another, he wanted to pull back. They'd only been together two months, and Mae was in the other room, and he knew *he* didn't have any condoms or lube. By the time Wil's fingers brushed over his nipples, and Wil's mouth moved down his throat, Zach was on that precarious edge of just not caring about anything other than what his body was demanding.

It was that moment Mae decided to remind them of her presence. From in the bedroom, a little sleepy whimper quickly grew into an ear-piercing wail. Zach all but jumped off Wil's lap, wide-eyed, flushed, and panting. What the hell was he doing?

He glanced at the movie. Given that Val's girlfriend's parents were now on the screen, eating dinner with everyone else, they had to have been making out for the last twenty minutes. He'd not even noticed the time. Zach glanced back at Wil, who was just as worked up as him, and another shriek from Mae set him in motion.

He wet his lips as he went into the bedroom, his whole body aching with the lingering arousal. Picking Mae up, he closed his eyes and took several deep breaths, rocking Mae to try and quiet her. Her diaper was heavy. She needed changing. Zach focused on that, picking up her changing blanket and spreading it out over the bed. "Just a minute, princess," he murmured, grabbing what he needed. "I know how uncomfortable a wet diaper must be."

Wil stood in the bedroom doorway, leaning against it with his arms crossed. "Need any help?"

"No," Zach said, pulling the old diaper off and tossing it into the trash. "She just needs changing."

"Does she need a bottle, too?"

Zach closed his eyes and let out a breath. "Yeah. Probably."

"You all right, Zach?"

"No." Zach wiped Mae, cleaning her thoroughly, and then powdered her skin. "I'm not ready, Wil."

Wil frowned. "Not ready for what?"

"For... for what... what on the couch was leading to."

Wil's voice was soft, calm. "What do you think it was leading to?"

Zach glanced over his shoulder at Wil. "Sex."

"Sex?" Wil's eyebrows rose.

"Yes, sex. What else was going to happen?" he asked, perhaps a little too sharply while he secured Mae's diaper.

Wil held up his hands. "I'll fix Mae's bottle."

Zach watched Wil head to the kitchen, and he hefted Mae up, patting her back. Why was he angry? Wil wasn't upset or put out, so why did *he* feel angry about things? Zach laid Mae back into her crib and left the bedroom. He went to the bar separating the kitchen from the living area and leaned against it, watching Wil. "You didn't want to have sex?"

"I didn't say that," Wil said, expertly putting together Mae's bottle.

"Then you did want to have sex?"

Wil huffed out a soft laugh, looking up at him. "It doesn't have to be black and white, you know. Was I turned on and looking forward to that point when we're ready to do more? Yeah. But I wasn't about to pull out a condom and take you right there on the couch with the movie going."

Zach felt his cheeks practically burn. Was he the only one whose mind had gone directly to sex? God, he felt young and stupid next to Wil, who was still so calm and collected. Almost infuriatingly so. He looked down at his socks. "I'm sorry I'm freaking out. I just... this whole situation... I'm not ready to deal with it."

Wil smiled when he looked up, and it was the most understanding, sweet expression that Zach could have hoped for. "That's okay, Zach. Really. Do we need to slow down?"

Zach licked his lips and shifted from foot to foot, uncertain. "I don't know. I *was* enjoying myself. Maybe not slow down, but just... cruise for a while until I can get hold of myself."

Wil's chuckle filled the kitchen, and it just made everything feel all right again for Zach, as if the sound alone had the power to melt away the tension from his shoulders. "All right. A nice, gentle cruise. Now, take this bottle and give me a kiss."

Wil leaned down, puckering his lips in a way that forced a smile onto Zach's face. He shook his head and walked over to Wil, meeting his lips in a quick peck before taking the bottle from Wil. He checked the formula against the inside of his forearm out of force of habit, but it was already at the perfect temperature. Of course. "You're too good for me."

"No, I'm not," Wil said with all the confidence Zach lacked. "You'd better get in there before she starts fussing again. I'll rewind the movie some so we can enjoy Agador and the 'seafood chowder' bit again."

Mae's whining and wordless mumbling drew his attention back to his bedroom, and he leaned up to press another kiss to Wil's lips, letting it linger just long enough to send a tingle down his spine. He smiled at Wil's appreciative hum. "I'll be back in just a couple minutes."

Wil nodded his agreement, and Zach went quickly to tend to Mae. "You're a lifesaver, little one," he confided in a whisper. "Can't go too far until we're sure." Mae gurgled up, clutching at the bottle as she suckled and blinked her big, hazel eyes at him. Mae was looking out for him, in her own way, making him remember what was most important. She was the center of his world, and he needed to keep her in mind whenever his body demanded more with Wil.

Mae seemed to forgive him his weaknesses, though. She drank her formula and burped like a pro, and when he did his best to sing her to sleep, she didn't complain that he was singing a slower, cuter version of Lady Gaga's "Alejandro" instead of a traditional lullaby. He sneaked back into the living room, and found Wil waiting for him with open arms. He'd take it a bit slower until he was sure, but kissing was still all right. With lips like Wil's, he could hardly help indulging, and as he cuddled with Wil on the couch and Wil rubbed at his hip, he almost forgot his own freak out. He'd think about it later. For now, watching the movie and sharing laughter and kisses with his boyfriend was more than enough.

# Chapter Twelve

"You really want to do this?" Zach asked for the fifth time. "I mean, I could have dropped Mae off hours ago—"

At the stoplight, Wil smiled and looked at him. "I'm sure. It's about time I meet your parents. I *want* to meet them, and you said they're eager to meet me."

Zach looked out the window as they drove through The Village, heading to his parents' house. In the backseat, Mae laughed and gurgled in her car seat. Wil had managed a Saturday night off work, and Zach had traded shifts with Piper. They wanted a single weekend where there was no work the next day, no baby needing attention, and they weren't stuck watching another movie on Zach's couch.

Wil had suggested they have a night out. It hadn't sat well with Zach. Anytime Wil took him—or Mae and him—out, it was always this big event. An event Wil never let Zach monetarily contribute to. At first, Zach hadn't cared. Hell, he didn't even know why he cared now. They were dating. Boyfriends. They'd made out more times than Zach could count. Wil adored Mae. So what was a couple dates a month where Wil spent money on them?

What, indeed. Zach sighed. "Are you going to tell me where we're going tonight?"

"Nope." Wil flashed him that boyish smile of his. "Surprise. After working two double shifts, I think you deserve a great night out. Do we have to pick Mae up tonight?"

Zach shook his head. "Mom wants to keep her tonight. I don't mind." He chuckled. "It means I'll be able to sleep in tomorrow." And sleep was a precious commodity for him now. "Turn at the next left. Yeah, there. Two streets down, on the right. The house number is 14382. It has this half-dead rose garden in front."

"Your mom not much of a gardener?"

"Have *you* tried growing anything in Florida?" Zach laughed as they pulled into the driveway. "It's impossible. She tried really hard with those roses, but... yeah. No. It didn't work. The pansies didn't last, either."

Once Wil shut the car off, Zach sat there listening to the engine tick softly. Mae slammed her rattle about and gave a squeal, and Zach let out a slow breath. This was it. He was bringing the boyfriend home. His first boyfriend. The silly stuff he'd tried in high school before Bethany wasn't like what he had with Wil, and this was serious. Serious-serious. His heart was pounding, and he knew he had to unbuckle his seatbelt, get Mae and her supplies, and actually go inside, but he just *couldn't* move.

"Zach?"

Zach's head snapped to the side, his eyes wide, and he stared at Wil. "Huh?"

"You still breathing over there? Or do I need to call the paramedics?"

Zach tried to swallow, but his mouth and throat were too dry. "I can't go in there. I can't risk you hating one another."

Wil reached over and squeezed his shoulder before fiddling with his hair. "You worry too much. Your parents are gonna love me, and I'm sure I'll like them, too."

"You're so sure of yourself," Zach whispered. "And here I am forgetting how to work my seatbelt I'm so nervous."

Wil chuckled and reached down, pushing the button that released the buckle of his seatbelt. "One step at a time. Get out of the car, and then open up the door and disentangle Mae from her car seat. I'll grab her bag of goodies." Zach hesitated, and Wil flicked his shoulder. "Out."

He might have been scared shitless, but his body followed Wil's orders without conscious input. He stepped stiffly from the car, but his attempt at a deep breath was foiled by cloying humidity. He coughed several times before opening the back door and reaching for Mae. The rest was automatic, and he cradled Mae against him, smiling at her nonsensical babbling and the way she tugged at her shoes. "She's going to want those shoes off the instant we get inside."

"Let's get in there fast. It's sweltering out here!"

The words were heartfelt, but Zach also knew it was a way to spur him forward, to get him to the door. His heart leaped into his throat again at the landing, as he looked awkwardly toward the door. Usually, he just let himself in. He had a key of his own, after all. But it just felt more formal with Wil there. Mae began to fuss and shift, not liking the humidity that made even the shade unbearable. Ring the bell or not ring the bell? Damn it, it was his home. There was no question. Zach turned the knob and stepped inside, the blast of the air conditioning a small blessing.

After they adjusted to the dimmer light inside the house, Zach's eyes landed on his dad sitting on the couch. To Zach, his dad didn't look a day over thirty, young and fit, and the minute Daniel Ayres' eyes fell on Mae, a bright smile curved his tanned face. Daniel stood, clicked off the television, and reached for his granddaughter.

"My!" Daniel laughed. "She's gotten so big."

"Maybe you should be in town more often," Zach said, handing Mae off to his dad. "She's rolling about, almost crawling now. Won't be long before she's a walking terror."

Daniel tsked. "My Mae could never be a terror of anything." He looked at Wil. Shifting Mae in his arms, he held out a hand to Wil. "I'm going to assume you're Wil. I'm Daniel, Zach's dad."

Wil grinned, shook Daniel's hand. "A pleasure to meet you, sir."

"Sir?" Daniel looked at Zach. "Manners, too. Maybe he can teach you some."

Zach rolled his eyes. "Where's Mom?"

"In the kitchen. Go on in. I'll keep Mae entertained."

Wil rested his hand on Zach's back. "Just take her sandals off. Her feet are fascinating to her."

"Noted," Daniel said, taking Mae back to the couch.

"Come on." Zach headed through the living room and into the kitchen. His mom was at the stove, and whatever she was cooking smelled amazing. "Hey, Mom."

Mindy turned and smiled. "Zach! I didn't hear you come in." Her eyes shifted to behind Zach. "Wil, I presume?"

Wil held out his hand to her. "Yes, ma'am."

"Lord, ma'am? Do I really look that old?" she asked, shaking Wil's hand.

"Not at all," Wil said. "You look like you could be Zach's older sister."

A little blush colored Mindy's cheeks, and Zach chuckled. "Thank you, Wil," she said, turning back to the stove. "Where are you two going tonight?"

Zach shrugged. "Wil's keeping it a big secret."

"I like surprising him." Wil gave Zach a little hug.

Mindy smiled. "You'll have to tell me all about it when you pick Mae up tomorrow, Zach."

Grumbling, Zach nodded. "I will. If I don't, you might refuse to send me home with leftovers."

"If holding leftovers hostage is the only way to learn about my own son's life..."

"Drama queen," Zach teased.

Mindy waved her wooden spoon at him. "This coming from *you*?"

"You two are adorable," Wil laughed. "I see where Mae gets it from."

Zach glared at Wil, but it was Mindy who said, "You're sweet. Maybe a little crazy, but sweet." She glanced at Zach again and tapped her spoon at him one last time. "Gossip for leftovers, Zach. And do you have time for a soda or anything?"

Wil smiled. "Unfortunately, no. It's a bit of a drive down to the restaurant, and if we're going to make the reservation, we'll have to get moving. Thanks for the invitation, though. Maybe some other night?"

Mindy's eyes lit up, and Zach stepped forward, trying to cut in before she could embarrass him too much. "Yeah. Some other night, Mom, and we'll figure it out later once we've finalized our school schedules and... and..."

"You'll have your people call my people?" Mindy rolled her eyes. "All right, all right. Off with you both. I'd love to have you over for dinner some other night when you're not sweeping my son off his feet, Wil."

"It'll be a pleasure, Mrs. Ayres," Wil said with a broad grin. He stepped forward for a moment as if he were about to whisper a secret into Mindy's ear, but when he spoke, his voice carried easily. "When you get us both over here, you can show me baby pictures or something equally embarrassing."

"I heard that!" Zach scoffed, though he couldn't help but laugh as he tugged Wil back to his side. "Come on. Embarrassing pictures can wait until the *second* date with the parents. Or the fifth. Maybe the fifth." Wil led him back out to the living room, and Daniel looked up. Zach finally passed over Mae's diaper bag. "I think everything you need is in there."

"If not, we have plenty of stuff in the nursery." Daniel chuckled as Mae stuck her foot into her mouth. "We'll be fine. Have fun."

"We will." Zach leaned down and kissed Mae. "Be a good girl. Daddy loves you." He hated leaving her behind, even with his own parents. It was like part of his heart was ripped out every time he left her somewhere. A tug on his hand, and Zach stood up, pressed close to Wil's side.

"I'll see you guys in the morning." Within moments, goodbyes were said and Wil had him back in the car. Zach shifted in the front seat, glancing back at Mae's empty car seat. He immediately wanted to go back in after her.

Wil turned on the car and put it in reverse. "It's all right," he said, reaching out to squeeze Zach's thigh. "Mae's safe."

"It's not about safe." Zach watched the house until Wil turned the corner, and then he focused on the road ahead. "I hate leaving her behind. It just tears me up inside."

"I understand, but you need time to be Zach sometimes, instead of just Mae's dad."

Zach frowned at Wil. "I'm always Mae's dad. That doesn't stop just because she's with my parents."

Wil sighed. "That didn't come out right, I'm sorry. I meant, having a few hours where you can eat, laugh, and be an adult isn't so bad. Mae's with her grandparents, who—from my very brief interaction with them—seem to be very nice folks."

A bashful smile made it to Zach's lips. "I did rush you, didn't I?"

"Just a little." Wil turned onto Dale Mabry Highway and headed south toward downtown. "It's all right, though. You were nervous."

"Weren't you?"

"Yeah, but I tried to play it as cool as I could."

Zach nodded and looked out the window. "I could tell my mom already liked you. Give it a couple months with frequent visits, and she'll call you the second son she never had." Part of the family. A warm feeling settled in Zach's chest at the thought. "Invite you to our small family gatherings. Nothing like your family, though."

Wil shook his head as they stopped at a traffic light. "My family's crazy. No one has time for anyone else because everyone's got someone demanding their attention. If it isn't a charity function, then it's a luncheon or a business trip or something else more important than a Sunday dinner."

"We don't have Sunday dinners at my house," Zach pointed out.

"No, but you do spend time with your parents. You bring Mae over at least twice a week." Wil shrugged. "Which probably says more about me than my parents. Maybe I don't make time for them. I don't know. It's just... the way things are. Crazy holidays, but pretty dull in between."

Zach nodded as he began to relax into his seat. Wil's life, while filled with so many family members, seemed to be missing the intimacy

Zach enjoyed with his family. Maybe he could share that intimacy with Wil, share his parents and grandparents. He smiled to himself and flipped on the radio. Alternative rock filled the car, and he was soon singing along. As he watched restaurants and businesses fly by in the night, he wondered —yet again—where Wil was taking him... and just how shocked he would be when they arrived.

# Chapter Thirteen

Zach stared at the building in front of them. No way. There was *no way* Wil had made reservations here. He eyes darted to Wil. "You've got to be kidding."

"Nope." Wil held out his arm. "Shall we?"

"Wil, Bern's is *expensive*." Zach threaded his arm through Wil's. "I... I can't imagine the cost. It's probably enough to pay my power bill *and* buy groceries for a week."

They entered the lobby of the restaurant, and Wil gave his name to the hostess. "Maybe, maybe not. I wanted to treat you to a great night out before school starts. My classload is pretty heavy, plus I have to work evenings. Between classes, homework, and work..."

Zach flushed. "I know. Once school starts, what little time I've had will vanish. All right. I suppose this *one* night is all right."

Wil kissed his cheek, uncaring of those around them. "Thank you. Enjoy yourself. And, if you don't want to stress over how much dinner will cost, I can always order for you."

"Like a gentleman?"

A laugh rumbled from Wil, and Zach's toes curled in his loafers. "Yes," Wil murmured. "Like a proper gentleman."

The hostess pulled a couple menus from the desk next to her kiosk and led them from the entry into a dining room. Zach's grip on Wil's arm tightened as he took in the formal space. The stone walls were made warm somehow by the wood beams accenting the ceiling, and everything was bathed in a soft, golden glow from lamps. It made him feel like a celebrity to be escorted down the red carpet of the restaurant to their table, and he had to stifle a nervous giggle when Wil even pulled out his chair for him. He sat and tried to get his breathing back to normal as Wil took his own seat. The effort seemed in vain, though.

"Hey," Wil said once the hostess had excused herself. "You're look-ing a little lost over there." He held out his hand across the white tablecloth, and Zach blushed as he reached over and clasped it. "Just breathe. It's a spe-cial night, but I don't want it to be memorable because you gave yourself a coronary."

Zach chuckled and scooted forward in his chair so he could lean closer to Wil over the table. "I've never been to a place like this. I feel underdressed, out of place. I should have worn a tie."

"You look fine," Wil said, leaning down to kiss Zach's knuckles. "If anyone's staring, it's because you look amazing in blue."

Zach smiled, glancing down at his dress shirt and slacks before looking at Wil again. "It doesn't hurt that I'm with the hottest guy in the room."

"Flatterer," Wil accused, but it got his knuckles another kiss before Wil let go to gesture at the menu. "Do you want to help choose the appetizer?"

Zach eyed the menu, feeling his pulse creep up again. "I'll give it a try, but no promises," he murmured, warily opening the menu and skipping forward to the appetizer page. He tried. He truly did try to just look at the names of the appetizers and their descriptions, but how could he miss the distinctive dollar sign and all the numbers after it? The first page was nothing but fish and shellfish, and his eyes skimmed over the contents before stumbling at the seared tuna and *escargot*. God, they served actual *escargot*, and there were words in French that he didn't understand; he skipped ahead and saw an entire page of caviar. He snapped the menu closed again, his eyes squeezed shut against prices that were the equivalent of an entire week's paycheck.

"Zach?"

He shook his head. "I can't, Wil. You're spending a fortune on me, and last week, you bought all that stuff for Mae. You *forced* me to go shopping for Mae." It was grating at him, the way Wil didn't mind throwing money at him every few weeks, and even though the anger seeped into his panicked voice, it didn't seem to phase Wil.

"Well, Mae's growing fast and needed a few new outfits."

"But I wouldn't have even *let* you do it if you hadn't threatened to buy nothing but pink stuff for her," Zach huffed.

"Hey, it was a gift, and you and Mae had a ball looking through things and picking out that polka-dot dress of hers." Zach didn't have a witty response to that, and when he nodded his defeat, Wil grinned at him. "Don't worry about the prices, Zach. It's a special night, remember? I'm taking care of it, and I can order so you can just enjoy all the food. Trust me?"

Zach took in a calming breath and let it out slowly. This wasn't the time for little frustrations. Wil was going to pay for it all no matter what he

did, so all he could do was resign himself to an amazing meal. "I trust you. I just... money shock. I'll get over it." He smiled and glanced around for a second before leaning forward, offering Wil a quick kiss that Wil eagerly accepted. Settling back into his seat, he let Wil order for him when the waiter came by to introduce himself. A Maine lobster cocktail and some of the house potato wedges for them to share, along with their entrées, and the waiter was off to get their drinks. Zach breathed a sigh of relief, but curiosity and his sweet tooth got the better of him after a couple minutes. "No desserts?"

"They'll take us to a different room upstairs for that," Wil murmured. "And they have a lot of choices I know you'll love, so be sure to leave a little room and take your time. A place like this won't rush us out."

"They have a whole dining room just to serve desserts?" Holy hell, Zach's head spun.

Wil squeezed his hand again. "It'll be all right. Enjoy it. Don't know when we'll be able to do it again," he said with a wink.

When their appetizer came—and it looked decadent and rich—Zach had to ask, "Why are fish eggs so expensive? That Russian caviar was almost *two hundred dollars* an ounce!"

"A lot of work goes into harvesting fish eggs." Wil dove into the lobster cocktail. "Most fisheries kill the female fish in order to harvest the eggs."

"It seems like such a waste." Zach frowned.

"Nah. They send the meat out to market, too. Nothing goes to waste."

"How in the world do you know about caviar production?"

"I know a little bit about everything useless."

That brought a chuckle out of Zach. "I bet you know a lot about many things that are quite useful, too."

"Maybe I do." Wil held out a forkful of the lobster cocktail. "Try it."

Zach fought the heat that threatened to creep up onto his cheeks as he leaned forward and took the bite into his mouth. He moaned softly as he chewed. The lobster was so fresh, and the sauce that Wil had dipped it into was just amazing. "What's in that?" he asked after swallowing, gesturing to the sauce, his mouth tingling with a pleasant burn.

"They make a fantastic ginger sauce, don't they? I've tried to make it on my own, but it just never tastes this good from my kitchen."

"You're welcome to try it out at my kitchen anytime," Zach offered with a grin. He had a few bites of the seasoned potato wedges, making little sounds of pleasure with nearly every bite. He couldn't help it; whatever they put into the sauces here was just magical. There was no way he could identify it off the top of his head, but he knew great flavors when he tasted them, and every bite was blissful. When Wil offered to feed him another bite of the lobster cocktail, he didn't even think twice, and they fell into a wonderful rhythm, exchanging small talk between little bouts of silence when eating with one another was a pleasure unto itself.

Their salads came next, but Zach knew if he ate too quickly or rushed into the main course, there was no way he would have room at the end of the night for dessert. The sweets at the end were always his favorite part of the meal, so he made a conscious effort to slow down and savor every bite. Not that savoring was difficult when the quality of the food was through the roof.

It didn't matter, though, how he paced himself. When their server set down his steak with the half dozen sides, Zach could only voice one response. "No way."

Wil laughed. "You can do it. There's no rush."

"I've never been fed so much! Wil, really, this is crazy."

"You told me I couldn't take you out for your birthday—even though eighteen is a big deal in my mind—so I have to get in the fancy dinner *now*, before school starts and before your birthday." Wil grinned. "This is, therefore, all your own doing."

Zach moaned. "I'll keep that in mind when my twenty-first birthday rolls around."

"I have three whole years to plan that celebration."

Warmth suffused Zach's cheeks, and he smiled to himself as he sliced into his steak. Wil was thinking three years into the future. Three years. Mae would be turning four, he'd be turning twenty-one, and maybe Wil would still be around. Zach's heart fluttered. Wil around three years from now, celebrating another milestone birthday with him. He *really* liked that idea.

# Chapter Fourteen

His mom bounced Mae on her hip, and Zach laughed as his dad brought in the elaborately decorated birthday cake with twenty candles—eighteen to mark his actual age, plus one to grow on and one more for luck—glowing on top. He was surrounded by his family and friends, Wil at his side as the cake was set in front of him.

"Make a wish!" Samantha crowed, and Sophia squealed in her high-chair.

Zach closed his eyes and thought for a moment. A wish. His birthday wish. *I wish... I wish for a better life for Mae and me.* He took a deep breath and blew out all the candles in one try, blushing slightly at the chorus of laughter and claps. Eighteen. He was eighteen today. Eighteen with a seven-month-old baby, but eighteen. An adult. A *true* adult, not just one by circumstance. As cake was sliced, ice cream dished out, and everyone talked around him, Zach shifted in his chair, a little disappointed.

Eighteen years old and he didn't feel any different than he had yesterday when he was still seventeen. Wasn't something miraculous supposed to happen today? Wasn't he supposed to feel differently now? He was an adult, able to vote and sign contracts without his parents, but...

"What's wrong?" Wil murmured, putting the biggest slice of cake in front of him.

Zach turned his head and smiled at Wil. "Nothing. I just... expected to feel different today."

Wil hummed and squeezed his thigh. "Because you're eighteen now. It's a big deal, even if it doesn't really *feel* like one now that you're here. I remember feeling sort of like that, a mix of excitement and let down. You don't suddenly grow three inches or become a billionaire or anything like that, but... you made it. Eighteen years is a long time to have been around, and it means you really get to make your own decisions."

Zach chuckled. "Like I haven't been doing that for a while now?"

"You're a special case," Wil laughed, nudging him. "The difference is that now you really start making your life your own. You decide what you want most out of life, and you go after it, even if it means no one is holding your hand."

Zach let out a slow breath. "That's kind of scary. You're taking away my appetite, you know."

Wil gave him a quick hug from behind. "Does it make it less scary if I promise I'll be holding your hand for a while yet?"

The thought did perk him up considerably, and he grinned, squeezing Wil's arms around him. "Actually, yeah. That makes me feel like I can take on the world."

"Good." Wil pecked a kiss to his cheek, and reached out in front of him, taking his fork from the plate and sticking it decisively into the center of his helping of cake. "The whole world can start with this piece of birthday cake. Conquer it, and you conquer yourself."

Zach laughed, and God, it felt good to just laugh. "How am I supposed to act like an adult when you're teasing me like that?"

"Who said you had to act like an adult on your birthday, huh? Now, eat your cake, birthday boy," Wil ordered with a grin. Zach couldn't find any reason to protest.

"You sure you don't mind?" Zach asked for the third time, hugging Mae to him. Everyone had already gone home, and he and Wil were the last to trickle from his parents' house.

Daniel reached for his granddaughter. "We're sure. It's your birthday. The little princess can stay with us. You can pick her up tomorrow after your shift."

Zach shifted from foot to foot, pressing a kiss to Mae's fuzzy head. "I don't want to impose." The party had been great, Wil had already loaded the dozen birthday gifts into the car, and Zach had pocketed the hundred dollar bill his parents had given him in a card. The plan had been to leave Mae with his folks and go back to his apartment, for some alone time together, and Zach knew what that could mean. "I don't know if I brought enough diapers, after all."

"Zach." Mindy smiled. "I have plenty of diapers. If you don't want to leave Mae, it's all right."

Wil frowned a little. "Something wrong, Zach?"

A flush crept up Zach's face. "No. I hate being away from her, that's all." Which was a half-truth, but he certainly couldn't say he wanted Mae home with him because Wil might be less likely to make a move on him. Besides, he *wanted* Wil to make a move, right? Zach handed Mae over to his dad. "My shift ends at seven. I should be here by eight to pick her up."

"We'll be waiting," Daniel said, settling Mae on his hip. "Everything will be all right."

Mindy leaned in and gave Zach a kiss. "Happy birthday, baby."

Zach grinned. "Thanks for the great party."

"Our only son turns eighteen, we have a great bash," Daniel said. "See you tomorrow night. We love you."

"I love you, too."

Wil gave a wave from the porch. "Thanks for having me. It was great seeing you all again."

"It was fun having you around," Mindy said. "Come by with Zach anytime."

"Will do," Wil said. "'Night!"

And then they were back in Wil's car, seatbelts fastened and Wil pulling out into the street. Zach stared at his hands in his lap, his heart pounding. They were on their way home. Alone. And he was eighteen. Eighteen meant Wil might want more than kissing. Was he ready for more than kissing? God, he didn't think so. Or did he? He jacked off almost nightly thinking about Wil, about what Wil might do with him when there wasn't the silent legal barrier between them. Yeah, he might have been on his own with a kid, but seventeen was seventeen, and he wasn't seventeen anymore.

"Hey, you all right?" Wil asked, his voice soft, careful.

Zach swallowed thickly and tried to play it casual. "Yeah. I'm good." His voice came out a little too high, though, and the words sounded clipped to his own ears. He didn't even have to look over to Wil to know he'd earned an odd look. He sighed, closing his eyes and fighting the urge to bury his face in his hands. He had to be cool. Calm was supposed to be the name of the game in these situations.

Wil's hand touched his leg, and he practically jumped out of his seat, his heart in his throat even as he inwardly cursed himself. So much for being calm. At least Wil wasn't as jumpy, his hand a steady, comforting presence at Zach's thigh. "Nothing to be so nervous about."

It sounded like a promise, but all Zach wanted to do was shout how there *was* something to be nervous about! He was eighteen. That meant a lot of things, but one of the big ones was just waiting at his apartment for them to arrive, like some predator ready for the right moment to strike. He saw it coming, but he didn't think he could dodge. He wasn't sure he *wanted* to dodge. He kept his mouth shut and did his best not to fidget as Wil drove one-handed the rest of the way to his apartment.

They practically ran from the car to the apartment door, trying desperately to get inside and away from the suffocatingly muggy night. Once they were safely inside, the cool air making their skin prickle, Wil breathed a sigh of relief and nudged one of Mae's toys aside with his sneaker, heading for the bookshelf housing Zach's DVD collection. "So, what'll it be?"

Zach frowned, rubbing his arms against the sudden chill of the cold air. Had he misread this whole thing? Did Wil really just want to cuddle up for a movie and nothing more? He wasn't sure why the thought disappointed him so much. He was scared of the alternative, but movie night happened all the time, and tonight was supposed to be special.

"What's that look for?" Wil asked, turning and slowly approaching him.

Zach felt his heart pound harder with each step Wil took. "What do you want to do?" he asked, unable to keep the confusion from his voice.

Wil gave him one of those gorgeous smiles and reached over to comb through his hair. It was an affectionate touch he was often given nowadays, but tonight it sent a shiver down his spine. "We can do anything you like. You're the birthday boy."

Zach just knew his cheeks were starting to flush up as he stared into Wil's eyes. "You mean you don't want to...?" God, he couldn't even say it, and the spark he saw glint in Wil's eyes just made him feel more embarrassed.

"I'd love to, Zach," Wil almost purred, but his eyes were serious as he continued, "but only if you're ready. I'm perfectly all right with a movie and giving you eighteen kisses. All I want is for this to be your best birthday yet."

"It has been," Zach insisted. "Having everyone at my parents', Mae laughing and happy, you being there with me, it's been a *great* birthday."

Wil drew his finger along Zach's jaw. "But?"

Zach's breath caught. "But... I'm scared, all right? I'm scared of this moment."

"You've had sex before," Wil said, eyebrow quirked. "Mae's proof of that."

Rolling his eyes, Zach sighed. "That was with Bethany. This would be with you. I might not be a virgin-virgin, but I'm a *boy*-virgin," he blurted out.

Wil laughed. Zach couldn't blame him, and he was soon laughing with Wil. "A boy-virgin?" Wil asked. He hugged Zach, kissing the top of his head. "I don't think I've ever heard *that* particular phrase."

"Well, it's the truth," Zach murmured against Wil's shoulder. "The most I'd done before you with another guy was hold hands and steal kisses behind the Ag building at school. Making out with you was... like... a *huge* step."

"I know." Wil tilted Zach's head back and kissed him softly. "We don't have to have sex right now, Zach. It's all right. Eighteen isn't a magic number. If you're not ready, then you're just not ready."

Zach shook his head. "But I am. I think. I don't know!" He was tying himself up in knots, and he wasn't sure that was an answer, either. He rose up onto his toes and brushed his lips against Wil's. "If we went into my bedroom and sat on my bed... and I kissed you..."

Wil moaned softly. "I'd kiss you back."

"And if I took my shirt off... helped you off with yours...?" Zach swallowed, staring up into Wil's eyes. "Would you touch me?"

"Yes," Wil breathed, his tongue darting out to brush along Zach's. "I'd touch as much as and wherever you allowed me to."

Zach slid his hands up Wil's back, gripped at Wil's shirt. "And if I can't go all the way?"

Wil smiled. "Then we go as far as you can, and when the time's right, we'll go the rest of the way."

"Okay." Zach let out a slow, soft breath. "Come into my bedroom?"

"I'd love to," Wil said just before their lips met fully.

The kiss lasted from the front entry of Zach's apartment all the way back into his bedroom. It took a little doing, but they managed to avoid the discarded clothes and Mae's scattered toys. Zach's toes curled each time Wil's tongue slid against his or Wil's hands squeezed his hips or ass. It felt so good, so right, even if Zach wasn't a hundred percent sure that they'd really have sex tonight. Maybe it would just be more of the heavy making out, just in bed this time. When Wil's hands gripped the hem of his shirt, and their lips finally parted, Zach was hard in his jeans, and when Wil pressed their bodies together, he could feel the hard heat of him, too. At least he wasn't the only one driven crazy by the kisses.

Zach lifted his arms, and once his shirt was lifted up and off him, tossed aside, he couldn't help but blush. Sure, Wil had seen him with his shirt off before. They'd gone out to the pool together with Mae, Samantha, and Sophia, and it hadn't seemed like a big deal to be in his swimming trunks. That had been a social gathering, and this was so much more intimate. Wil was going to touch his bare skin, and the moment of anticipation made his pulse flutter.

Wil's fingers hovered over his skin, and their eyes met for a moment before he breathed, "Go ahead. I... I want you to touch me." It seemed to be exactly what Wil needed to hear, and he choked back a groan as Wil's warm hands finally ran broadly down his torso from neck to jeans. He pulled Wil down into another kiss, and his knees went weak when a brush of thumbs against his nipples forced a moan from him. He was soon drowning in Wil's kisses, pressing eagerly forward into hands that were so gentle in their touches to his skin. He pulled back only to keep from collapsing, and even then, he could feel a smile on his face. He started tugging Wil's shirt up, laughing breathlessly. "I think... I need to sit."

"We can do that," Wil chuckled. The moment after he peeled Wil's shirt the rest of the way off, Wil grabbed him and yanked him down to the bed. He was forced to straddle Wil in order to catch himself from landing in a heap, and something told him that had been Wil's intent all along. The pressure of his jeans was torturous, but the position put their lips at the perfect level for kissing, and he couldn't help but kiss Wil as he worked up the courage to touch along the lines of Wil's torso and the light muscle definition he'd admired at the pool whenever he thought Wil wasn't looking.

When his lips were numb from all the kissing, Zach sat back, panting, staring down at Wil beneath him. Wil was sexy. There was no denying it, or the effect Wil had on his own body. Zach was uncomfortably hard, and he could easily feel the line of Wil's cock against him when they rubbed together. That, Zach thought, was one hell of a turn-on. He licked his lips as he looked down at Wil's chest, and his fingers trailed along the golden-hued skin, his thumbs brushing over Wil's nipples. The moan Wil uttered was enough to send a shiver down Zach's spine.

"You're gorgeous," Zach whispered. "Would it sound stupid to say I've been fantasizing about this moment for months?"

Wil hissed when Zach's fingers pinched at his nipples. "No more stupid than if I admitted the same thing." Wil's hands slid up Zach's thighs, his thumbs brushing near his crotch. "You look so good right now."

Zach couldn't help his flush. "Yeah?"

"Yeah."

Wil pulled him down for another kiss. It was sweet and slow, and Zach was soon thrusting against Wil. He almost stopped the minute he realized he was doing it, but the low moan Wil let out bolstered his resolve. He pulled away from Wil's sinful lips and trailed kisses down his throat, his fingers playing with Wil's nipples, trying for more of those gorgeous sounds. His heart was racing, his body hard and ready, but still he hesitated to let his fingers move lower, to finally touch what he could feel through their jeans.

Wil wasn't nearly as uncertain, and he was glad of it. While he hesitated to touch, he could feel Wil's hands kneading at the muscles of his hips, lower back, and ass. When he pulled back to take a breath, Wil panted against his lips, "May I touch you?" Touch him? Wil was already touching him, and it felt amazing. His pause must have conveyed his thoughts, because Wil chuckled, and his hands moved forward, whispering over Zach's groin. "Touch you here?"

Zach groaned, wiggling his hips up to meet Wil's hand. He could say no, stop things from going any further, but he didn't want to. He wanted to feel Wil's hands all over him, and that definitely included the skin still hidden beneath his jeans. "Yes," he breathed, a smile quirking his lips upward. "Please."

Wil grinned and leaned forward to kiss and nip along his neck, and when Wil suckled over his pulse, it nearly distracted him from the tug and pull of denim over his groin. Nearly, but not quite. He was almost light-headed by the time his fly was down, and he trembled when Wil nudged him up so his boxers could be pushed down a bit. His cheeks flared with heat, and a wave of nervousness overcame him when Wil pulled back from his neck and looked down. Wil had to be more experienced than he was, had to have seen at least a handful of guys naked. How would he compare? He'd never felt so self-conscious about his size in his entire life.

"S-sorry I'm not..." He couldn't even finish the sentence. He was just sorry if he was a disappointment after making Wil wait for so long.

"Don't be sorry," Wil murmured, his voice so warm, so soothing as he looked up into Zach's eyes. "You're perfect. Just perfect."

The words alone would have been enough to make him flush, but they were joined by a light caress of Wil's fingers along his shaft that made him gasp with pleasure. The light touch was followed by the heat of Wil's palm closing around him, and he cried out at the first stroke. It felt far too good, and he just knew he was going to embarrass himself and come in seconds if Wil kept touching him like that.

"Wil—" was all Zach could choke out before his back bowed sharply and he came all over Wil's stomach. The pleasure of it was immense, but it was tempered by pure, unadulterated embarrassment. He flushed brightly. "I'm so sorry!" he said, reaching for tissues. "God, I'm such a dork, and I—"

Wil stopped him, their faces near one another, and he was smiling. "Zach, calm down." He kissed Zach softly, sweetly. "It's all right. You're new at this. I didn't expect you to last long the first time. It's cool. I was the same way."

"You were?" Zach whispered.

"Yeah, I was. I promise. I blew the minute my ex had his hand down my jeans. Made a huge mess, and I had to find a way to explain the wet stain to my sister when I slunk back home." Wil nipped at Zach's lower lip. "You wanna know the bonus to being new at it all?" he purred.

Zach shifted on Wil's lap, moaning softly. "Yeah, I do."

"It means you have amazing rebound time," Wil said, his eyes sparkling.

"And what about you?" Zach said, rolling his hips forward against Wil's groin.

Wil groaned. "Me? I think I could do with a hell of a lot less clothing between us."

Zach laughed, much more at ease with Wil's encouragement. He wiggled his way back off of Wil's lap, and stood next to the bed. His jeans and boxers were down at his feet in seconds, and he attempted to hide himself for just a moment by bending down and distracting Wil with another kiss. He wasn't sure if Wil wanted to undress himself or not, but Wil's hand closed around his and guided him to the fly of his pants. He could feel the hardness pressing up against the denim, and it made him shudder. "You're so hard."

"And it's all your fault," Wil moaned. "I want you to touch me. Are you afraid to?"

Zach swallowed against a dry throat. "To touch you?" Wil nodded, and he blushed. "A little. Kind of scared I'll disappoint you."

Wil pulled Zach's hand up to the button and zipper of his jeans, and then tipped Zach's face upward so their eyes met. "You won't disappoint. I don't think it's possible for you to disappoint me, Zach. Try not to be afraid. I'll like anything you do."

Zach still wasn't sure, but it was now or never. He wanted to impress Wil, to make the night just as memorable for Wil as it had been for him. With a steadying breath, he smiled and flicked open the button of Wil's jeans. Wil arched back to give him a little space, but he could feel Wil's eyes on him as he slowly pulled the zipper down and hooked his fingers over denim and cotton to pull everything down past Wil's hips. He couldn't help but blush when Wil's erection sprang free.

"You okay?" Wil asked, and Zach blinked, suddenly realizing he had been staring for a while, his hands having stilled completely in pulling Wil's clothes off.

"You're—" His voice cracked like a twelve-year-old's, and he flushed deeply as he cleared his throat and tried again. "You're larger than I thought."

Wil grinned, and it was a smug grin at that. "Really?"

Zach nodded. "Yeah." He pulled Wil's jeans and boxers the rest of the way off, and then kicked off his socks. He bit his lower lip. "I... I'm not sure what to do."

"Touch me." Wil took Zach's hand in his and brought it to his cock. "Please?"

It was the 'please' that did it. Zach wrapped his fingers around Wil and stroked. The sound it pulled from Wil went straight to Zach's cock. He hadn't believed he could get hard again so soon, but the combination of Wil's sounds, the heat of his skin, and just how erotic this moment was brought the blood rushing back to his cock. Zach licked his lips, pumping his hand up and down, unsure of what else he should do. He needed direction, but he didn't want to *ask* Wil.

"Kiss me?" Wil asked, arm outstretched. "I'd love to feel you against me."

"Against you? Like... laying on top of you?"

Wil smiled. "We could do that, if you like, or I can be on top. Either would feel amazing."

"I think I'd like you to be on top," Zach murmured. Wil knew more than he did, and he'd much rather follow Wil's lead rather than stumbling around blindly. "I like the idea of just... rubbing against each other. Does that sound too half-assed to you?"

Wil sat up, cupped his cheek, and pulled him into a slow, deep kiss. "Not half-assed at all, but you will have to let go of my cock so I can switch places with you."

Zach laughed, blushing again, and released Wil's cock. "God, I am such a dork."

"But I like you that way," Wil assured him, shifting until Zach was spread out in the middle of the bed. Wil eased his legs apart, and it left Zach feeling utterly exposed for a few seconds. Wil was quick, though, and lowered himself down, pressing their bodies against one another fully for the first time.

Zach gasped and gripped tightly at Wil's hips. He'd never imagined it could feel this good, this *right*, to simply be laying down with someone. He could feel Wil's erection perfectly, hot and silky against his skin, pressed right alongside his own revived cock. The warmth, the pressure, the puff of Wil's shaky moan against his lips, everything was just wonderful. He arched up, his lips seeking and finding Wil's. He hadn't known what he wanted, but now that he had Wil so close, he knew this was it. He felt safe, secure, and with the way Wil kissed him, he had never felt so cherished.

Wil rocked into him, rubbing their cocks alongside one another, and Zach's startled moan was quickly devoured by Wil's kisses. He'd never thought just being naked with someone else could be so erotic, and when Wil's tongue did one of those wicked curls against his, he pulled back to gasp and shudder.

"Feel good?"

Such a simple question, but it made Zach grin as he panted up at Wil. "God, yeah." Another perfect shift of Wil's hips made him moan, and he arched his neck, closing his eyes, enjoying every moment. Wil's lips trailed over his neck, and his pulse fluttered up to meet the touches. A nip to the tender skin made him shiver, his grip on Wil's shoulders tightening.

"Ever had a hickie before?" Wil breathed against his ear.

Zach laughed, though it trailed into another moan when Wil blew gently against the lobe of his ear. "N-No."

"Mmm, you will in a minute," Wil promised before returning to his neck.

The nips were stronger now, and they were joined by suction that made Zach's toes curl. He cried out, rubbing against Wil, who continued to thrust against him, pressing him firmly into the mattress with each rock of their hips. It was like Wil knew exactly where to touch him, how to send pleasure directly to his cock, and he made sounds he hadn't thought were possible to make as he was pushed higher and higher.

His throat began to throb, and Wil didn't let up. The thrusts were harder, a little faster, and his hands clung to Wil as he cried out. He was drowning, his heart pounding and lungs aching as he panted. It was too much. Everything crested, his knees squeezing against Wil's hips as he bucked against Wil, came thickly between their bodies. His head swam, his throat burned, and he didn't know if he ever wanted to come back to his senses.

Wil grunted against his throat, shuddered above him, and a goofy smile curved Zach's lips as the wet heat of Wil's come joined his own. It was sexy and messy and Zach couldn't believe it had taken them this long to reach this point. He kissed Wil's shoulder, neck, ear. Heaven. He was in Heaven. "I love you," he whispered against Wil's ear, because it just felt *right* to say it then, in the aftermath of something so spectacular.

Wil lifted his head, stared down at Zach, his fingers stroking along Zach's flushed cheek. "I love you, too," he breathed. A smile graced Wil's face at that moment. "Happy birthday."

Zach laughed, the sound tapering into a purr. "The *best* birthday," he said before pulling Wil into a lazy, satisfied kiss.

# Chapter Fifteen

Zach let out a slow breath, willing himself to relax now that Samantha had arrived. Sophia was acting like a little lady, playing with Mae and mimicking her as she shuffled, wobbled on her knees, and rolled all around the living room. He'd cleaned up the living and dining area as much as possible before Samantha had dropped by, and he was glad for the effort as Sophia toddled around. His eyes focused on Mae, though, and how she kept trying to scoot herself along the floor. It dawned on him then that Mae would be crawling soon. *Crawling.* Zach couldn't believe she was becoming mobile. It felt like only yesterday he had to hold her head up for her, and now she was on the cusp of crawling and walking and oh, God, he was getting worked up again.

"Breathe, Zach," Samantha laughed. "You look like you're going to have a heart attack."

"She's just growing up so fast, Sam. I don't know how you do it, running around and keeping up with Sophia. When Mae's her age, I'm going to be exhausted. How am I supposed to balance everything? I feel like I'm part of some circus act, juggling all these different parts of my life, but if I drop one, I feel like I'll drop them all."

Samantha leaned over and gave him a hug. "You're not going to drop anything. You're doing a great job. Kid, relationship, school, work. Plus, you know you can send Mae over to my house for a night off every so often. I know you want extra time with your gorgeous boyfriend."

Zach blushed and gave Samantha a playful shove. "That's a tempting offer. If you ever need someone to look after Sophia, you know I'll do it in a heartbeat, right?" Samantha watched Mae so often, Zach was starting to feel guilty. He didn't want to take advantage of her.

"I'll keep that in mind," Samantha said, nudging Zach with her foot. "Maybe when I have a new boyfriend to whisk me off to expensive restaurants..." She chuckled. "Until then, I'll live vicariously through you. Now, you *have* managed to at least cross paths with him a couple times since school started, right? If I had a man like that, I'd have him on a pretty short leash." Samantha's eyes grew dreamy. "Hell, if I had *any* man..."

"You'll find someone, I know it." Zach then ran his hands through his hair. He might need a good trim, but he didn't have nearly enough hair to hide the goofy smile that formed as he thought about Wil. "We've gotten together a few times," he admitted. "It's always amazing. Spending time with him, I mean."

Samantha gave him an odd look, and then realization dawned, and she *oohed* and *ahhed* at him. "Somebody's been getting some!"

"Shut up!" Zach laughed, his face far too warm at the thought of the last time Wil had come over. He'd never known a tongue could do all the things Wil's had done to him. He only hoped his pitiful attempt at returning the favor had been as nice as Wil had insisted. He knew he definitely had room for improvement, though, but that would mean getting in more practice, which was much more difficult than he'd hoped with both their school and work schedules at odds with one another. "I just wish we could get more time together. Alone time."

"Always the best kind of time," Samantha agreed.

"I mean, I love it when we do stuff with Mae or go out for dinner, and he does this really sweet tickle game with Mae that can bring her out of even the worst tantrum. He takes me places I'd never be able to afford on my own, and while I like it, I sometimes just want to yell at him how unnecessary it is for him to spend so much on us. All I want is him close. I want him even closer than he's been, you know?"

Samantha eyed him for a few seconds, making him feel like some sort of bug under a microscope. "You haven't gone all the way with him yet, have you?" There wasn't any judgment in the question, but it still made him flush up redder than a tomato, which earned him an almost evil cackle. "You haven't! I knew it!"

"Just because I have a kid doesn't mean I move fast," Zach sputtered. Mae and Sophia drew his attention to the corner of the room. Nothing to really be concerned about, but he preferred them be more in his line of sight. He leaned forward in his seat on the sofa and called out, "Sophia, honey, try to get Mae back over this way. Mae! Come to daddy, Mae!"

Mae laughed and pawed in his direction, and Sophia helped Mae up onto her hands and knees. Zach laughed with Samantha as Sophia half-dragged poor Mae their direction. He finally stood up to spare his daughter any more of the good-natured help. Zach gave Sophia a kiss on the cheek, and then swept Mae up into his arms. God, Mae was so much bigger than the shrieking little newborn he swore she'd been just last week. Time really did fly, and as much as he wanted her to thrive, he also wanted her to remain his baby girl forever.

He sat on the couch next to Samantha and tickled Mae's belly, earning him a shrill laugh and a toothless grin. "Mom says Mae should start teething any day now."

Samantha shook her head. "When Sophia was teething, I thought I'd go crazy. Nothing I did really helped. Dad said I should try whiskey, but... come on. I wasn't going to give my five-month-old booze."

"Five months?" Zach frowned, looking down at Mae. "Mae will be eight months in a couple of weeks. Shouldn't she have teeth by now?"

"Every baby is different." Samantha nudged him. "Don't worry. Before you know it, you'll have a screaming baby you can't soothe because her mouth is driving her crazy."

Zach sighed. "I just want her to be happy and healthy."

"She *is,*" Samantha said. "Just look at her. She's squirming and laughing and happy. She's also so close to crawling. Sophia didn't crawl until she was almost a year old." She smiled at Sophia, who brought her one of her dolls. "You were just a late bloomer, weren't you?" Sophia grinned and ran back to the pile of toys on Zach's floor. Samantha chuckled and turned back to Zach. "Mae is doing great. Don't worry."

"I always worry," Zach said, putting Mae back on the ground. She wobbled on her hands and knees, and then inched forward once before collapsing. She did it several times before Zach stood and helped her sit up so she could play with her toys. "I can't help it."

Samantha nodded. "I've noticed. Mae, work, school, bills, your parents, your car, your boyfriend." She watched him go into the kitchen, and her voice rose as if he wouldn't be able to hear her around the partition. "So... you've messed around with Wil, but not actually had sex?"

Zach flushed, looking at her through the cut-out that made the breakfast bar. "We've had sex." He frowned. Even if they hadn't 'gone all the way' like Samantha put it, they'd still made love. "My ass may be virgin territory, but it doesn't mean what we've done doesn't count. It counts a lot."

"Oh," Samantha breathed, and he watched a blush creep up her cheeks. "I'm sorry, Zach. Sometimes, my mouth just runs off before I even have a chance to think about what it's saying. Of course it counts. Now, excuse me while I insert my foot into my mouth."

"I just want you to know that it's important. Like, important-important," Zach murmured. "We've been taking it a little slow, and I like that. What we do is really nice. I don't want to just leap forward, like everything we have now isn't good enough. Not only that, but I have to be sure

90

there's a safety net, you know? Baby on board." He gave a fond look to Mae and watched her grab one of her rattles with both hands. It went straight into her mouth, of course, but the sight made his heart nearly burst with love for her.

"You're afraid you'll fall for him?"

The question made Zach chuckle, looking over his shoulder at Samantha. "I think it's safe to say I've already done that part."

"Then why the fear of going all the way? He's an awesome guy, has a plan for his life, and treats you and Mae like royalty. I don't think you could ask for a better candidate if you've been saving yourself." Samantha grinned. "Besides, how will you know for sure you're not just a flavor of bi-sexual instead of gay if you never try it? I still might be able to win you over and we could live happily ever after with our 2.5 children and a white picket fence!"

Zach reached over and swatted at her. "It would never work between us, darling," he fired back. "We just don't fit together the way I like."

"And I can just imagine what that way might be with Wil around," she said, bringing the conversation back to Wil, her earlier question still left hanging.

Zach shifted, leaning back against the lower half of the sofa. "It's just a big deal, that's all. I mean, I know it was a big deal for Bethany when she let me inside her body. It's intimate, takes a lot of trust, and I... want to be sure I can trust him not to leave once he's had me."

Samantha picked up one of Mae's plastic, puffy books and flipped through the handful of pages. "Have you thought about, you know, *talking* to him? If you're afraid, the best person to confide in is the guy you're thinking of having sex with."

Zach blinked a couple of times as her suggestion sank in. "Talk to him?" Could it be that simple? Just... talk it out with Wil?

"Yeah," Samantha laughed. "Talk to him. About sex. I'm sure you can manage that much. If the two of you are doing things already, he's probably expecting it."

Zach watched Sophia babble at Mae, who laughed, squealed, and shook her rattle. He smiled. "I guess you're right."

Samantha grinned. "Aren't I always?"

With a roll of his eyes, Zach gave her a shove. "Come on. Let's get their lunch together." He'd call Wil tonight and see if they could arrange an evening together to talk. He didn't know when it would be, but now that he'd decided on a course of action, he felt a hell of a lot better.

# Chapter Sixteen

"I am so behind," Zach muttered.

Devain looked up from his notebook. "How behind?"

Zach rubbed his face, his head pounding. "Three assignments behind in Criminology, one assignment behind in Ethics."

"Why?" Piper opened her soda and took a long drink. "I thought things were going well."

"They were." Zach poked at his cold taco. "At least, I thought they were. I took three extra shifts at Walmart, and Mae's been sick twice with an ear infection *and* some sort of stomach bug that's going around the daycare. I haven't had much time to sleep, let alone work on assignments. On top of that, I haven't had a chance to see Wil in almost two weeks. He's taken extra shifts at the pharmacy," he grumbled.

"How long do you have to catch up?" Devain asked.

Zach glanced around his little study group. "Until the end of the month."

Jamie shook his head. "A week? For your current assignments and what's past due?"

"Shit," Piper breathed, the word partially muffled by her soda bottle. "It's a good thing your parents could take Mae for tonight, then. You have to hit the books *hard*."

Zach almost laughed, but there wasn't much mirth in the grunt that escaped him. "As if I haven't been doing that the last two hours. Three, if you include the hour before you guys got here with Taco Bell, since I was working on this instead of baking something for everyone to snack on."

"Hey, it wasn't a problem," Devain assured him with a smile. "You've been doing everything all at once. Time to just prioritize and tackle one problem at a time. Stop looking at the four assignments all at once and just work on one until it's finished." Zach looked at his spread of notepads and folders before Devain leaned over, glanced at everything, and pointed to the second folder to his right. "That's the one you're closest to being done with, so let's finish that one off first. Then, you get to reward yourself by reheating that taco and actually eating before we start on the next one. You two," he added, glancing left and right at Piper and Jamie, "can keep working on math. Just 'cause you have different teachers doesn't mean you can't help each other out."

There was stunned silence from all of them until Piper began to fan herself. "Am I the only one who loves it when he gets all tutor-y on us?"

Zach laughed softly and flicked her forearm with his pencil. "First it's the athletes, and now it's the geeks. What group are you going to crush on next semester, hmm?"

"Hush." Piper giggled before schooling her expression into something much more serious, her eyes zoning in on her textbook. "I'm doing math."

"And hoping the tutor will reward you for being a good student?" Jamie snorted.

Devain nudged Jaime. "Well, if I offer to kiss anyone who finishes all their math assignments, I have a feeling that'll motivate her more than you."

"Don't offer that unless you mean it," Piper warned with a grin before attacking her math problems with renewed vigor.

Zach just smiled, relaxed a little by their banter and the thought that Piper might actually have a thing for Devain. They were both nice people, both motivated, and they deserved to find someone they could get close to, go out with, and have their troubles kissed away by. Like Wil. He sighed at the thought of Wil, feeling the need to see him again after such a long stint apart.

"Hey," Devain murmured, snapping Zach out of his little daydream. Devain was sitting next to him now, everyone having shifted into a new arrangement. God, he was so distracted! "You're going to have to focus for me. Tell me about this assignment and where you're having trouble."

Zach dropped his pen and rubbed at his face, sighing. "I'm supposed to write up a summary about Aristotle's Virtues and Happiness, and then write a fifteen-hundred-word paper about the connection of virtue to happiness, and how one might detract or add to the other."

Jamie whistled. "What class is this for?"

"Ethics. I missed one of the classes, which included a discussion on the work—which the professor graded everyone on—and so she gave me this in order to make up the credit lost." Zach glared at the textbook. "I had to take Ethics. I wasn't all that interested in the material or the class."

"Ethics are a part of Criminology," Piper said. "I'd hate to think about you as an unethical criminal profiler."

"I'd probably make more money if I was unethical," Zach muttered.

"Maybe make more money, but you wouldn't be happy." Piper gave his foot a nudge under the table. "You had to know Ethics would be a part of it. If you didn't like the courses, why be a profiler?"

Zach looked up from his paper. "I like the idea of taking dangerous criminals off the street. Working for the FBI would mean, more or less, a desk job. It would be safer for me while letting me help people. I didn't want to be on the street or anything, putting my neck out there. Not when I have Mae. This was the way I could still work in law enforcement but not wind up dead on the street."

"So it was the lesser evil?" Jamie asked.

"Sort of. I mean, once I chose the course, I got really excited about it." Zach leaned forward. "I like most of the classes. I really can't wait to get to all the psych stuff. It just feels like I'm dragging my heels with all this foundation stuff when I want to be learning the interesting, important things."

Devain quirked an eyebrow at him. "Ethics are important, even if they aren't interesting."

Zach flopped back against his chair. "I know, but it doesn't mean I have to like it."

Devain pointed to the paper, drawing Zach's attention back to the current assignment. "Well, how many words do you have so far on the Ethics paper?"

Zach glanced up at Devain's dark face. "Just about a thousand."

"So you're almost done." Devain poked him. "Finish it. You don't want to flunk out your second semester, do you?"

"No." Zach frowned. "Of course not."

"Then do the work, Zach." Devain motioned to everyone else. "We're all working just as hard. No, we may not have a kid, but we do all have jobs. We have families. We have draws on our time, too."

Anger welled in Zach. "Draws on your time? How much sleep did you get last night, Devain? Eight hours? Ten? I got three. Three! Mae was up half the damn night with colic. Then, I had to get up and go the hell to work, all while having this shitload of work waiting for me when I got home. I know you're all working hard, but don't compare your hard work with mine."

Piper shifted in her seat across from them. "Zach," she murmured. "We're only trying to help."

"I know," Zach said, looking away from them. He felt tears sting his eyes. He was so tired, and, dammit, he missed Wil. "I know. I'm sorry." He looked back at Devain. "I'm really sorry, man."

Devain smiled, patted him on the back. "Stress is a bitch."

"Yeah, it is." Zach nudged Devain. "But you're right. It's just a few hundred more words."

"And then you have your—" Jamie lifted up another textbook and read the Post-it note on the cover. "'Pick three crimes from the list and discuss their economic impact on the local level' assignment."

Zach threw a pencil at Jamie, laughing softly. "Thanks for the reminder."

"Just trying to help." Jamie grinned at him, and their help didn't seem so intrusive at that moment. "Which three crimes are you going to pick?"

"I have no idea. I don't even want to think about crime and money and the impact on a city."

Devain shook his head. "Is there any part of this you want to think about?"

"When my advisor talked to me about criminology, he forgot to mention all the foundation classes I'd have to take." Zach rubbed at his face. God, he was tired. "If I wanted to be a cop, all I would have had to do was finish high school."

"But you didn't want to be a cop, remember?" Devain asked, crossing his arms.

A small smile tugged at Zach's lips. "Yeah, I know. Besides, I like the idea of being a criminal profiler. Being an FBI agent sounds a lot more appealing than a Hillsborough County sheriff."

Jamie pointed at Zach. "You still have to have the local work experience, right? I didn't think you could come out of college and go right to the FBI."

Zach rolled his eyes. "Yeah, I know. I'm going to be a peon here for a couple of years, and then I have to climb the ranks up through the FBI. Then, after about ten years and a Masters degree, I'll be able to apply to NCAVC." When the three of them stared at him cluelessly, he grinned. "National Center for the Analysis of Violent Crime. In Virginia. It's where the type of special agent I want to be is assigned." The years stretched out in front of him as he thought about it all. It sent a shiver of fear down his spine to be planning his entire life from here on out at eighteen. "By the time Mae's going to college, I hope I'll have the job I want."

"Wow," Piper breathed. "That's... intense. I think you could be a doctor in a shorter amount of time."

"No." Zach laughed. "I don't want to mess with people's insides, thank you very much. I'd rather pick apart their brains in a clean, quiet office."

"If that's what you want to do, then you need to get past college. What else do you have?" Piper asked, poking around his books.

Zach let out a slow breath. "I have to do the study guide questions for Ethics. We have our first exam next week. That shouldn't be too bad. I have all the notes and material. I also missed a second class for Ethics, and let me tell you, Professor Wall is *not* happy with me. She told me I could miss one more class this semester, but to make up for the second absence, I have to write a 3,000 word paper on morality, religion, and altruism. I can sum up the whole thing in one sentence: Altruism doesn't exist, religion formed mass morality, and we are only kind because it serves Ego."

Devain let out a low whistle. "Bitter much?"

"Exhaustion and pent-up sexual frustration," Zach said, his cheeks heating a little.

"Sexual frustration isn't a problem for me," Jamie said. "Jack is waiting back at the apartment, keeping the bed nice and warm."

"Lucky you," Piper said as she kicked him under the table. "Some of us don't even have a Friday night date to look forward to."

"My Friday night is just work. Work at Walmart, work on assignments, and then work to make sure Mae is amused, and then hopefully healthy enough to fall asleep without a fuss." Zach couldn't help but feel frustrated when all his schedule looked like was one endless pile of books, pills, and bills.

"Ever heard the saying 'All work and no play...'?" Jamie murmured, his eyes worried as they peeked through his bangs at Zach. God, that look made him feel like shit for saying anything. He didn't want them worried about him. All his complaining must have just sounded like whining to his friends.

"Makes me a dull boy, I know," Zach huffed. He tried to find a good excuse, but there wasn't one. "I can't help it. Just stressed out."

"Then make sure you get that boyfriend of yours over here for some serious de-stressing, and pronto," Piper ordered. "You need a break.

We'll hit the books hard the next few hours, and then you'll have a bit of breathing room."

Devain smiled at him. "Take a swig of caffeine, and start on those last five hundred words. Think of it as just being a few more paragraphs. You can do it."

"I'll even look through the list and try to brainstorm an interesting combination of crimes for you to write about," Jamie offered with a grin that made Zach wary.

"Why does that make me nervous?" Zach asked him, and when Jamie tried for an innocent shrug, he shook his head and laughed. "All right. Work now, play later." Devain was right; he could do this if he just put his mind to it and stopped letting himself get distracted. He took a few gulps of Mountain Dew and let out a slow breath before rereading the last paragraph of his essay and starting on the next.

Zach groaned softly as he leaned his forehead against the cabinet flanking his stove. If he wasn't careful, he was going to fall asleep with his pasta still on the stove, and that was a recipe for disaster. The last thing he needed was a fire in his kitchen. He deserved the reward of a starchy, homey, late-night meal, though, and the beefy bolognese sauce he'd tossed together would be delicious on the pasta. Now that everyone had left from the long study session, he was happily soaking up the relative silence of his apartment.

He stirred his boiling pasta, making sure it wouldn't stick to the bottom of the pot. As the timer he'd nearly forgotten to set beeped, he forced himself upright and transferred the pasta into a strainer. Within minutes, he had himself a big bowl, the leftovers safely stowed in the fridge for another time. He flopped onto his bed with his bowl, his eyes lingering on his cell phone and the empty crib as he took bite after bite.

He'd spent all afternoon and evening without Mae, and there was something deep inside him that ached at the thought. What if he'd missed one of those wonderful moments, one of those landmark events that most people videotaped or stuck into a baby book? Mae was going to be crawling up a storm soon, and that meant she was nearly walking. She was going to start speaking coherently, and he was just waiting for that moment when she would call him Daddy for the first time.

The ache in his chest only got worse when he looked at his cell phone again. It had been way too long since he'd gotten together with Wil. Sure, they were busy and all, but he was going through withdrawal here!

Would Wil even be around to take his call? He glanced at the clock on his nightstand. Two o'clock. It *was* Friday night. No classes for Wil tomorrow, but maybe an early open at the pharmacy. Zach sighed and poked at his pasta again as he debated. Finally, he snatched up the phone and quick dialed Wil's cell. The worst that could happen was he woke Wil, so he might as well try. They hadn't talked in days, and he missed Wil.

The phone rang three times before Wil's sleepy voice answered. "Zach?"

Suddenly, Zach felt like a compete idiot for waking Wil up. "Hey, Wil. Sorry to wake you."

"It's all right." Wil yawned. "Is Mae all right?"

The concern made Zach grin stupidly. "Yeah, she's fine. Nothing bad's happened. She's with my parents tonight, and I was thinking of you. I had a long study group. Nearly half a dozen assignments to work on, so I needed no distractions."

"That many? Are you behind?"

Zach took a bite of the pasta to buy himself some time, and then he muttered, "I *was*. Not anymore. Devain didn't let me stop working until everything was done."

"Things okay?" Wil sounded like he shifted in bed, and Zach could just imagine Wil, sleep tousled and half-naked.

"I just... I miss you. It's been two weeks since I last saw you. You live ten minutes away, and I can't find any time to even drop in on you at work."

Wil chuckled. "I know how you feel, trust me. When is your next day off?"

"Tuesday. I have my online class, but I can watch the lecture and do the classwork in the morning." Zach's heart began to race. Did this mean they'd finally have a chance to see each other?

"I have class Tuesday afternoon, but I can take Tuesday night off from the pharmacy."

"No, Wil, don't take time off," Zach said, his hopes sinking.

Wil snorted. "I miss you and Mae, Zach. One night isn't going to kill my future career. How about I come by around five on Tuesday with some food?"

"I can cook," Zach murmured weakly, not wanting Wil to spend yet more money on him.

"Nah. I don't want you to have to cook and clean. It should be a fun night for us. I'll pick up something and head over after my class lets out. Sound good?"

Zach smiled, excitement bubbling in his chest, and he decided fighting over takeaway food wasn't worth it. He was going to see Wil in a couple of days. "It sounds great. Now, go back to sleep."

"Will do." Wil paused. "I love you."

Oh, could Zach turn any redder? He bit his lip for a moment, and then replied, "I love you, too. Night, Wil."

"See you Tuesday."

"Tuesday."

"Bye, Zach."

Zach clicked the phone off and continued to grin at it on his night-stand. Thank God he'd called. Tuesday night. He could make it until then. At least, he hoped he could. No one died from going without kisses and cuddling, right?

# Chapter Seventeen

Five o'clock on the dot, Wil knocked at Zach's door. Mae on his hip, Zach all but bounced to the door and threw it open. He grinned up at Wil. Two and a half weeks! He couldn't believe it had been two and a half weeks since he'd last laid eyes on his boyfriend. Zach stepped aside and waved Wil in. "I was just about to feed Mae."

Wil's hands were full of takeout bags from TGIFridays, and Zach inwardly winced. That didn't look like cheap, quick food. "Wonderful. We can all eat together."

"You didn't have to pick up something so... elaborate," Zach said, trying to keep his annoyance to himself. He shut the front door and locked it before heading with Mae into the small dining nook.

"It's nothing." Wil set the bags on the table. "I was starving, so I may have gone overboard." He turned and held out his hands for Mae. "Can I hold the little princess? God, I've missed you both!"

Zach handed Mae's squealing, squirming body over to Wil. "She's so happy to see you."

Wil held Mae in his arms, smiling down at her flushed, happy face. "I'm thrilled to see her. She looks bigger."

"She is." Zach went into the kitchen and gathered up dishes for dinner. "She's gained five pounds since you last saw her. I think she eats *everything* I put in front of her."

"Good." Wil jiggled her until she laughed. "It's great to see her so healthy."

Zach nodded to her highchair. "Buckle her in, Bozo, so we can eat."

"Yes, sir!"

Wil settled Mae in her highchair, promising softly to tickle her after her supper settled. Zach shook his head, handing plates, glasses, and flatware to Wil, and then he went back into the kitchen to fetch Mae's meal and the pitcher of tea. By the time he returned to the table, Wil had uncovered quite a feast, and Mae was slamming her hands against the tray of her highchair.

"You're both starving, huh?" Zach asked, sitting down and uncovering Mae's dish of mashed sweet potatoes, pureed chicken, and apple-

101

sauce. He brandished her favorite little spoon. "Time for num-nums," he declared.

"Num-nums?" Wil sat down and dished out the food onto the plates.

Zach flushed. "Shut up. Small words are easier for babies to learn."

Wil gave him a look. "Don't dumb it down. Talk to her like you would me. It'll ensure she has a large vocabulary."

"Speaking from experience?"

"Yep. All my nieces and nephews were early speakers. I attribute it to none of us using baby talk with them." Wil grinned. "But you're adorable saying 'num-nums', so I might have to concede that word."

Zach laughed and fed Mae a spoonful of the chicken. "He thinks I'm dumbing you down by saying 'num-nums'. What are you thoughts on that, princess?"

Mae banged her hands on her tray again, grinning as she reached for the section of her dish with the sweet potatoes. She babbled at them as she took a handful and brought it to her mouth.

"I think that was a definitive 'screw you' in my general direction," Wil said, laughing.

"She'll forgive you in five minutes," Zach promised, letting Mae have a little fun with her plate. Wil watched for a moment before stabbing a small piece of lobster and offering it to him. He glanced at the plate. God, was that salmon actually covered in lobster bits? It looked expensive, but that first bite erased any protests from his mind.

They fed one another, chatting happily about school and work and family, everything that had kept them apart. Wil shared a couple amusing stories about customers at the CVS, and he laughed more between bites of Parmesan-crusted salmon than he had for the last two weeks combined. The food was amazing, and even after his stomach was full, there was plenty for at least one extra meal. After they packed everything into Tupperware, Zach burped Mae, cleaned her up, and deposited her wriggling form into her playpen.

They chose a movie at random from his DVD cabinet and soon plopped themselves on his well-worn couch. Of course, the movie was the least important thing in the world to Zach. He was too busy cuddling Wil to care what was going on in the film. Cuddling led to lingering touches. The touches then led to kisses, and before long, they were making out. It just felt so good to be close again, and Zach couldn't help but bask in Wil's presence, wanting every moment to count. It was only when Wil's hands slid under his t-shirt to touch his bare skin that he pulled back with a gasp.

His mind felt hazy, but the thought of sex reminded him of the conversation he'd had with Samantha. He almost pushed away the idea of talking when Wil dipped forward to nuzzle and nip at his throat. Once the thought was there in his mind, though, it niggled at him. He groaned softly, gently pushing Wil back from his neck.

"Something wrong?" Wil asked, and his voice was low and husky in all the right ways.

Zach bit his lower lip for a moment. "No. I want to keep going, trust me. I just... I promised myself I'd talk to you first."

Wil sighed, but before Zach could curse himself for bad timing, Wil just smiled and kissed him sweetly. "Whether you mean to or not, you're being a tease, and I think I like it." Zach felt his cheeks grow hot, but Wil just chuckled and gave his hips a squeeze. "Now, what's up? I have a feeling it's important."

"It is." At least, to Zach it was. "I... I have this feeling that we're about to have sex any minute, but we've never really talked about sex. Only that you'd wait until I was ready."

"You saying you're ready?"

Zach shifted on Wil's lap. How did he always end up astride Wil? "I'm saying I *think* I am, but there are things that I worry about."

Wil smiled at him, gave his hips another squeeze. "Such as?" he encouraged.

"Such as... I've never done it before. You'd be the first. I don't want to give in, make love with you, and then have you dump me." Even as he said it, Zach thought the insecure words sounded stupid. "I mean, you obviously have experience, and I know you've been dating guys since high school, but I haven't. You're my first serious boyfriend, and you say you love me, and God knows I love you, but it's a big step, and there's Mae to think of, and I don't want you to just have me and go on your merry way, and—"

Wil pressed a finger to Zach's lips, stopping him mid-ramble. He was smiling, his blue eyes sparkling with amusement. "You need to take a breath sometime," he teased.

Could Zach blush any brighter? He didn't think so. "I know. When I get nervous, I ramble, and once I start rambling, I can't stop, and then I get all self-conscious about the rambling, and then I get *more* nervous, and

—" He stopped short, grinning like an idiot. "See? I'm doing it again. I'm just... nervous."

"I know." Wil combed his fingers through Zach's hair. "But you don't have to be. I love you. Sex, while nice, doesn't *have* to be a part of loving you. If you aren't ready, Zach, then you just aren't ready."

Zach shifted against Wil. "What I'm saying is, I think I am, but I want to know if you'll be around in the morning? And the week after that... and the month after that?"

"Yes," Wil said. There was no pause, no hesitation.

"Yes?" Zach blinked. "It's that simple? Just... yes?"

Wil's lips curved into a faint smile. "Yes, Zach. I love you. I love Mae. I'm in this for the long haul, and that isn't going to change whether we have sex now or six months from now."

The idea of waiting six more months to know Wil like that seemed excruciating to Zach. He flushed again, swallowed against his dry throat, and the wet his lips. "We love you, too, and... I want to. Tonight."

There was no mistaking the eagerness and arousal that sparked in Wil's eyes. His hands shifted to cup Zach's ass through his jeans. "You're sure?"

Zach felt love rush through him. Even aroused and having waited this long for him, Wil was still hesitant, still putting him first. It made the small things like busy schedules and overpriced dinners fade into the background. Zach smiled broadly as he nodded. "Yeah. I'm positive."

Wil moaned softly, and one hand came up to cup the nape of Zach's neck and pull him forward. He wasn't about to resist as his lips met Wil's again in the sweetest kiss he could ever remember receiving. It began almost chaste, but excitement and arousal soon had him deepening it, curling his tongue against Wil's until they were forced back for air.

"Will Mae be all right in her playpen for a bit?" Wil breathed.

Zach looked over at Mae, who was absorbed in her toys, trying to push one of the rings from her stacking toy into the shaped slots of her shape sorter that looked like a cookie jar. He couldn't help but smile at her. "She could play for hours with those things, even with the sound switched off. She shouldn't need her diaper changed for another hour or so."

"And then, I can tickle her as I promised," Wil chuckled. "Let's set up the baby monitor. We can leave the door open and the monitor on so we'll hear if she needs anything."

That Wil worried about Mae touched Zach, made him smile, and he kissed him again before climbing off Wil's lap. He took out the baby monitors from a box he kept near the playpen and handed one to Wil. "You can set that one up in the bedroom. I'll get this one."

Wil nodded, pecked his cheek, and headed into Zach's bedroom with a backward glance that was filled with promise. It made heat coil and churn in Zach's gut, and he tried to calm his racing heart as he set up the other monitor in a mesh pocket connected to one of the playpen's spokes. He leaned down to kiss Mae and murmur, "Daddy will be right back, princess. You just holler if you need me." He smiled as she gurgled up at him and babbled a few words, showing him her toy. "Where does that ring go? It goes on the stick with the other ones, doesn't it? Such a smart girl!"

Another kiss, and he tore himself away. Every step toward his bedroom made his pulse beat faster and faster. He was nearly breathless when he managed to reach the door frame, and his heart clenched when he looked inside. Wil had set everything up, turned down the bed, and taken off his shirt. He'd even lit the three-wick candle Zach had on his dresser. He tried to say something, but his throat refused to work.

A blush crept onto Wil's cheeks as he looked around. "Just thought I'd set the mood a little. Too cheesy?"

Zach shook his head. "No. Just cheesy enough." He crossed to Wil and wrapped his arms around Wil's waist. "I don't know why I'm so nervous. We've done some... stuff... before."

"This is a little different," Wil said, combing back Zach's hair with his fingers. "It'll be all right, though. I promise." He ducked down and drew Zach into a kiss, and the one kiss led to another. And then another. By the time Wil had Zach's shirt off and was sprawled under him on the bed, they were both flushed, hard, and panting. "Doing all right?" Wil asked, lips teasing Zach's throat.

"Yeah," Zach whispered. God, he was doing more than all right. The room was too hot, or maybe it was just him. It didn't matter. He wanted out of his clothes.

The getting undressed part wasn't difficult. It had only been a few weeks ago that he'd been nervous about Wil seeing him naked, but since then, he'd enjoyed every moment of nudity with Wil. Clothes fell away, and Zach gasped as he arched up against Wil, flesh to flesh, and felt the hardness of him. As Wil left another hickey on his throat, the nervous fear began to crawl back along his skin. Wil seemed big against him, and, if things went the way Zach was sure they were supposed to, that thickness was meant to go inside him. While logic—and porn—said it was very possible for them to fit together perfectly, an irrational part of Zach's brain whispered the impossibility of it.

Wil kissed his way down Zach's chest, and Zach cried out as Wil's teeth tugged lightly at a nipple. It was sharp, bright, and the pleasure sizzled through him. Zach gasped and arched up against Wil. "God!" He squeezed his eyes shut while tangling his fingers in Wil's hair. They'd always kept things pretty simple, but this was anything but simple. Wil's mouth did things that made Zach's toes curl, and when hot, moist breath ghosted over his cock, the world narrowed to just them.

He looked down the length of his body at Wil nestled between his legs. A flush pounded in his cheeks, and he opened his mouth several times. No sound would come out. Wil grinned at him, and then he dragged his tongue from Zach's balls up to the tip of his cock. Zach forgot to breathe. His head swam, and when Wil licked him again, his vision went a little hazy. He took in a great, shuddering breath, and then he moaned. "Wil."

Wil met his gaze. "Yeah?"

"I think I'll come if you keep that up," Zach whispered.

A grin graced Wil's handsome face. "That's all right. We have all night." He ducked down then and drew Zach's cock between those lush, smiling lips, and Zach bucked, whimpering in the back of his throat as pleasure coiled tightly in his groin.

All night. Zach couldn't imagine a full night of nothing but this pleasure. He'd never survive it! His head fell back as he surrendered himself into Wil's care. Lips caressed him, and Wil's tongue lapped at the slit of his cock. Every kiss, every lick, every stroke of that strong hand on him, just pushed him higher. He teetered on the edge for a moment, but Wil withheld nothing and sent him flying without hesitation.

Zach cried out as heat and pleasure exploded through him. All that existed in that bright moment was Wil. The swell of love inside him demanded voice beyond a simple cry of pleasure. The last of his release was milked out of him as he babbled words of affection he wasn't even sure Wil could understand. He couldn't understand them himself. He couldn't even think straight. Wil was there to catch him when he collapsed, though, and he soon found himself silenced by a kiss that made his toes curl all over again.

"Shh," Wil soothed, his lips curved in a smile against Zach's. "It's all right. I know."

Another kiss, and Zach realized he could taste himself on Wil's lips, the tang of his own bitter come mixed with the sweet spiciness of Wil's tongue. It pulled another moan from him as he wrapped lethargic arms around Wil, holding him close. The aftershocks were amazing, like tendrils of gold spreading out and tingling over his skin. It seemed the pleasure didn't really end at all, simmering low in him as Wil rocked against him, silently reminding him of the act they were building toward.

Zach carded his fingers through Wil's hair, his heart pounding in his ears as he stared up at Wil. That soft smile, the gentle flush of flesh, and that hard, insistent shaft moving against him, they all told Zach how much Wil wanted him. How much Wil was a part of his life, part of *Mae's* life, and it scared the hell out of him how much he wanted Wil to stay a part of their lives. He swallowed thickly as Wil's hand stroked from his throat to his hip, the touch so loving, tender. "Are you here to stay?" he whispered, Mae's babbling easily heard over the monitor.

Wil's eyes closed for a moment, and he hummed softly before they opened again. They were such a dark blue, like the ocean at night, and the heat Zach saw in them made his cock twitch with renewed interest. "Yes," Wil murmured. "I'm here to stay, Zach. I love you. I love Mae. Things might be a little complicated, but we'll sort through it all."

Tears stung Zach's eyes, but they didn't fall. "I'm a little afraid," he confessed. "I haven't had someone mean what you mean to me... and I haven't... you know... with a guy. Will it hurt?"

"Yes." Wil brushed his lips over Zach's. "But I'll try to make sure the hurt doesn't last long."

Zach let out a slow breath as Wil's fingers began to fondle him, and the exhale became a moan. "And then it'll be good?"

Wil chuckled. "Even when it hurts, I hope it'll still be good." He ducked down and drew Zach into a long, wet kiss. Wil's hand never stopped moving over Zach's cock and balls. The kiss seemed to go on for-ever, and by the time Wil drew back, Zach was hard again, shivering on the bed under Wil. "You ready?" Wil whispered.

Was he ready? Fuck, no, but he was pretty sure he'd never feel ready-ready. Zach took a deep breath and nodded. "As ready as I'll ever be," he admitted. "If it's anything like the blowjob..." But he knew it wouldn't be. Not quite.

His heart leaped in his chest as Wil shifted, eased his thighs apart. Heat suffused his cheeks, and the vulnerability that washed over him as Wil settled there between his legs was almost painful. Zach licked his lips as his whole body tensed, but Wil only stroked up and down his thighs, dipping in to suckle the head of his cock. Zach moaned, his eyes fluttering, and he relaxed bit by bit as Wil touched, kissed, licked, and soothed him. It was going to be enormous, life changing, but Zach was willing to rush headlong into it so long as Wil was the one he was rushing with.

He heard the cap of the lube pop open, and looking down sent a shiver through him. When had Wil managed to get a condom on? He wasn't sure how Wil could give him so much pleasure and still multi-task like that, but the sight of Wil stroking himself until the condom glistened made his breathing ragged with need and fear. "It won't..."

Wil glanced up at him through blond strands of hair. "It will," he promised with a smile and soothing touch. "Just remember to breathe. I'm with you every step of the way."

Zach nodded, taking a deep breath and trying to let it out slowly. Slow was easy, but smooth was impossible. Every breath trembled as soon as Wil's slick fingers began massaging at his opening. It wasn't that Wil had never touched there before, but just that he knew how much further they were about to go. He reached for Wil's hair, giving his nervous hands something to play with as he concentrated on breathing. In... out... in... and out. In... and oh, God, the first finger was inside him. His exhale was little more than a long groan.

"Easy," Wil soothed, licking up the length of him again. "Let me in. I won't do more until you're stretched and ready."

It was a sweet promise, and despite the slight discomfort of Wil's finger inside him, Zach nodded. He had no idea how long Wil worked him up, sucking at him until he was squirming, gasping on the edge of release, only to use that frantic moment to pull back, deny him, and ease another finger in. Tears stung his eyes when Wil's lips left him once more, his body practically thrumming with need. Wil's face appeared above his then, and those fingers slipped from his body. Eyes almost black in the dim light of his room stared down at him, Wil's face flushed, beautiful. Zach's mouth went dry, and his heart pounded in his chest. This was it. This was *the* moment he'd been fantasizing about.

"Wil—"

"Shh." Wil brushed his lips over Zach's. "If you want to stop, we can."

It was a generous offer, and one Zach seriously considered. Even now, Wil wasn't going to push, wasn't going to ask for more than Zach wanted to give. But Zach *wanted* to give this. He wet his lips and combed his fingers through Wil's hair. "I don't want to stop," he whispered.

Wil's smile was both loving and lusty. "Shift your hips," he murmured, kissing Zach between words. Gentle hands guided Zach, spread his thighs a little wider, and then there was the blunt press of Wil against him. "Look at me," Wil said, voice low and breathy.

Zach hadn't realized he'd closed his eyes, but at Wil's prompting, he immediately opened them. It was such a big moment, and that firmness rubbing against him where he'd only ever had fingers was as frightening as it was exhilarating. Zach panted softly, his hands gripping at Wil's shoulders. There was that moment of pause on the cusp of something so great, Zach couldn't fully comprehend it, and then Wil was pushing inside him.

The pain was sharp, his breath catching as his toes curled. Wil's lips moved, and Zach was sure sound was coming from between them, but all he could hear was the rushing of his blood in his ears. It hurt. Not so badly that he cried out or tried to pull away, but it was uncomfortable, strange, and he wasn't sure he liked it much. His face screwed up as Wil settled inside him. He shifted on the bed, but it didn't help, and a small whimper spilled from his lips. His hands actually ached from how hard he was gripping at Wil's shoulders, and finally Wil's words filtered into his ears.

"Zach." His name was tight, the timbre of Wil's voice off, a little breathless. "Zach, you have to breathe deeply or else you'll pass out."

He was breathing wrong? Was that why his head was spinning? Zach blinked several times. Yes, he was. He was hyperventilating. He looked up at Wil's face again, concentrated on Wil's dark eyes, and tried to slow his breathing. As he forced deep breaths in and out of his lungs, his body relaxed slowly around Wil, and the odd, full feeling lessened. "Wil..."

"I know." Wil leaned down and kissed him slowly, deeply. "It gets better. I promise."

He wasn't sure how, but he nodded, still preoccupied by his own breathing. Wil's muscles shifted beneath his hands as he moved inside Zach. It was a small thrust, couldn't have been more than a fraction of Wil's length that actually moved, but it felt monumental. The inward caress was the very first he would ever receive, and yet the discomfort and strangeness of it made him tighten and forget all about his breathing. It was so big, so much to take in. Another whimper escaped from between his clenched teeth.

An answering moan drew his attention upward again. "Breathe. If it's too much, we'll stop. It's okay." But the strain in Wil's voice didn't sound okay to Zach. Was he hurting Wil? Was he clenching so tightly it was painful? The thought sobered him, renewed his determination, and he started the deep breaths again. He wanted to help, and the tremor in his breaths slowly eased again, his body releasing its death grip on Wil.

"I'm all right," he finally managed, though the words still wavered a bit. "I'm all right. Don't stop."

Wil's fingers danced along his hairline, smearing through the sweat that beaded on his forehead. The touch was tender, reassuring in a way Zach's hazy mind couldn't define. When it was joined by another little thrust inside, he couldn't help but gasp. Wil took advantage and sealed their lips together while rocking forward, and all Zach could do was moan. It wasn't as bad as before. The discomfort was fading, and the newness somehow went from strange to painfully intimate as their bodies shifted with Wil's slow, careful pace.

The kisses seemed endless, adding a layer of possession on top of everything else. Zach's arms wrapped around Wil's neck, and soon his hips began to arch up into each thrust. The minute he became an active partici-pant in their dance, everything changed. The slight angle, the depth, the in-tensity. One moment he was clumsy and awkward, and the next he was crying out into Wil's mouth, pleasure tingling along every nerve. Wil's lips curved against his, and he rolled his hips just so against Zach. It offered a deep thrust coupled with Wil's stomach moving over the ridge of Zach's cock, and Zach thought he'd never felt anything as pleasurable in his life.

"Wil!" he choked out.

"You like that?" Wil whispered, smirking into their next kiss.

Zach moaned, his knees gripping tightly at Wil's hips. He wanted to say yes, he loved it. That it felt like nothing he'd experienced in his short life. He wanted to shout that he never wanted it to end, that this was every-thing he'd ever dreamed of and more. All he could do, though, was make desperate noises he fed into each kiss, his hands clinging to Wil as they sank into a perfect rhythm together. Zach had been on the edge long before Wil had slid inside him, and while that arousal had wilted a little at the beginning, now it raged through him. He gasped, squirming beneath Wil each time Wil's stomach rubbed against him. His toes curled, and his fingers tightened in Wil's hair.

"God, Wil—" was all Zach managed before he bucked and cried out, coming between their sweaty bodies. It made Wil's cock feel so much thicker inside him, his body clenching around Wil over and over. Wil groaned low and deep, their bodies pressed flush together, the full length of Wil's shaft jerking faintly inside him. Zach stared up at the ceiling with wide eyes, the pleasure rolling through him coupled with the shock of the moment.

Wil's lips peppered sweet kisses over Zach's flushed face until their lips met. The kiss was lazy, slow, and Zach's body trembled. He couldn't help it. Everything seemed to slam into him at once as he lay there beneath Wil, their bodies glued together by come, his ass throbbing, and Mae's quiet babbling coming in through the baby monitor. He swallowed several times, his sinuses stinging, and he was hardly aware of the warm trickle as tears slid down his temples to wet the pillow.

"Hey," Wil said, his voice so gentle. "Zach, are you all right?"

Zach squeezed his eyes shut and let out a long, slow breath. "Yeah," he managed. "It's just... a lot, you know?" He scrubbed at his eyes for a moment. "Just... you and school and work and Mae and this... this moment. This big moment, and... it's a lot," he finished weakly.

Wil smiled that smile of his, the one that told Zach everything would be fine, that he was completely understood. "Yeah, I know," he said, fingers brushing away Zach's tears.

"Will you stay the night?" Zach asked.

"I'd love to." Wil kissed him once more. "I need to pull out and toss the condom. If Mae's all right in her playpen, we can take a quick shower together."

Zach laughed. "My shower's pretty small."

"I don't mind close contact," Wil said with a wink.

In that moment, Zach didn't think he could love anyone more than he loved Wil, except Mae. He pulled Wil down for one more bout of kissing, and only then did he let Wil pull back, separating their bodies. As more of Mae's babbling filtered in through the monitor and Wil stood by the door, removing the condom and tossing it into the trash can, Zach realized he was happy. Sore. Sticky. Tired. But he was happy, and he couldn't help the goofy smile on his face as Wil helped him up, snatched the monitor, and dragged him into the bathroom.

# Chapter Eighteen

Awareness came very slowly to Zach. The warmth of his bed made it so easy to stay in his dreams. They were good dreams, filled with light and all those pleasant emotions that made his skin tingle and his chest tight with happiness. There was light outside the dreams, too, though. That was the first vague sense that pulled him upwards. He hadn't pulled the blinds tight enough, or maybe he'd fallen asleep with the light on again.

But then his sense of smell registered. Biscuits and sizzling bacon. Wait, bacon? He twitched in his half-sleep, his head turning to the side, and then another smell filled his nose. Wil's unique spicy scent washed over him, and his toes curled as he mindlessly buried his face in the pillow. Rolling over made the empty space next to him almost startlingly apparent, and his eyes opened as he slammed into reality.

Wil had stayed the night. Wil was here. They'd had sex, showered together, and Wil had put Mae to bed and held him as he fell asleep afterward. Wil must have let him sleep in, and those amazing smells meant Wil was making breakfast.

Oh, God. This was it. This was the morning after. He'd never really thought beyond the losing-his-virginity part. Wil had woken up next to him and was now using his kitchen. A quick look at Mae's crib revealed she was already up as well. He was usually so in tune with Mae, and yet he'd been so worn out that he'd slept through her waking up and shifting about in her crib. Then again, last night had been unlike anything he'd ever experienced before.

A flush stole across his face, making him feel too warm against the pillow and sheets. Stretching only made the blushing worse, though. He was still sore, still a bit sensitive, and it was such a good feeling! He hid in the covers for another minute before rolling out of bed. He pulled out a pair of sweatpants and slipped them on with trembling fingers.

What was he supposed to do? What was he supposed to say to Wil after last night? He hesitated at the doorway, shifting from foot to foot, his stomach working itself into knots. Bathroom. His bladder was incredibly full, so he might as well buy himself a little time. Zach rushed from his bedroom to the bathroom, shutting the door silently behind him. It didn't take long for him to relieve himself, wash his hands and face, and drag a comb through his hair. He stared at the closed door for as long as he dared, and then he opened it, stepping out into the living area.

Mae was in her swing by the table, and when she saw him, she began to bang her hands against the little tray in front of her. "Bbbllphhl!"

"Mae," Wil said from in the kitchen. "You need to be quiet or you'll wake up—"

"Too late." Zach smiled as Wil turned around. "The smell woke me." He walked over to the swing and picked Mae up, settling her on his hip. He nuzzled her soft hair, inhaled her unique baby scent, and smiled. Damn, he felt so good, even if it was coupled with an awkwardness he couldn't quite shake. He headed into the small kitchen and watched Wil pull out a tray of biscuits from the oven. They had the smell of instant ones from a can, but he didn't mind. "You didn't have to do this."

Wil set the tray on the stove. He turned and wrapped an arm around Zach's waist. "I wanted to. I haven't been able to cook breakfast for you yet. I wanted to take advantage of the opportunity." He smiled and kissed Zach softly. "Sleep well?"

"Better than I have in a while." Zach shifted Mae's weight. "I just... I don't really know what to do now. You know, since we've..." What did he call it? Fucking? Sex? Fornication?

"Made love?" Wil offered.

Color crept over Zach's cheeks. "Made love, yes."

Wil bent down a little, brushing warm lips over his hot cheeks. "Well, I'd say we start with breakfast. Mae already had a bottle, but she keeps looking at me like she expects more. Can't blame her, though, with how good it all smells."

"I am hungry," Zach admitted, angling his neck so their lips met in a kiss that lingered perfectly, calming a few of his nerves. Mae squirmed in his arms and started babbling again, and he chuckled. "Yes, Mae, it's time for num-nums. Daddy's going to follow Wil's lead and give you your own little feast."

"She deserves it just as much as you do," Wil agreed, bending to give Mae a little kiss and tickle her into a fit of happy giggles.

The whole thing just made Zach's heart want to burst with joy, and he found himself walking Mae to her highchair with a bounce in his step. Once she was secured with the tray in front of her, he returned to the kitchen, going to the fridge for the infant applesauce he always kept in stock for Mae. He glanced over at Wil, who was softly humming to himself as he flipped a fried egg with an effortless flick of his wrist. "You really fed Mae her bottle while I was sleeping?"

"Sure did," Wil grinned, and when he caught a glimpse of Zach's expression, he chuckled. "A lot of little cousins, remember? This isn't my first rodeo. Besides, I wanted to let you sleep. I really tired you out."

Oh, there was a smugness there now, and it made Zach laugh and nudge him as he passed Wil to get to the pantry. "Brag away, but I'd like to think I gave as much as I took." His voice became a bit softer as he asked, "I... did okay, right? I didn't embarrass myself too much?"

Wil plated the last egg and put the hot pan into the sink before wrapping both arms around Zach's waist and pulled him forward, ignoring that Zach had a box of Cheerios in one hand and one of Mae's miniature, sectioned plates in the other. The press of their abdomens and Wil's box-ers-covered groin brought another infuriating blush to his face. With his hands full, he couldn't hide his face, but Wil just kissed along one of his cheeks. "You were perfect, Zach. I'm not just saying that, either," Wil purred. "You were amazing."

Pride made Zach's heart speed in his chest, and he couldn't help the relieved smile that curved his lips. "I love you." The words were simple, but he meant them.

"I love you, too." Wil kissed him again. "Now, let's eat."

It was so domestic, like those dinners they sometimes had. But this was more than a quick meal shared while Mae watched them from her highchair. Despite all they had done before since his birthday, he'd given more of himself last night than he had before. Maybe the importance of it was all in his head, but it was still important. They'd taken this giant step together and this was *the morning after*, when things changed. Wasn't that what his mom had always told him? Sex changed everything. It had with Bethany. Hell, that had changed his entire *life*. Was this going to change his life, too? Yes, it would. It would change his life, and it would change Mae's. That gave him pause. He watched Wil set down the plates, pour orange juice, and poke Mae's nose. She laughed at him, grasped his finger, and gave him that slobbery grin of hers.

In four short months that felt like a lifetime, he'd fallen in love with Wil and brought him into Mae's life. He licked his lips as anxiety twisted his gut. Zach was sure he could survive a broken heart, being disappointed and hurt if Wil left, but Mae... Mae was different. Mae was his daughter, and he was supposed to protect her from disappointment and hurt and heartbreak. He sat down in his chair and spooned some applesauce into Mae's plate, and then added some Cheerios for her to munch on.

"Hey," Wil said, fork poised over his eyes.

Zach blinked, flushing from his neck to the tip of his ears. "Hmm?"

"You look like someone just killed your dog. Want to tell me what's going on in that head of yours?"

"I... just... all this," Zach said, waving his hand around. "You. Me. Mae. Sex. You spending the night and making me breakfast in the morning."

Wil's smile fell. "Oh. Did... Should I have not made breakfast? If I wasn't supposed to take care of Mae..."

Zach's stomach twisted, and he prodded at his egg. "It's not that. Well, it is and it isn't. This is all really new. I've never had this with anyone, so I don't know what it all means, how things will change, or even *if* things will change."

"Change as in what?" Wil prodded gently.

"I don't know, just change," Zach murmured. "Big changes like spending the night and raising Mae together and moving in and... and meeting extended family for more than a while-I'm-in-town brunch."

"Would those changes be unwelcome?"

"No. I mean, I don't think so." Zach fidgeted with his fork. "I don't know. I just have all these pictures in my head, you know? They're like blueprints of what we're supposed to do, all the steps normal couples are supposed to take, and I don't know if I'm ready for any of it if that's what's actually coming. I hadn't thought past that moment last night with you, and everything is just here now, and so big, and how do we—"

Fingers against his lips suddenly silenced him, and he blushed when he realized that Wil was practically standing to lean over the table and hush him. "It's all right, Zach. You do today what you did last night and every day before that." Zach blinked at Wil, and his expression made Wil's face crack into a smile. "Breathe. You breathe."

Zach let out a breath he hadn't even realized he'd been holding, an echo of laughter in the huff as he shook his head. "How are you able to take everything in stride? How can you be so calm and take care of Mae with one hand while the other makes me breakfast?"

Wil gave a nonchalant shrug. "I just think that we can get through the big stuff fine as long as we help each other along the way," he said, his voice the most soothing Zach had ever heard it. A smirk ticked up one side of Wil's mouth. "And it helps to be ambidextrous."

The joke brought another laughing exhale from Zach as he let the worst of his tension bleed out of him. His shoulders relaxed, and he reached out to squeeze Wil's hand. "I just worry about everything. I want what's best for Mae, and changes are hard to take, hard to plan for. I want to keep you close, but I'm not sure how close is too close, you know?"

"I understand," Wil said, squeezing his hand back before letting it go and pointing to Zach's plate of food. Zach took the hint and started eating. Eggs were never good cold, and Wil had made them especially for him. Wil took a bite and chewed a bit before adding, "We have a lot going on right now. Thanksgiving is around the corner, finals, and then there's Christmas, and our families are demanding time. Working retail's a fucking nightmare right now, and we're trying to hold things together and move forward in our relationship. There's a lot on our plates and that's okay."

Mae babbled and pawed at her plate, managing to get some apple-sauced Cheerios into her mouth. Zach chuckled. "Yeah, the holidays are crazy."

"So, it's okay. Overwhelmed and weird and great," Wil said with a smile. "It's all okay."

Zach let out a long breath. "Right now, I think I'll just enjoy today." He looked at Wil and smiled. "You, me, and Mae. I'll enjoy us." Maybe it wasn't that simple, but Zach was going to *make* it that simple. He had today, and tomorrow he could worry. Worry about Thanksgiving, about Christmas, about the new year, about all the what ifs that made him bolt upright in bed in the middle of the night. Today, though, was for celebrating a milestone. "How about, after breakfast, we clean Mae up and go to the beach? Water's too cold, but she'd have fun playing in the sand."

Wil grinned at him, blue eyes sparkling. "Sounds perfect."

"Yeah," Zach said, eyes turning to Mae and her giggling, her hands pressed to her smiling face. "Yeah, it does."

# Chapter Nineteen

There wasn't much of a breeze or chill in the air when Zach stepped out of the building his final exam had been held in. That was one of the sad things about Florida: it didn't matter if it was Christmas Day or the Fourth of July, the weather was pretty much the same. The only differ-ence was that in December, the sky was more or less gray. Always gray. He looked up at the clouds, wondering if there would be any rain to follow them. At least the semester was over. One less thing for him to worry about. Except he would worry until the grades were posted. He had to pass. He'd worked so hard, even taking the last week off to ensure he studied enough.

He paused outside the door and dug into his bag, looking for his keys. Zach also couldn't help but look at his cellphone, wondering if Wil had called or texted him during the exam. They'd made love, and then ev-erything had exploded. Thanksgiving had meant they'd both been pulled in by family, and once that was over, final exams and work. Working for Wal-mart, especially during December, was a harrowing experience, if you asked Zach, and he earned every minimum wage dollar he received.

No message. He sighed, plucked his keys from the bag, and looked up. He then almost dropped his keys. Wil was standing at the end of the walkway, holding three balloons and a bouquet of colorful flowers. Zach's face heated with a flush as he forced his feet forward, a goofy smile making its way to his lips. "What's this for?" he asked when he stood in front of Wil.

"For surviving finals." Wil held out the flowers. "For being a great dad and an awesome boyfriend. Because I love you. There's dozens of rea-sons, the foremost being we haven't spoken much, let alone seen each other, since before Thanksgiving."

Zach grinned as he took the flowers and immediately wrapped his arms around Wil's neck. "You're romantic and sweet and cheesy as hell, but I love you even more because of it," he laughed before closing the distance between their lips. The kiss was soft, lingering, and it made his heart feel light. "I did it," he murmured as he pulled back a fraction for air. "I really made it through the semester."

"You did," Wil chuckled, leading Zach out to the parking lot. "Thanks to a lot of hard work, great study buddies, and a little help from the people who love you most."

"Fishing for a compliment?" Zach laughed.

"Actually, I was talking about your parents. If mine hadn't had sticks up their asses, I'd have joined you and yours for Thanksgiving. Probably would have given my mom a heart attack even though it would have meant one less mouth to feed in such a huge family."

"The big family gatherings." Zach remembered that detail. Sisters, nieces, nephews, cousins, second-cousins. The breadth of Wil's family was daunting.

"Huge," Wil confirmed with a wry smile. "Something I've inherited. Christmas, I'm all yours after ten. I told them we can do the whole breakfast and presents thing, but it's a special day for you and Mae, too."

Warmth surged through Zach at the thought of sharing Christmas with Wil at his side, not to mention the way Wil had just referred to Mae and him as family. He stopped at his car and unlocked the passenger door, tossing his bag inside. "So, you'll be coming over to my apartment for late morning presents and Christmas cookies?"

"That's the plan, unless you do things differently with your family."

Zach grinned. "Now that I'm out of the house, I think we're saving presents until we do Christmas dinner. It won't be a huge event or anything, but it'll be Mae's first Christmas, and I know my parents are going to want to record every second." He pulled back just a little from Wil. "You sure you want to be subjected to all that?"

"Are you kidding?" Wil squeezed around Zach's waist. "I wouldn't miss it for anything."

"Ten o'clock Christmas morning, you, me, and Mae."

Wil nosed his cheek. "Yes, but... if you have no plans for today..."

"Only plan I have," Zach murmured, turning so his lips brushed against Wil's, "is going to the tree lot on Fletcher and picking out any tree under forty dollars."

"Want some company? We can even splurge and find a tree under a hundred."

Zach frowned. "A hundred dollar tree?"

Wil nodded. "Anything under fifty will be puny."

"I only budgeted forty for the tree." Zach unlocked the driver side door.

"I can cover the difference," Wil said, following him around the car.

Zach sighed. "Look, I know you mean well, but..." Wil frowned, and Zach hated that look on Wil's face. He looked down at his scuffed shoes. "How about you go to the lot and pick the tree, and I'll go to Walmart to get the decorations since I have an employee discount. Mom is bringing Mae by in a couple hours. We'd have enough time to set up the tree before she shows up."

Wil hugged him, made him look up. "Everything okay?"

Briefly, Zach thought to bring up all the money Wil effortlessly spent on him, on Mae, but it was so close to Christmas. It was a happy season, Mae's first, and he didn't want to ruin what Wil meant to be a generous, loving thing. He smiled. "Everything's fine. Go to the lot. I like Fraser firs. They smell best."

"Smell best?"

Zach nodded. "They smell like Christmas." He kissed Wil. "Go get the tree. I'll meet you back at the apartment."

"Will do." Wil hugged him again. "Congrats on the final final for 2012," he murmured between one kiss and the next.

"If we're quick," Zach found himself saying, "maybe there will be time between finishing the tree and Mom showing up for us to celebrate the final final."

The soft little moan that rumbled up out of Wil made Zach's stomach flutter, and a tingle made its way down his spine to his groin as Wil purred, "I'll do my best to hurry, then. I wouldn't want to miss the opportunity."

"You do that," Zach chuckled as he forced himself to pull back. He reached up, pulling one of the balloons down to place between them. If he didn't get a little distance between him and Wil at that moment, he feared he might never get in his car. "Thanks for the flowers and balloons."

"You've earned them. You've also earned a great night of Christmas tunes and tinsel," Wil added with a grin, and Zach fell in love with him all over again at that. "Go," Wil insisted before he could get a word in edgewise. "I'll see you back at your place soon."

With parting kisses, he stuffed the balloons into his car. He gave Wil a wave out the window and hummed "Carol of the Bells" to himself as he turned out of the parking lot, the weight of final exams finally lifting from his shoulders.

The holiday section of Walmart had been the bane of Zach's existence as an employee, but there was something exciting about actually shopping for his own decorations. It took away the flatness of knowing how every shelf was stocked. It erased the headaches he'd endured making sure every label matched when they had switched the displays around to drive shoppers to specific items. He might have known exactly where to look for each kind of decoration he wanted, but still, he lingered in the aisles. He leaned against his cart and tapped the handle in time with the music playing softly over the sound system.

He perused the shelves. Did he want LED lights or normal ones? Blinky or constant? He even stopped in front of the old-fashioned flicker lights that gave off an orange glow that imitated candles. If he was getting a nice tree, he knew he had to get a few nice ornaments, too. Sure, he had a few he'd kept from his parents in a box at home, but none of them were exactly color coordinated. For a moment, he wondered if Wil had any ornaments to add. That brought a smile to his face. Over time, maybe he and Wil would build up their own collection of ornaments with Mae.

It was amazing, the way he could picture himself with Wil for years to come. It was also scary as hell. In such a short time, he'd become attached, and so had Mae. He was lucky, though, to have a stable relationship with an awesome guy, even if Wil kept spending way too much money on them. But, it was a giving season, and he could forgive a little splurging to make Mae's first Christmas great.

It would be a wonderful Christmas if he just allowed himself to stop worrying. He didn't have school to worry about for the next few weeks. In fact, he'd felt so good about finishing the semester that he'd signed on to take an extra class in the spring. If he could get through his degree just a little faster with Wil's support, then that was exactly what he wanted to do. Mae was nine months old now, and he knew she was only going to become more active. The sooner he finished his schooling, the better things would be for Mae. That was all that mattered.

He snatched up a few boxes of multi-colored lights and one strand of blinky, white lights. They would be fun to look at on the tree at night. He then moved on to the ornaments and tree toppers, a bounce in his step as he looked through the angels and stars. His parents always had an angel on top of the tree, but there were some really beautiful blown glass toppers that were more abstract, with bulbs and glitter and fiberoptics. What would

Wil want to top the tree with? He wondered if Wil's family had a tradition they followed with toppers like Zach's family did.

If he'd met Wil's family before, he might have asked them. He could have called them up and conspired with them to surprise Wil with something he'd like. But, as things stood, he hadn't even met Wil's parents, not to mention Wil's two older sisters and their huge families. He frowned as his fingers trailed over the lines of a delicate, glass star. Why didn't Wil introduce him? He didn't like to think that Wil might be hiding him or embarrassed by him, but what other reason could there be for him holding back?

Zach chewed at his lip as he debated between the fiberoptic angel and a silver, glittering snowflake. Tradition won out, and he snatched up the pretty angel, tossing it into his buggy. Lights and tree topper, now he actually needed to decide on ornaments. He glanced at his watch. This was taking too long. If he didn't get a move on, Wil would be waiting in front of his apartment with a tree, sticky with sap. He stared at the wide selection of glass ornaments and plucked several of the brighter color packages. It was going to be one colorful Christmas, he thought as he hurried to the front of the store. Now, if only he could figure out why Wil was hiding him from his parents, his holiday would be complete.

# Chapter Twenty

Mae crawled across the floor toward the brightly lit tree with the handful of colorful packages under it. Zach rushed over and picked her up, swinging her into the air with a smile.

"No, princess, not yet. We have to wait for Wil." Zach cradled her against him and looked at the clock again. Quarter after ten. It was Christmas morning, so Zach figured Wil's family was keeping him. "How about some num-nums, hmm? I got you that guava stuff you love so much."

As he walked into the kitchen, a knock at the door sounded. His heart leaped into his chest. He snatched up the jar of guava baby food and rushed to the door. A quick peek out the peephole, and he unlocked the door. "You're late," he announced to Wil, and then his smile fell.

Wil stood outside in the damp, cool mist of Christmas morning with his arms full of presents, plus a bag of presents at his feet. It made his measly contribution seem absolutely pathetic. Never mind that he'd been saving for Christmas since August, blown the food budget on ornaments and stockings. He forced the smile back onto his face when Wil peered around the mass of gifts.

"Sorry," Wil said, stepping into the apartment. "You wouldn't think there'd be traffic on Christmas morning, but Fletcher was busy. Got caught up. But, I'm here now!" He set the load of packages on the counter, retrieved the bag, and closed the door. He turned to face Mae and Zach, a bright smile on his face. "Merry Christmas to my two favorite people." Wil leaned in and rubbed his cool nose against Mae's cheek, making her squirm and giggle in Zach's arms.

"Merry Christmas." Zach lifted his face in anticipation of the sweet, slow kiss Wil offered. "I'm glad you made it. We were getting worried."

"Nothing to worry about. If clingy relatives can't keep me away, then nothing can," Wil purred against his lips, kissing him again an instant later.

Zach smiled, though Wil's comment brought back that niggling in the back of his mind. Wil had been careful not to mention his family much over the last couple weeks, or that's the way it seemed to Zach. Then again, Zach might have been overly conscious of it. Just a little. Suspicion had a

way of making him obsessive. "So," he began, shifting Mae from his hip over to Wil. "Your family is doing well?"

"A mile a minute, as usual," Wil chuckled, tickling Mae until she was a squealing, kicking mass in his arms. "It's a whirlwind every Christmas. Too many people trying to coordinate with a single person's watch."

"That person being your mom?"

"How'd you guess?" Wil's tone was equal parts sarcasm and humor. Zach laughed as he set down the jar of baby food. He then picked up a few of the boxes from the bar and motioned for Wil to follow him to the tree. "She's always getting on people about being punctual," Wil said, "but when half of your eight cousins have families of their own, it's pretty much impossible to get everyone to the table at seven thirty sharp."

"Sounds like more excitement than my mom and dad would ever be able to handle," Zach mused as he arranged Wil's presents under the tree they'd decorated together. He had to remind himself not to count the gifts, not to compare his number to Wil's. He already knew Wil outnumbered him; he didn't need to know just how much. Wil handed him the presents from the bag as well, and he did his best to hide a blush when he read the labels, seeing several presents with his name on them. "Does your family know about me?"

Wil paused before handing him the next present, and Zach cursed his lack of basic tact. "Of course they know about you. I talked to them about you less than an hour ago. My parents, my sister..."

"They know I'm a guy? That Mae is here, too?"

Wil frowned now, and Zach's throat tightened as fear made his pulse race. "Zach, what's wrong? What are you getting at?"

"Nothing!" Zach hurried to make that frown disappear. "It's nothing. Really. I just wanted to make sure they actually knew about us. I mean... Isn't it time they got to meet me? We've been together for six months, and you've never brought up visiting them or even going out for coffee or something."

A soft smile slowly replaced the more severe expression on Wil's face, and Zach let out a sigh of relief when Wil spoke again, his tone soft, almost embarrassed. "I was going to wait until later to bring it up, actually, but consider yourself officially invited to my parents' New Year's Eve party next week."

"I am?" Excitement bubbled inside Zach. "Me and Mae?"

"You're invited, but I didn't know if you wanted to bring Mae. It is a New Year's Eve party."

Zach slowly sat on the floor with Mae between his legs. "You... don't want your family to meet Mae?"

Wil crouched, frowning again. "Yeah, I do, but I thought a busy New Year's Eve party with guests and champagne and a three A.M. bedtime weren't really Mae's bag. But, if you want to bring her, I don't mind."

"You're right." Zach laughed, the sound tight as he shook his head. "I'm just being stupid. I thought you might be ashamed of us. Like you didn't want your family to know you're dating some poor store clerk who has a baby."

"No." Wil kissed him. "That's not it at all. I wanted us to be good before I dragged my parents into it. If I were honest, I'd say I'm a bit embarrassed by my parents, not you. My mom still thinks my being gay is a phase. Let's not bring up that I've been out to them since freshman year of high school. It's a phase until I meet the right girl."

Zach tsked. "A phase?"

"Yep. Don't you know, I can be cured by the right woman with the right breeding." Wil winked. "Now, how about we open gifts and stockings and watch *Rudolph* with Mae, hmm? It's a lot more fun than talking about my parents."

"You really went all out on Christmas presents," Zach said, reaching for the stocking he'd made Wil. "I feel kind of shitty for barely affording what I did get."

Wil shrugged. "It's the thought, Zach." He took his stocking. "My mom chooses a couple of things for everyone, but she has a personal shopper who does most of the gift shopping for the family."

Zach blinked. "Your parents don't buy all your presents themselves?"

"Nope." Wil began pulling out the various candy and small, wrapped trinkets from his stocking. "Awesome, Zach. I love coconut Santas!"

"I hoped you would. You always get the Almond Joy ice cream, so I guessed you like chocolate and coconut." Pride filled Zach. He'd been watching Wil for a while now, trying to memorize his preferences. "I was tempted to clear Walmart out of them for you." He picked up Mae's stocking and began to unload it for her. Zach looked up and smiled as Wil snatched up the digital camera from the bookshelf and looked it over.

"Mom and Dad gave that to me yesterday as an early Christmas present so we could document our first Christmas morning," Zach explained.

Wil crouched again and began snapping pictures. "Your parents are awesome, Zach. I think if I'd come home and told them I was going to be raising a baby on my own, my parents would have had me committed."

"Oh, I'm sure it passed through Mom's and Dad's minds," Zach said, dancing the small, stuffed rabbit from Mae's stocking in front of her. "But, I knew what I wanted, and I wasn't going to be talked out of it. I was having a baby, and I refused to give up."

"One of many reasons why I love you."

Zach smiled, and Wil took another picture of him with that smile on his face and Mae chewing on the ear of her new bunny. Present after present was unwrapped, gushed over, and pictures taken. By the time they were done, Mae had a new spring wardrobe and a dozen new toys and books, Zach had new clothes for work and several books, and Wil had a couple new movies and a framed picture of Zach with Mae. It was perfect. A little much, but Zach didn't regret a thing. Mae crawled about in the discarded paper, babbling to herself, and Zach cuddled with Wil on the floor against the couch.

"I'll ask my parents to look after Mae during the party," Zach murmured, his eyes always on Mae. "I'm sure they won't mind."

"You mean they don't like to get all lushed out on New Year's?" Wil asked with melodramatic flair. "Shocking!"

Zach laughed. "I know. My parents would probably share a drink between the two of them and call it quits. I saw my mom tipsy once, and she felt guilty over it for days afterward, worried she was being a bad role model."

Wil's arms tightened around him. "If you ask me, your mom and dad did a perfect job with you. You're smart, dedicated, loving, and cute as hell."

The last was purred against Zach's hair, and he chuckled as he turned his head, looking away from Mae for an instant to wrinkle his nose at Wil. "Cute as hell?"

"Yes." Wil grinned. "And it's a quality your daughter has definitely inherited. Right, Mae?" Mae looked over at the sound of her name, grinned broadly and squealed happily, waving a handful of ribbons at them amidst the wrapping paper. "See? Cute as hell."

Zach just laughed and settled against Wil again, unable to do anything but smile. He wasn't sure how long they stayed like that, but when Mae finally made her way over to them, crawling into their arms, Zach looked up at the clock and hummed at the time. "Are you ready to go see Grandma, Mae? Are you ready for more presents and Christmas kiwis?"

"Kiwi?" Wil chuckled as they slowly righted themselves and started to gather Mae's things.

Zach added a couple of her new toys to her bag with a grin, bouncing Mae on his hip. "She's never had kiwi before. I thought it would be something new for her to try today. Mom promised she would pick up the best ones she could find at the store."

"Sounds like tonight is going to be full of amazing firsts for all of us," Wil murmured, dipping low to catch Zach's lips in a kiss before helping him to his feet.

Zach's heart fluttered in his chest, and he squeezed Mae as happiness spread warmly through him. "It will be."

# Chapter Twenty-One

Zach bounced Mae on his hip as he listened to Wil's cellphone ring and ring. When the voicemail picked up, he hung up the phone. "Dammit." He looked around his apartment as if it held the answer to his current predicament. The clock on the wall told him Wil would be here soon, and what the hell was he supposed to do with Mae? He picked up the phone again, dialed Wil's cellphone, and waited. Voicemail again. Zach barely resisted the urge to throw the phone against the wall.

"Okay, princess," he murmured, heading into the bedroom. "I guess you're coming with Wil and me to a party."

He set Mae down on her changing table and opened up drawers. Mae squirmed and kicked, shoving her hand into her mouth as she watched him. As much as he loved her, he hadn't thought he'd be meeting Wil's family with his daughter. Not yet, at least. But nothing big ever went quite right for him, and his mother's last-minute cancellation had thrown a wrench into his night. Teeth gritted, he chose one of Mae's best dresses, some cute ruffled socks, and her Mary Jane shoes. It would have to do.

After changing her diaper, he set to dressing her, teasing her belly when she tried to put up a bit of a fuss. He slid on a white bow headband that really stood out against the soft, dark wisps of hair she'd begun to grow the month before. She looked beautiful, and Zach hoped it was enough to impress Wil's parents. He quickly slid on her Mary Janes, straightened her dress, and then picked her up. Just as he was settling her against him, a knock sounded at the door. He rushed over and opened it, tears in his eyes when he saw Wil.

God, Wil was dressed to kill, and it made Zach feel horribly inadequate in his slacks and shirt. He wanted to cry. He wanted to throw up. Instead, he blurted out, "Mom has the flu, which means Dad has it too, and we didn't want to risk Mae catching it, so I have Mae tonight. I tried to dress her up and I tried to call you in case you wanted to reschedule, but your voicemail kept picking up and I didn't know what to do and now we're both dressed and you're here but I need to get her bag together and I haven't fed—"

Wil pressed two fingers to his lips and smiled. "Calm down. Every-thing's fine. Mae is beautiful, and you're gorgeous." He stepped inside. "Now, what do you need?"

Zach let out a slow breath, trying to tamp down the knot of anxiety that had settled in his stomach. "Mae's bag has to be packed, and I haven't fed her yet."

"Okay. Not a problem. You make a bottle, grab a couple jars of food, and I'll put her bag together." Wil kissed his cheek. "She can have her bottle on the way there, and if she's fussy, we can take over the kitchen and feed her again."

A slow, hopeful smile found its way to Zach's face. "Really?" It couldn't possibly be so simple.

"Really. Go on. Fix her a bottle." Wil gave Zach's ass a swat before heading into the bedroom.

Zach adjusted Mae on his hips and grinned at her. "Wil, it seems, is in charge."

"Damn right!" Wil called out from the bedroom.

Zach laughed, and it was such a relief that the nausea began to sub-side. He stepped into the kitchen and began making Mae a bottle. Maybe tonight was going to be awesome after all.

Every ounce of calm Zach had managed to gain with Wil's help the last half hour was lost completely. Every house on this street seemed bigger and more impressive than the last. It might have been normal for Cheval, but Cheval had to be the most upper-class place within an hour's drive of his apartment. There had been a drug bust just across the street from his apartment; here, they had gated communities and *armed guards*.

He was breathing a little unevenly when they pulled up to the huge, two-story house. By the time he walked up the pathway of the manicured lawn, he was ready to have a heart attack. Mae squeaked in his arms, squirming against his hip, and he whispered a breathless apology to her. "Sorry, princess. I know I squeezed you a little too hard. Bear with Daddy. Be a good girl and don't cry."

Mae looked up at him, her eyes telling him she was seriously debat-ing giving a good wail. He stopped in his tracks and shifted her, his heart pounding in his chest as he nestled her against him and peppered her cheeks with little kisses. He forced his voice to a soothing coo and smiled at her. "It's an adventure, princess. You like adventures, don't you? Yes, you do!"

"Problem?" Wil asked as he joined them halfway up the path, his hand automatically petting Mae's hair in an effort to quiet her. He shifted Mae's diaper bag on his shoulder, and Zach almost demanded to have Wil hand it over to him.

"My fault," Zach admitted. "I'm jittery. That's all."

"Nothing to worry about," Wil insisted for what had to be the hundredth time that evening. It was a phrase he was sure Wil was tired of saying, but he couldn't help but take comfort in the constant support.

He took a deep breath in and exhaled slowly before nodding. "You're right. Tonight's gonna be great. And they're gonna love you, aren't they, Mae?" Mae finally cracked a smile, and that bolstered his courage enough to start walking again. He was about to raise his hand to knock on the door when Wil simply stepped past him and turned the knob. "Shouldn't we...?"

"I used to live here," Wil chuckled. "My mom still keeps my room aired out, just in case. It's all right. Come in."

Zach shifted on his feet, and butterflies fluttered in his stomach as he stepped over the threshold. He couldn't help but stare. The entryway was spotless, and the hardwood floor gleamed in the warm light that seemed to draw him in toward the center of the house. There was a wide, curved staircase partially blocking the view, and he leaned down to murmur to Mae, who was looking around curiously. "See that staircase, Mae? That's where princesses like you come down to make grand entrances with billowing dresses and sparkling tiaras."

"Sounds like a flashback to my high school prom," a female voice sounded from behind him.

Zach jumped, tightening his arms around Mae. He was strung *way* too tightly. One more surprise like that, and he might just have a nervous breakdown. He stared at the woman, and his protective grip on Mae relaxed a little. She had the same blue eyes as Wil, but her long hair was a pretty chestnut brown color. She was dressed to the nines, though, and it made her almost otherworldly to Zach. He swallowed, unable to make his voice work.

"Chelsea, stop that!" Wil chuckled. "You know better than to sneak up on a man with a baby."

"It's the men who usually have the problem with it, not the babies." Chelsea laughed, pulling Wil into a hug and giving Zach a wink before stepping back to grin at Wil. "Just like you to be late. Mom's gonna strangle you."

"Look who's talking, sneaking in behind us."

Chelsea held up the camera in her hand and wiggled it almost accusingly. It looked expensive to Zach, like one of those professional, digital ones that made fake shutter noises and had a million different settings. "Brian insisted he needed this from the car. I swear, he's just documenting everything to pick through later and use as blackmail."

"He'd better watch it, then," Wil warned, turning to Zach and slipping an arm around his lower back. "Zach here is a criminology major, and his partner, Mae, is sharp as a tack. No funny business will get past her."

Chelsea raised both hands in playful surrender. "I consider myself warned." Her posture relaxed, and she held out her hand to Zach. "Hey, Zach. I'm Chelsea. Glad you could make it out. My baby brother won't shut up about you and Mae."

"Chels." Wil blushed, and it was such a rare sight that it put Zach instantly at ease.

Zach smiled as he took Chelsea's hand and shook it before shifting Mae a little on his hip. "It's nice to meet you. I hope you don't mind me bringing Mae. It's her first big party."

"Not at all," Chelsea said with an easy smile. "Though, you won't find any other kids here tonight. This is the one night I hire a sitter and have a couple cocktails."

"Chelsea is the proud mother of a girl and twin boys," Wil explained.

"Fraternal twin terrors," Chelsea corrected. "My girl is a piece of glitter-bedecked cake compared to those two. I'd thought to tie the score with Jess, but I think I've had as many as I want."

Jess... Zach had heard that name before, and it clicked into place a few seconds later. Jessica was Wil's eldest sister, which made Chelsea the middle child. She still looked a good deal older than Wil, though, and having three kids just blew Zach away. "You look amazing for a mother of three," Zach said, and then blushed as he quickly amended. "I mean, you look amazing in general. That dress is amazing."

He stopped himself before he said the word 'amazing' another dozen times. It made Chelsea beam, and so his embarrassment was worth it. "This old thing?" she teased before giving a little twirl. "No, it's actually new. I wanted something fun. I think I'm channeling my daughter. She loved all the beading."

Mae giggled and clapped her hands in Zach's arms, and he kissed Mae's forehead, the last of his nerves starting to melt away with Mae's good cheer. "I think Mae likes it, too. Wait a few more years, princess. I don't know if I want to think of you in something so slinky yet."

"Slinky. That's a good word for it," Chelsea agreed before gesturing. "Come on in. There's a whole party, not just me. Is Mae all right, or will she need a change or meal sometime soon?"

"I think she's a little overwhelmed by everything new," Wil answered for him. "But she might start getting fussy in a bit. Permission to commandeer the kitchen?"

Chelsea all but snorted. "If you can manage to get Jess out of there, sure. I think she'd rather hide in there all night and supervise than be the social butterfly."

"Only room for one of those in this family," Wil chuckled, and when Chelsea wrinkled her nose at him, he urged her forward toward the party. "Go. I'll make the rounds with Zach in a bit."

Before Zach could even say goodbye to Chelsea, Wil pushed him past the stairs along a hallway. "Your sister seems nice," he muttered.

"She's great. Acts more like sixteen instead of almost forty."

"And she's the middle one?"

Wil nodded. "Yep. I was the happy accident that pushed Dad's retirement plan back by eighteen years."

The kitchen Wil ushered him into was easily as big as Zach's apartment. Food was laid out on shining trays, and several servers moved in and out through another door. In the middle of it all was a woman, tall and full-figured, with her tawny hair pulled up into an elegant sweep. She seemed to have everything under some sort of chaotic order that baffled Zach, and Wil moved past him to hug her from behind.

"Watch it, Wil," the woman said, a tremor of a laugh in her voice. "This dress wrinkles easily."

"Then you shouldn't have worn it to a party with mandatory hugging and kissing." Wil stepped back. "Looking good, Jess. Where's Josh?"

When Jess turned, Zach could see she wasn't simply full-figured. She looked about ready to pop! Wil hadn't told him Jess was pregnant. Zach shifted on his feet, and when he moved Mae from one hip to another, he felt the cool heaviness of her diaper. Great, she was wet, and he didn't see an easily accessible bathroom to change her in.

"He's in the living room with Daddy. You're late."

Wil rolled his eyes. "I'm always late."

Zach frowned a little. Wil was the most punctual person he knew.

"Well, Mom's not thrilled. She wanted to prance her pretty prince around her friends." Jess looked over to Zach. "You must be Zach," she said with a smile. "I'm Jessica. Wil's eldest sister."

"It's pleasure to meet you," Zach murmured.

Jess' eyes lit up. "Oh, you brought your daughter." She walked over to him, and he couldn't believe she could be so graceful in such high heels while quite pregnant. "I'm having my first girl next month." She pressed a perfectly manicured finger to Mae's nose and made a sound, which earned a slobbery grin from Mae. "I have four boys at home."

"Four?"

Wil popped an olive in his mouth. "I told you I had a big family. Thank God Chels figured out what causes babies and *stopped*, unlike Jess."

"I know what causes babies, little brother, as I do believe it was part of the reason my graduation was ruined."

"Your graduation?" Zach asked, looking between the two of them.

"Mom went into labor with me the day before Jess graduated from Harvard. Mom and Dad missed it." Wil grinned. "Jess hasn't let me forget her selfless sacrifice."

Zach laughed, but Mae began to fuss. "She's wet, Wil. I need to change her."

Wil nodded. "Sure thing." He kissed Jess on the cheek. "Tell Mom and Dad I'm here. I'll be down in a bit."

"Uh-huh. Should I let them know you brought Mae?"

Wil paused at the door of the kitchen, his hand on the small of Zach's back. "Yeah," he said after a pause. "No point trying to hide it."

Jess and Wil shared a look Zach didn't fully understand, but as Mae began to kick and whine, he didn't want to ask after it. If they didn't get Mae changed, there would be a squealing, kicking, crying scene he'd rather avoid. "Where can I change her?"

"My room will do the trick." Wil led him upstairs. Upstairs was a little more understated than the main floor, but it was still richly decorated with beautiful art, one sculpture, and several pieces of antique-looking fur-

niture. Wil opened the third door on the left. "My childhood room," he announced, following Zach into the room.

Once more, he was reminded of Wil's privileged life. Not that he
needed another reminder. He swallowed as he looked around the beautiful,
large room with two walls of windows. There was a queen-sized bed in the
center of the room, a desk, several bookshelves, a small entertainment center, and... "Do you have your own bathroom?"

"Yep. All the bedrooms are en-suite. Mom never liked the idea of
us using the bathrooms guests used. Let me a grab a towel for you to
change Mae on."

Wil disappeared into the bedroom, and Zach stood stupidly in the
middle of a room full of books, magazines, electronics, and fine fabrics. It
looked as if the room were ready for Wil to come back at any moment. He
slowly walked toward the bed. "Big bed," he called.

"Came back from freshman year to find Mom had bought a new,
bigger bed. I liked my old double better." Wil appeared with a thick towel.
"I think she wanted me to live at home again."

After Wil had laid the towel out, Zach set Mae on it. "I'm glad you
don't. We might not have met if you were living here."

Wil hugged him from behind, kissed along his shoulders. "And
that's a tragedy I don't even want to comprehend."

Zach smiled and pulled Mae's diaper off, cleaning her as he relaxed
in Wil's grip. He was pulling Mae's dress back in place when a sharp knock
sounded at the bedroom door. Within seconds of the knock, a heavily per-
fumed woman and a sharply dressed man who could have been Wil in
thirty or so  years walked in. Zach smoothed Mae's dress and picked her
up, cradling her against him. He tried to summon up a smile as Wil turned
to face the pair.

"Mom. Dad." Wil kept an arm around Zach's waist. "We would
have been down in a few minutes. Mae just needed a change. Mom, Dad,
this is Zach and his daughter, Mae. Zach, Mae, meet my mom and dad,
Carol and Bill Eastland."

Carol smiled at him, but it was strained. He could also see how
tight her skin was, caked with make up. Chelsea and Jess were in or near
their forties, and they both looked radiant and happy, but Carol seemed
like a woman trying very hard not to look her age. Bill was gray around the
temples, wrinkles across his brow and around his eyes, and his smile was
more genuine than Carol's. Bill held out his hand for Zach to shake.

"A pleasure to meet you, Zach," Bill said, his voice much deeper than Wil's. "Junior's told us quite a bit about you."

Zach looked over to Wil. Junior? Wil grinned. "Named after Dad. Second William in the family."

"It's a pleasure to meet you, too, Mr. Eastland. You, too, Mrs. Eastland." Zach juggled Mae a bit in order to shake Carol's hand.

"Call us Bill and Carol," Bill said as Carol released Zach's hand. "We weren't expecting your daughter."

Carol's eyes, a cooler blue than Wil's, watched Mae. "I don't believe the party is an appropriate place for an infant. Was there no one to leave her with? A babysitter?"

Zach opened his mouth, his cheeks heating up, but Wil beat him to it. "I know, Mom, but the babysitter got sick at the last minute. No time to change plans. Besides, Mae's a good girl. She won't be a bother."

"Wil." Carol smiled tightly again. "I just don't think this party is quite the right... place... for Mae."

Wil shrugged. "Then I'll go down to the kitchen, poach some food, and the three of us will hang out up here. No biggie."

"You're not going to say hello to our guests?" Carol blinked. "We told everyone you were coming."

Zach gave Wil a nudge. "Go on," he said, even as he wanted to break down in frustrated tears. "Do the rounds. You can bring some food up in a bit. I have Mae's food. I can feed her."

Wil's jaw tensed, and he stared at Zach. "You sure?"

"Yeah." Zach smiled, swallowing down his embarrassment and hurt. "Go on. We'll be up here." He didn't want to point out *he* was the one with the kid, not Wil, and Wil shouldn't be punished because he couldn't find a babysitter at the last minute. "Go on."

Wil didn't move, and Zach was almost certain he saw anger flash in Wil's eyes. Wil almost never got angry, and to see it—even briefly—unsettled Zach. "I'll be back up here in half an hour."

"Wil—" Carol started, but Wil shook his head.

"That's enough time to do a round, shake everyone's hand, and beg off, Mom. Zach's my New Year's date." Wil smiled at him then, and to see it was a huge relief for Zach. "And he happens to have brought my very favorite girl with him. Half an hour's all I've got to give before counting down to midnight with my dates."

Bill chuckled. "Sounds good to me. Come on, Carol. Time's a-wasting. Nice meeting you, Zach. I'm sure we'll see you in the morning." Bill led an unhappy Carol out, murmuring, "Give the boys a minute, dammit," and then shutting the door behind them.

"Wil, you don't have to come back up," Zach insisted.

"Yeah, I do." Wil dipped down to kiss him. "I want to count down to midnight with you. Kiss you when everyone downstairs cheers. I'm not going to let my mom ruin that for us, okay? We just get to celebrate privately."

Zach tried to muster up a smile. "And what is this about tomorrow morning?"

"I told them we would spend the night, but only if you want to. We can go home when everyone else does, if you'd like."

"Nah." He smiled. "I think we can be happy here for tonight."

Wil kissed him again. "Half an hour."

"Half an hour."

Zach watched Wil leave, and then he looked around the room of a rich boy with a mother who didn't much like him. This wasn't his world. It would never *be* his world. He and Mae stood out like sore thumbs. He hugged Mae and went to the diaper bag, determined not to brood too much. "Time for num-nums," he said, bouncing her on his hip. "And then we can see what's on Wil's awesome television, hmm?"

Mae babbled and sucked on her hand, watching him with her big eyes. He couldn't help but smile at her. Even if Wil's mom couldn't accept him and Mae, Bill seemed to, and so did Jess and Chelsea. Maybe, just maybe, things wouldn't be so bad. He glanced at the clock on the nightstand. Ten-thirty. As he settled down on the floor with Mae and her supper, he wondered just how long Carol would make half an hour be.

Zach glanced at the clock for what had to be the dozenth time since the half hour was up. He'd seen the number change every single minute since then, and he couldn't help but grow more upset as time went on. It had to be Carol who was keeping Wil. Wil wouldn't let him sit alone up here with Mae all New Years Eve, would he? Zach chewed his lip as he watched the clock flicker to eleven-thirteen. Eleven-fourteen.

He stood up, ruffling Mae's hair gently as she played with her little colorful shaker with all its rings and beads that he'd stuffed into her bag at the last minute. He couldn't leave Mae alone, but a minute just to ask the closest person where Wil was wouldn't put her in any danger. He paced another minute, but seeing the clock flicker to a quarter past eleven made up his mind, and he went for the door. He nearly had the doorknob turned when approaching voices stopped him in his tracks.

"I told you, Mom. Half an hour, and that's it. Zach and Mae are waiting for me."

"We have guests downstairs!" That was Carol's voice, and Zach swallowed back his pounding heartbeat, slowly letting go of the doorknob.

"It's an open bar." Wil sounded exasperated through the door. "They don't care if I'm here. They care where the closest waiter is."

"Don't you talk to me that way, William," Carol hissed. "This is my house and my party. That boy—"

"Zach," Wil ground out.

"Zach," Carol amended, "brought an infant here with him. It's completely inappropriate, and he should have known better than to inconvenience everyone. Honestly, first you walk out on Christmas, and now New Year's, and for what? A high school dropout with a baby."

Zach recoiled from the door like he'd been slapped. He'd gotten his GED. He was in college now and standing on his own two feet. Summing him up as a dropout just wasn't fair! He wanted to defend himself, but he couldn't move, couldn't do anything but clench his hands into fists.

"Mom." There was a warning in that word, but Carol didn't seem to hear it. Or she didn't care.

"He has a child, William. He's just a kid who lives in the slums, and he got some poor girl pregnant by the time he could drive!"

Zach could just picture her: no wild, flailing waves of her hands, just her arms crossed and those eyes glaring, accusing. Zach couldn't help himself and leaned against the door, his ear pressed to the crack.

"Mom, that's enough," Wil snapped, his tone forceful while still managing to sound respectful at the same time. Patient. Wil was always so patient. "You don't know a thing about Zach. You have no right to speak badly of him, and I won't stand here and listen to you bitch about me having a boyfriend over when Jess and Chels are allowed to have their husbands here in addition to your three dozen friends. Even if it were a family event, Zach and Mae are family to *me*."

"He was with a girl," Carol insisted, and Zach winced against the door frame. "He could get along fine with a girl, and so could you if you'd just let me help you find the right one. It's just a phase. The two of you shouldn't encourage one another."

A sigh sounded significantly closer to the door. Wil must have moved. Zach straightened from the door, taking a couple steps back as Mae gurgled and slapped two of her plastic play rings against each other. Even a couple steps back, he could hear Wil on the other side of the door.

"Dad invited Zach, and Mae's part of the package. If you don't like it, take it up with him. I'll be up here the rest of the night, and I don't want to be disturbed. Is that understood?"

Zach didn't hear a response, but after a second of silence, the click-ety-clack of Carol's high heels retreated almost harshly down the hallway. He all but ran back to Mae, dipping down and doing his utmost to hide his flushed face. His eyes were teary as the door opened, a little clatter telling him Wil had brought a tray up with him. He couldn't look. If he looked up, if he so much as blinked, he'd lose control and cry. He didn't want that.

"Hey," Wil said, kicking the door closed. "I didn't expect Mae to still be awake."

"She's excited," Zach mumbled, hating how thick his voice was.

"Zach?"

He couldn't look up, and he shook his head. Don't look up. Don't blink. Don't talk. If he just stayed still, staring down at Mae through his tears, he wouldn't break down like the irresponsible child Carol thought her son was involved with. Zach didn't hear Wil put the food down, didn't even notice his approach, but suddenly, Wil arms were around him, turning him, holding him.

"I guess it was too much to hope you didn't hear that," Wil said against his hair.

"I'm sorry," Zach managed, and then the tears slid down his cheeks. New Year's wasn't supposed to be full of tears and hurt and cruel words. It was supposed to be champagne and smiles and kisses. "I shouldn't have come when Mom canceled on us. I should have stayed home. I've ruined your m-mother's p-party and m-made her m-mad at you."

Wil tilted his head up, forced their eyes to meet. "No. Don't do this. My mom's issues are hers. She sees everything in black and white. If it doesn't conform to her viewpoint, then it's a phase. You didn't do any-thing wrong, and I wouldn't want my New Year's Eve to be without you." He gently brushed away Zach's tears. "No more crying. Nothing's ruined." That reassuring smile of his curved Wil's beautiful lips. "You, me, and our

princess? We're going to watch the ball drop, toast with champagne, and share many kisses."

Zach gave a watery laugh. "You, me, and Mae? Alcohol and tongue-kissing?"

"Well, how about we put Mae into the bed, and *then* have champagne and kisses?" Wil kissed him softly, murmuring, "Don't worry about my mom. She'll come around. She hated Brian the first time Chelsea brought him home, and now she monopolizes his time."

"Really?" Zach asked, hope creeping in.

Wil nodded. "Really. Now. Let's put Mae to bed, turn on Times Square, and eat all the goodies I brought up. We don't need an open bar and a room full of drunks."

Put that way, Zach had to agree. "You're too good to be true."

"Nah." Wil stepped back and swept Mae up from the floor. "I come chock full of four exes, a large family, an old-fashioned mother, and three more years of schooling."

"When you say it like that, you're a single guy's nightmare!" The uncertainty after Carol's harsh comments in the hall seemed to evaporate under Wil's good mood. "What have I gotten myself into?"

Wil set Mae on the bed and began to undress her. "I don't know. It's going to be a hard road."

As Zach watched Wil get Mae ready for bed, it didn't seem as if it was a hard road they walked. It would be, and he had no illusions otherwise, but as Wil blew against Mae's belly and she squealed with delight, Zach didn't care. Screw Carol. Screw school. Screw the world. So long as he had Mae and Wil, he'd be happy no matter what.

# Chapter Twenty-Two

Zach added the last book he'd need to his shopping cart online. If he were lucky, the books would arrive before the spring semester started in a week. Mae was crawling all over the living room, and before he knew it, she'd yanked down his backpack, spilling its contents all over the floor. He cursed and stood up.

"No, Mae." He set her in her playpen. "Daddy is trying to order books." Mae's face scrunched up, and she began to cry. "No, no, oh, baby, please." He picked her up and rocked her. She was flushed again, and he hurried into the bathroom. Snatching up the ear thermometer, he checked her temperature.

101.6 degrees.

Wonderful. She was sick. Again. She'd been sick just after Christmas, too, and now—not a week after New Year's—she was sick again. He ground his teeth together and rummaged in the medicine cabinet. Of course. He was out of Baby Tylenol. Mae screeched louder and pounded him with her fists. Taking a deep breath, he carried Mae into the kitchen so he could grab his shoes, keys, and wallet. She was crying so hard that, the minute he slipped his shoes on, she threw up on both herself and him.

"Goddammit!"

He picked up the phone and hit the second speed dial number. It rang twice before Wil's sleepy voice picked up. "Zach?"

"I hate to wake you up," Zach said, his voice a little too sharp, "but Mae's sick. I don't have any Baby Tylenol in the house, and I was going to run out, but she's crying so damn hard, she threw up everywhere."

"Hey, hey, calm down." Wil coughed. "I'll run by Walmart. I'll be over in twenty minutes."

Zach nodded, trying to keep his own gorge down. "I'll leave the door unlocked."

He hung up, kicked off his shoes, and headed into the bathroom. Now he'd have to do laundry tonight, or else the whole house would smell like puke. And he'd probably be up all night with Mae. Which meant he'd have to call off work tomorrow. He resisted the urge to curse again, getting Mae into the bathroom. He stripped her, and then stripped himself, piling the soiled clothes into the sink.

"We don't have the luxury of me taking off work whenever you're sick," he said, but Mae's red, tear-streaked, puke-smeared face only made his heart break. "Come on, princess. It's a cool shower for us. Wil will be here soon, and then you'll feel a lot better." He just hoped it wasn't *another* ear infection. She seemed to come down with those every other month.

In the shower, he sat down under the stream and cradled Mae between his legs. Carefully, he used the no-tears soap and washed her from head to toe. Her screaming subsided into pained whimpers and sniffling as she looked up at him. Guilt rose up in Zach, black and ugly. "I'm sorry," he said, wiping a sud from her cheek. "I know you didn't mean to knock over the backpack, and I should have put it out of your reach. And you don't mean to get sick. Daddy shouldn't have yelled." He kissed her forehead and prayed he'd make it through the first five years of her life without completely losing his mind.

Keeping her cradled between his calves, he washed himself under the spray. He tried to be quick. The water was too cold, and soon Mae began to fuss again. "I know it's cold, but I can't put you into hot water. Do you know what that would do to your fever?" The last thing he needed was to make everything *worse* with a hot bath. He rinsed, shut off the water, and rose with her. Grabbing her towel first, he wrapped her up before grabbing his own.

In the bedroom, he set her down in the bed, and she started squirming and pulling at her right ear. Zach bit the inside of his cheek. He was about to let himself cry right along with her—as pathetic as that would have been—when Wil appeared in his doorway. He looked up at his sleep-tussled boyfriend, and his voice cracked when he said, "She has another ear infection."

"You sure?"

Zach nodded. "She only tugs at her ear like that when it gets infected."

Wil held up his Walmart shopping bag. "The Tylenol should at least help some of the discomfort until we get her to a doctor."

"A doctor." Zach scoffed. "A doctor. Wil, I can't *afford* a doctor."

"I thought Mae was on Medicaid or Medicare or something."

Zach dried Mae off, anger and frustration bubbling in him. "She is, but it doesn't work like that. I still need an appointment. If she's bad enough that an appointment can't be managed, then I need to take her to the ER."

"Then let's go to the ER." Wil took the Tylenol out of the bag. "They can see her."

"For an ear infection." Zach shook his head. "Wait six hours, get a shot of antibiotics and a prescription."

"What would you like to do then, Zach?" Wil snapped. "If she can wait until the morning, we can take her into an urgent care clinic. And be- fore you start, I can cover it."

"You can cover it? You mean, like you cover dinner? Her clothes? Her toys? My gas?" Zach stood up, the towel slung around his hips as he began to shout. "How about my fucking books, Wil? You going to cover that, too? My cell bill? How about my damn lab fees? You seem to have an endless wallet and nothing to spend the money on!"

"Hey!" Wil frowned. "I'm just trying to help."

Those words, the same words *everyone* said to him when he put up any kind of fuss. What little calm he had left went up in a puff of smoke. "Help by throwing money around. I can take care of me and Mae myself!"

Wil took a step back, and Mae wailed, writhing on the bed. "You need to take care of your little girl," Wil said, voice deep, unreadable. "Here's the Tylenol you needed. I'm heading back to my apartment and go- ing back to bed." He tossed the package to Zach, and before Zach could say anything, Wil was gone.

Mae screeched, her whole body shaking, and Zach closed his eyes, counted to ten. He opened up the package, checked the dosage, and used the syringe it came with to draw up the right amount. He sat back down on the bed and pulled Mae into his lap. "This will make it feel better, princess," he said, trying to keep his voice even, calm.

It took three tries to get the medicine down, and then he had to clean her up again. An hour later, Mae was cried-out in her crib, sleeping uneasily, and Zach was naked at his computer. He had to order the books. After adding the books into his timed-out shopping cart *again*, he put in his address and debit card number.

And the site rejected it.

He tried again.

When that didn't work, he logged into his bank account. He wanted to hit something. $23.76. That was all he had. He didn't get paid again until next Monday, and he was going to miss work. While he could call his mother, she'd bailed him out last time, even paid his tuition for spring. He was pretty sure they didn't have more money to lend him.

Lend. Ha. There was no lending. Lending meant he would pay it back. At this rate, he was going to be back home, living in his old room, with Mae taking over his parents' office. He let out a slow breath, picked up the phone, and chose the second speed dial option. The phone rang twice, and then Wil's voice—clipped and tight—filtered over the line.

"What, Zach?"

Zach swallowed. "I'm sorry. I shouldn't have yelled at you."

"No, you shouldn't have."

He hadn't expected Wil to make this easy on him, but he missed the soft warmth of Wil's voice. "Please, come back. We need to talk. *I* need to talk."

Wil was quiet for a moment. "I'm still in your parking lot."

Zach closed his eyes and smiled to himself. "Please," he murmured. He walked into the bedroom and snatched a pair of sweats from a drawer. "Come back up. I won't yell."

The line went dead, and a minute later, Wil knocked at the door. Zach pulled his sweats on, and then went to the door and let Wil in. "You sat in your car for an hour?"

"I was hoping you'd call. I was going to give you another fifteen minutes, and then go home."

"I think... we need to talk."

Wil sat heavily on the couch and rubbed his face. "Yeah, we do."

"I'm sorry I shouted." Zach sat beside Wil on the couch. "I shouldn't have. I just... I don't want you to think I'm incapable. That I'm just some... deadbeat dropout with a kid," he said, Carol's words echoing in his head. "You mother doesn't like me. I can hope all I want that she'll come around, that she'll like me like she does Brian,

but—"

"She won't."

Zach sat there, staring at Wil in dumb shock for a moment. "What?"

Wil looked up. "She won't. That's why I haven't been around since New Year's. Mom and Dad called me after I dropped you off and told me to come back to the house. They wanted to talk."

"And... it didn't go well." It wasn't a question; Zach could see the tired, worn expression clear on Wil's face. "I'm not allowed at family func-tions?"

"No." Wil sighed and leaned forward. "It's worse. Mom..." Another sigh. "Mom said if I keep seeing you, they won't pay for fall semester. They've already paid for spring, but they'll pull their funds. They won't pay for the apartment, the books, the fees, the tuition, anything."

Zach felt his world crumbling around him. "Oh."

"I thought Dad was on my side, but he worried that, as Mae got older, my... priorities would change." Wil shook his head. "There was a lot of yelling, but in the end, it's *their* money. I do what they say, or they take it away from me."

Zach couldn't find his tongue. It took several seconds for it to sink in. He had an irrational moment of wishing he hadn't heard that, as if not hearing the words would mean Wil hadn't said them or was lying. Wil never lied, though, and there was no unhearing it. He squeezed his eyes shut against the sickening feeling in his stomach. "So... you're being punished for being with me."

"Zach..."

"No, Wil," Zach protested weakly, opening his eyes again, but he couldn't bring himself to meet Wil's gaze just yet. "That's basically what it comes down to, whether you like it or not. And... maybe they're right."

"What?" Wil's fingers cupped his chin and tugged, forcing their eyes to meet.

"Maybe your mom and dad are right," Zach repeated, trying to keep his voice from wavering. It killed him to say such a thing, but he couldn't help but entertain the idea. "What she said at New Year's keeps echoing in my head. That whole argument I overheard... I can't stop thinking about it. Your mom doesn't want me around you, and she'll never see me as her son, much less Mae as her granddaughter. I'm making a mess of your life."

"No, you aren't!" Wil said instantly.

It was almost too quick a response, and Zach convinced himself just as quickly that it wasn't true. Wil might not lie, but he might believe something that just wasn't right. "I'm a pull on your time, your finances, your emotions." Zach laughed, but the sound was strained, mirthless. "I call you at three in the morning to get medicine for my daughter, Wil. Without me—"

"Don't." Wil's voice was hard, putting a halt to Zach's line of reasoning before he could even finish. "Just... don't go there, Zach. I don't want to think about that, and it's useless because I'm not leaving you just because my parents dangle the financial bone in front of me! You're... You're just talking crazy!"

Zach's face flushed, and he looked down, feeling such a deep sense of shame and helplessness. He didn't care what Wil said; he was having a negative impact on Wil's life. Wil thought he was crazy. Wil's mom probably thought he was a no-good freeloader taking advantage of her only son. Everything was just falling apart at the seams, and his hands began to tremble.

It took several tries before his voice would work, but when it did, he managed to keep it from cracking. "Maybe you should just go. Go to your parents and tell them it's over between us, that you'll continue your schooling as planned without me involved."

"No." It was Wil's voice that cracked ever so slightly, and Zach opened his mouth to continue only to be cut off. "Zach, that isn't what I want."

"You don't want to finish school? I don't believe that. You have three years left." Zach held out his hands helplessly. "I certainly can't spare a dime to help you make it through those three years. I can't just let you muddle through living in this shitty apartment in this shitty neighborhood with shitty healthcare while compromising your schooling. You should go and accept their terms and live a better life than the one I can offer."

Something flashed across Wil's face. Anger? Pain? It was there, and then gone again in an instant, far too fast for Zach to identify. All he saw was a mask, a calm coolness that sent a tendril of fear tingling down his spine. In that moment, Wil looked like his mother. "You said you wanted to talk. Do I get to say my piece at all?"

Zach swallowed thickly, pushing back the tears he knew were rising again. "I know what you would say. You'd just say we'd find a way through, but I don't see a way through this. I don't see how anything can work between us if you don't have your parents' support to get through school."

They stared at one another for what felt like an eternity, and the longer the silence lingered, the more frightened Zach became. If Wil wouldn't listen to him, then he'd have to *make* him listen. He began to fidget under Wil's stare, and he couldn't take it anymore, whispering, "Don't reject their help."

"What about Mae? She has an ear infection and a fever," Wil reminded him, and the strain in Wil's voice made it impossible for Zach to keep his own in check.

147

His lower lip trembled as he glanced at the wall separating his bedroom from the main room, as if he could see right through to Mae's crib. She was sick, and panic at his finances started to creep up on him again, making his trembling all the worse. "I... I don't..."

"If you let me do nothing else, just let me take care of this, okay?" Wil's hand was on his shoulder. They were arguing, and still Wil was offering him support. He was weak to take it. He should have felt ashamed, but he clenched his jaw and nodded his defeat. "We can fight, we can yell and scream at one another, but no matter what's going on here?" Wil pointed at the sofa between them, and then to the bedroom. "It doesn't touch what's going on in there. Mae's my priority right now."

It made Zach want to cry. Wil was devoted to Mae. Wil was the perfect boyfriend, but he just couldn't let Wil throw away his future and his schooling. He forced himself to stop thinking of his own wants. What Mae needed right now was to see a doctor, and Wil wanted to help him like he'd always helped. He couldn't say no. He couldn't let pride get in the way of Mae's health. "Mae is the one who matters most," he finally agreed in a shaky whisper. "She has to get medicine. She has to get better."

Wil let out a long exhale and nodded, squeezing his shoulder. "Then I'll come by in the morning. Nine o'clock sharp. We'll head over to the minute clinic and make sure Mae gets what she needs. We'll take care of us after her."

"Yeah," Zach nodded, quickly swiping at his eyes with his sleeve when he felt a couple tears escape. "Mae first."

"Zach..."

It sounded like Wil was going to say more, but the pause lasted so long, Zach actually looked up again. It made him feel so small, Wil looking at him with that mixture of concern and what had to be hurt. "Yeah?"

"Get some sleep. You need sleep in order to be well enough to look after Mae. Get a few hours while Mae's out, and we'll get her to the doctor first thing in the morning. All right?"

Zach wanted to laugh. Sleep? Sleep was something for those who weren't single fathers, those blessed people who weren't on the brink of being broke every damn week. Sleep was something he hadn't really enjoyed since that wonderful night with Wil and Mae in a fantasy house with fantasy furnishings at some fantasy date that couldn't have been just two days ago. He wanted to laugh, but he wanted to weep even more. Neither was really an option. "All right," he breathed with a nod.

When Wil stood, he followed, and there was something empty in the way they shared a ritualistic kiss goodbye at the door. How could a kiss from the man he loved hurt so much? With the door shut behind Wil and the deadbolt in place, Zach finally let himself cry. He didn't want to hurt Wil. He didn't want to hurt Mae, either, but the choice before him seemed so clear. Wil was right about one thing: he'd need his sleep if he was going to have the strength to do what was necessary. For Mae and for their relationship.

# Chapter Twenty-Three

"He took Mae to the doctor, helped you buy your books, and you *broke up* with him?" Samantha shook her head. "You've lost your mind, Zach."

Zach sighed as he helped Samantha fix lunch in the kitchenette her parents had installed. Samantha had chosen to live in her parents' attic, and while it was a little warm, it wasn't unbearable. "No, I haven't. I'm doing what's best. Wil doesn't need to lose his entire future because he was stupid enough to get involved with me."

It had broken his heart to say goodbye to Wil after they'd come back from the walk-in clinic. He had antibiotics and pain medicine for Mae, and Wil had signed the credit card slip. It had all been done in tense silence broken only by Mae's crying. She knew they were fighting, that they were upset, and adding an ear infection to the emotional stress couldn't have been fun for his little girl. He looked over to the carrier where Mae slept peacefully. He supposed it was best for him to have had the falling out now before she could remember Wil.

They hadn't even kissed after he'd thanked Wil for everything. Wil hadn't even tried. Zach cut the sandwiches in front of him in half diagonally, and then in quarters. Sophia liked her sandwiches in quarters, and he wondered if Mae would, too, when she was Sophia's age. Samantha added pickles and chips to the plates, and they went into the living room.

"You need to get over yourself." Samantha sat down on the couch and pulled Sophia up to sit between them. "You're not asbestos."

Zach snorted. "Have you asked Carol?"

Samantha rolled her eyes at him and helped Sophia with a triangle of the sandwich. "You're basing your entire life off a five-minute interaction with a woman who had already decided not to like you before you ever showed up? Please. You have more intelligence than that. You're in *college*, Zach. You have your own apartment. You've held down your job while going to school. And, come on, you're an awesome dad. Mae has never wanted for anything."

"Except, if Wil hadn't stepped in, I wouldn't have been able to take her to the doctor."

"That's not true. You could have gone to the ER." Samantha smiled at him. "You might not have liked the wait or the condescending attitude some of the nurses have, but you would have endured it, gotten her the medicine she needed, and gone on. Wil just gave you a bit of a shortcut that saved you some trouble. There's nothing Mae needs that you haven't—and couldn't have—provided in some way."

Zach stared down at his sandwich, not very hungry. "I've missed half the week at work. I shouldn't have, but between Mae being sick and the break up... I just haven't wanted to do much more than get out of bed and take care of Mae."

"The break up is your own fault," Samantha said, merciless in her tone. "Wil was willing to choose you, but you wouldn't let him." She chuckled. "And this from the guy who wouldn't let *anyone* tell him how he was going to live his life once Mae showed up. You did to Wil what you fought against anyone doing to you." She poked him with a pickle spear. "You chose for him, and the repercussions are your fault."

Zach's stomach twisted. "But Carol—"

"Sounds like a bitch." Samantha frowned at him. "Come on. Bethany's mom wasn't exactly the greatest well of support, and she has nothing to do with her grandkid. Would it be nice if Wil's folks wanted Mae? Yeah. And, hell, who knows, three years down the road, maybe they will. But you won't know until you try."

"You sound like me when you started dating Jimmy." Quick to take the heat off himself, Zach grinned. "How are things with Jimmy?"

Samantha blushed a bit. "He's great. Nothing like the guys before him. He likes playing with Sophia. Jimmy just... doesn't feel like the kind of guy who'll run because Sophia grows attached."

"Good. You and Sophia deserve a guy who appreciates you for the awesome package you are."

"Kind of like you had with Wil?"

Dammit. She was good. Zach shifted on the couch, helping Sophia with a bite of a particularly large potato chip. "What's done is done. I broke up with him, and he's back at school." The look she gave him made him squirm. "Sam, I don't want him to choose us and, when it gets hard or he loses out on school, that he starts hating us. I couldn't live with that. I can't ruin his life!"

"Did he say it would ruin his life?"

"Well, no, but he wouldn't know that."

Samantha quirked an eyebrow. "And you do?"

Zach wanted to snap back, to say he did know it, that he'd know better than anyone else, but the lie wouldn't pass his lips. He clenched his jaw, glaring at Samantha for a minute. She took it in stride too well, and that just made him all the more frustrated. "I come with baggage, okay? Wil doesn't need that when he's trying to travel light through college."

"My, my. You're just full of excuses today," Samantha huffed.

"I'm not making excuses."

"Yes, you are. You're determined to excuse yourself for making a decision that Wil should have had a say in."

"I have my reasons," Zach said, scrambling for some kind of foothold in their argument.

"They're the wrong ones," Samantha maintained. "You don't dump someone for doing everything right. You don't decide they're too good for you and just let them go. As if Wil were biding his time and gnawing at some sort of chain you've had around his neck." Samantha shook her head and took a bite of her sandwich, barely swallowing before continuing. "You kick someone to the curb for being abusive, for not caring about you or about Mae. You send 'em packing if they ever so much as threaten to harm you and yours. And you let them go if they're too much of a child to be part of your and your daughter's life. Those are good reasons."

"From my very own love guru, the one who's been through it all," Zach snapped, instantly regretting his biting tone and the hurt the words caused to flash in Samantha's eyes. Guilt rushed in so fast, all the fire in his own gut was instantly extinguished. "I'm sorry, Sam. I didn't mean it that way. I'm just..."

"You're grasping at something that isn't there," Samantha finished for him flatly. "And now, you're being a jerk about it."

Zach winced and reached over to touch her hand, relieved that she even allowed it. "I'm really sorry. You have experience, and I shouldn't have just... shit on it. You're trying to help, and I've always liked that you're brutally honest with me." God, he felt like such an asshole for opening his big mouth. Samantha had been through a lot, and he had no right to throw it up in her face like that, as if it was all a joke.

Samantha let out a slow exhale. "I have to be brutally honest when I think you're making a huge mistake. I don't blame you for getting defensive, but you have to question whether or not you're wrong, okay?"

Question if he was wrong? He couldn't be wrong about this. It was important, and it would change everything for him and Mae. For Wil, too. "I'm stressed. I don't want to think about—"

"Da!"

All conversation stopped as Samantha and Zach looked to Mae in her carrier. She clapped her hands sloppily, squealing, but then she said it again.

"Da! Dadada!"

Zach's heart clenched in his chest, and he slid off the couch to kneel in front of Mae. "Mae! You said 'Dada'!"

Samantha was laughing. "Her first word! And it's you!"

All the stress, all the second-guessing drained away in that moment as he swept his daughter up. Zach hugged her close. "Good girl, Mae!" Mae laughed, her face a drooly mess, but it didn't matter. She'd called him 'Dada', and Zach was in heaven. Samantha and Sophia pressed close, and Zach kissed Mae again. He'd never forget this moment. Never.

His mood hadn't fallen all day, and he talked happily to Mae as he opened the door to their apartment and let them in. "Dada's so proud of you! When we see Grandma and Grandpa on Friday, you'll have to show them how well you speak." Mae yawned, dozing in the carrier. He shook his head. "I know, Daddy's being crazy, but you said 'Dada', and Daddy's thrilled."

As soon as he was inside and had Mae set down, he picked up his cellphone. He barely stopped himself from pressing the second speed dial number. It hit him hard at that moment. He couldn't call Wil. He couldn't share this great moment with the guy he'd fallen in love with because he wasn't good enough for Wil. In a heartbeat, his mood evaporated under the harsh glare of reality. Wil wasn't his to call and gush at. They couldn't go out and celebrate. There was no excitement to funnel into lovemaking as they relished this first step of Mae's.

Zach tossed his cellphone onto the counter and sighed. He was tired. Mae was tired. He might as well give her a bath, take a shower, and go to bed. He actually had work in the morning and online classes in the evening, which meant an early drop off at the Catholic daycare and a quick rush after his shift ended. At least Mae was feeling better, and they'd upped his hours at work. He might have lost Wil, but life kept going, and if he didn't get his shit together, he'd be left behind.

He hefted Mae out of her carrier. "Come on, princess," he murmured, kissing her temple. "Time for a bath, and then bed."

He didn't have Wil, but he had Mae, and he would eventually make peace with his choices. Wil was better off without them, even if Zach knew *they* weren't better off without *him*. It was just another of those lessons, he supposed, about self-sacrifice and doing the right thing. He nuzzled Mae as he turned on the shower, and then set about stripping them both. She babbled at him, slipping 'Dada' in every now and then, and Zach began to smile once more. They'd been a family before Wil, they'd be a family after him.

Zach figured if he kept telling himself that, one day he'd believe it.

# Chapter Twenty-Four

"Welcome home, stranger," Mindy said, holding the door open for Zach and Mae.

Zach laughed. "It's not my fault you wound up with the flu."

"I go almost a decade without a sniffle, and the one night you need me to babysit, I wind up with a 103 degree fever." She shut the door behind Zach. "How's the little lady?"

"Much better since her last trip to the doctor." Zach beamed. "She said 'Dada', though. Isn't that awesome?"

Daniel popped his head into the room. "My granddaughter is already talking?"

Zach put Mae down onto the floor, and she immediately took off, crawling up a storm. "Well, I don't know. She pointed at the mailbox and called it 'Dada', too."

"She'll make the connection soon," Daniel assured him. "Once the words start, it's a quick slide down the slope to adulthood."

"A bit of a jump, Dan," Mindy said, bumping Daniel with her hip. "She's crawling and you're already writing her off as an adult!"

Zach flopped down onto the couch, grinning. "It doesn't feel like she should be turning one soon. March is going to come way too fast for my liking."

"We'll have a big party. Invite Samantha, the kids from daycare, your co-workers, Wil." Mindy pulled Mae away from entertainment center. "It'll be a blast."

In just one moment, the wind in Zach's sails deflated. He'd actually woken up this morning without the urge to cry, and now the feeling was back. When he'd gone weeks without seeing Wil before, it had been bearable because he knew they'd see each other at the next available moment. But this... this was hell. He missed Wil, wanted to share so much with him, and he couldn't. There was no next available moment for them, and it tore Zach apart. He cleared his throat, eyes on Mae's little crawling form. "Wil and I broke up, Mom."

He didn't have to look up to know his mom's eyes were wide with shock. She froze next to him before a hand came to rest on his shoulder. "Oh, honey. What happened?" she asked, sitting next to Zach on the couch, followed swiftly by his father. God, it was so embarrassing to have to explain everything!

"Nothing. Nothing *bad*, I mean. Not really." Zach fidgeted for a second, trying to find the words to sum up what had happened when he visited Wil's family. "New Year's was great only because we stayed away from Wil's parents the whole night. His mom and dad are worried I'd distract him from his goals and—" He had to stop to keep his voice from cracking. No. No, he wasn't going to cry. He'd cried enough already. With a deep breath, he continued. "They threatened to pull their financial support unless we stopped seeing each other."

He glanced up to see his father frowning. "And Wil chose their funding over you and Mae?"

"I can't believe it," Mindy breathed, and she sounded so heartbroken that Zach instantly tried to clear things up.

"Wil didn't... I mean..." Zach looked down at Mae again as she crawled under the coffee table. "*I'm* the one who broke it off. I couldn't let him sacrifice his entire life path because of me and Mae."

An awkward silence followed in the wake of that admission, and Zach began to worry he'd have to beg them to say something when Mae managed to prop herself up on the far side of the coffee table. It was just low enough for her to reach, and she squealed her triumph. It was a short-lived victory, though, as she wobbled. She fell backward with a yelp, taking every magazine and sheet of paper within reach down with her.

"Mae, honey." He couldn't help but chuckle as he went to her rescue, thankful for the distraction from the silence. He beeped her nose, gave her belly a tickle, and replaced the fallen magazines, his cheeks flushed as he avoided the twin expectant gazes still leveled at him.

"Zachary."

Oh, no. He was getting the full-name treatment. He barely managed not to wince as he looked up through his dark bangs. "Yes, Mother?" he asked solemnly, out of habit, knowing he couldn't ignore his mom when she addressed him like that.

In the end, it was his father who responded. "What, exactly, happened, son? Wil was given the choice, and you—"

"—made it for him?" Mindy finished incredulously.

"It's complicated," Zach tried to reason, unconsciously shielding himself with Mae. Of course, his princess didn't much appreciate the restriction and squirmed until he finally let her go. She promptly crawled away to explore, and he swallowed again. "Look, I don't agree with pretty much everything else Wil's mom leveled at me when she thought I wasn't within earshot, but they're right to worry about Wil's education. I can't let him endanger all that to live with me in the worst neighborhood in town."

"There are options for students who need financial aid, Zach," Daniel pointed out.

"That's right," Mindy agreed. Apparently Zach was outnumbered, though he hadn't expected anything different. "If he wanted to stay with you, why did you argue with him?"

Zach shook his head. "There are options for students like *me*. Financially independent from their parents and make no money. Wil... Wil's parents are wealthy. He's not financially independent. Financial aid isn't going to help him. They'll tell him to go back to his parents! And then where will he be?"

Softly, Mindy said, "He will be where he wants to be. Zach, you can't make these choices for Wil. He has to weigh the options, and he has to accept the consequences of choosing his path."

"Mom." Zach drew his knees up to his chest. "He wouldn't want to hurt me. He'd stay just to stay. We'd be an obligation."

"And you know this how?" Daniel asked.

He didn't, and that was what kept nagging at him. He didn't know if, should the worst of the worst happen and Wil had to put off his education, he and Mae would be nothing more than a bitter obligation. Zach didn't want that. The handful of months he'd had so far, from the outings to the special nights to the sex to the days in with Mae, were what he wanted. Love and happiness and everything he'd seen his parents enjoy.

"Zach?" Mindy called.

Zach looked up. "I don't know," he whispered. "I'm just... afraid to try and then find out that nightmare will be our reality."

"You're young. So's Wil." Daniel leaned forward. "It's going to be hard at the start no matter what. Maybe doubly for you and Wil because there's school and a baby, but it's never easy. Things worth having, they're never easily achieved."

Mae crawled toward Zach and sat back onto her butt. "Da! Bahda."

Zach laughed. "Is that so?"

She slapped her hands on her knees several times, bouncing up and down on her bottom. "Da! Dadada!"

"I think Mae is making her wishes known quite clearly." Mindy stood up. "How about I go start some supper, hmm?"

Zach watched his mom leave the living room, and then he gathered Mae into his arms. "I don't want to hurt Wil, and I don't want Mae to be caught in the crossfire," he murmured.

Daniel nodded. "I understand, Zach, I do, but life is about taking chances. You took the chance that led to making Mae. You took the chance at being her father. You took the chance of doing most of it on your own. You took your chances up to this point. Now, you need to let Wil take his."

"And if it all falls apart?" Zach asked, looking up from Mae's wispy dark hair. "What if he winds up hating us?"

"If you worry about all the 'what ifs', you'll never live." Daniel smiled. "Do you miss him?"

Zach let Mae go, and, her message delivered, she crawled toward the doorway leading from the living room into the kitchen. "Mom! Mae's on the move!"

"Zachary," Daniel said, bringing his attention back to the question.

"I do," Zach said. "I just... I want to do the right thing."

Daniel stood up and held out his hand for Zach. Once Zach was on his feet, his dad gave him a tight hug. "The right thing is what you and Wil decide to do *together*. You understand, son?"

Zach nodded, and they walked from the living room into the kitchen. "I understand." He stopped at the end of the kitchen, shaking his head. Mae sat on the floor; Mindy had given her a wedge of lemon, and Mae was making the most ridiculously cute faces. "Mom."

"What?" Mindy grinned. "I gave you a lemon wedge about this time, too."

"And did I make the same faces?"

Mindy laughed, turning on the water. "Yep."

"Sadistic."

Mindy gave him a wink. "Mother's prerogative."

Zach shook his head and took the lemon wedge from Mae, tossing it into the garbage. "Evil grandmother. Let's find you something yummy in the pantry, princess. Oh, stop making that face! Mom, you're terrible. Her eyes are watering."

His parents laughed, and he soon joined them as he cleaned her hands and face, found her one of the popsicles she liked so much. Nothing was fixed, but Zach had an idea of what direction he needed to go in. He looked at his parents, love making his chest ache, and without thinking, he said, "I love you both."

Mindy kissed his cheek. "We love you, too. We just want you happy, Zach."

A smile made it to his lips. "I think I finally know how to get to happy again. But, that can wait until *after* dinner. It smells awesome, and I don't want to miss out." And with that, the topic of Wil dropped, and food and school and his dad's next business trip cycled through the conversation. Mae made a mess of herself with the popsicle, and his mom dropped the bowl of peas, but it was home, and Zach was glad he had the refuge he did. Not everyone had such a safe haven, and that made him wonder about Wil. Did Wil have this love, this acceptance, this safe place with his parents?

Something told Zach that, no, he didn't, and it made him want to extend his refuge to Wil. Make him a part of his family. Truly a part of it. By the time they sat down to eat, Mae in her highchair and everyone else around the table, Zach knew exactly what he had to do. Once he knew, he found it a lot easier to laugh, to smile, to enjoy his life. His dad was right. He couldn't live in the 'what ifs' anymore.

# Chapter Twenty-Five

Zach puffed out a soft breath as he put his car into park, letting the engine idle rather than turn everything off straight away. The sun had been down for over an hour, but even in January, the heat was uncomfortable, and he wasn't about to subject himself or Mae to it. Plus, if he turned his car off, he'd have to hurry up the stairs, and he just didn't have the courage to take those steps and knock on Wil's door. Instead, he just stared up toward Wil's door as the AC blasted his face.

He'd taken special care planning this visit, and yet he wasn't even sure if he could go through with it. Wil had told him which classes he planned to take, so his school schedule was easy enough to piece together online. A quick phone call to the pharmacy, and he'd known when Wil would most likely be home studying. Still, going up there meant facing Wil, facing down everything he'd said and done the last week.

What would Wil say? Would he even answer the door if he saw who it was through the peephole? The thought of being turned away began to twist Zach's stomach into knots, and he closed his eyes, feeling the cool air against his face and breathing deeply to fight the panic. He imagined his dad sitting there in the passenger seat and mentally repeated a few of the things his parents had said during his last visit home.

"Da!" Mae's voice broke his concentration as he rehearsed what he would say if Wil opened the door.

He unbuckled his seatbelt and twisted, watching Mae shift around in her harness, searching for him. It was the sweetest thing, seeing her desire just to see him and know he was close. "I'm here, Mae," he cooed, reaching over and petting her hair over her little headband. "We're going to see Wil, and he'll take one look at you in that pretty purple dress he gave you for Christmas and open the door just to cuddle you."

He must have said something right, because Mae giggled and slapped her hands against the pads of her car seat. Just seeing her so excited bolstered his courage. He had to think of Mae, and talking to Wil would be giving Mae a chance at happiness just as much as the two of them. He finally killed the engine and stepped out into the muggy air. Once he had Mae free of her car seat, he walked up the stairs with her bag slung over one shoulder.

He could feel the sweat gathering on his forehead and neck as he paused in front of Wil's door, and it was only Mae's fussing that finally spurred him to knock. His heart was in his throat, pounding out a beat that just made the Florida weather ten times worse. When the door opened, he forgot to breathe. It had been over a week since he'd seen Wil, and just see-ing him standing there filled some void in Zach he hadn't fully realized was there.

"Zach." Wil's tone was surprised and wary all at once, but he watched Wil's eyes dart down to Mae and there was no mistaking the soft-ening of his expression. It only lasted for a couple seconds, but he could tell seeing Mae gave Wil pleasure, and hope sparked in Zach's gut, even as Wil asked, "What are you doing here?"

All his rehearsed lines flew out the window, and he shifted on his feet for a second, moving Mae from one hip to the other. "I... Wil... Do you have a few minutes, 'cause I wanted to come here and see you and apolo-gize and we need to talk and—"

"Zach... *Zach.*" It took the second repetition of his name to actually make him stop rambling. The smallest of smiles tugged at the corner of Wil's mouth, and Wil opened the door wider. "Come in, before Mae has a fit and you faint from lack of oxygen."

A flush moved up Zach's neck and face. "Thanks." He stepped into the apartment, the cool air a relief. "Am I interrupting?"

"No. Steve and John are at the library, and Kevin is with his girl-friend. It's just me and Frank until midnight." Wil led him through the common area and into his room. "Do you want something to drink? Does Mae need anything?"

Zach stood in Wil's bedroom, looking around the small, simple room, and thought... *this* was Wil. Not the impersonal room in a lavish house in the exclusive neighborhood. This was the man he had kicked out of his life. A few photographs—one of him and Mae included—and some knick-knacks, his desk covered in books and papers. He swallowed and looked up at Wil. "Mae needs you," he whispered. "I need you."

"Zach—"

"No. I... I made a choice for you. I thought you were trying to fix everything with money because you pitied me. I was angry because I wasn't living up to my own expectations, and your mom's opinion of me hurt. Confirmed things I'd tried to deny." Mae stuck her thumb in her mouth. "But she was wrong. Me and Mae? We aren't going to ruin your life by loving you. I work hard to better myself. I take care of Mae, and I work, and I go to school, and I love you. Can that be enough? Is that worth turning your back on your parents' money? Are we enough to risk everything for?"

Wil shut his door and leaned against it, sighing. "You kicked me out. You told me to go, and then you didn't call. You didn't even text to let me know Mae was doing all right. You disappeared without letting me choose my own way, and now you're asking me if you're enough?"

Zach's heart began to sink. "I wanted to do what's right for you. I didn't want you to grow to resent us... to hate us."

"I could never hate you," Wil said, his voice low, an edge of anger. "Your lack of trust in us—in *me*—hurts."

"I was wrong."

"Yes, you were." Wil shoved off from the door. "I'm almost twenty-two. I've been to Europe. Japan. Canada. I have worked very hard to get where I am today and not be totally dependent upon my parents' money. You don't know me, Zach." His voice softened. "I know everything about you, but you know so little about me. Why? Why haven't you asked the questions? Why didn't you trust *me* to make the right decision for myself?"

Zach, in that moment, felt so tiny and self-involved. He hadn't asked the questions. He'd only soaked in the tidbits Wil had given him here and there. And when it came down to it, he hadn't trusted Wil when he should have. He licked his lips. "I don't know. I *want* to know. I know about your parents. Your sisters. How many nieces and nephews you have. Your birthday. But... I didn't know Jess was pregnant, and I didn't ask about your first boyfriend, and I don't know about your financial planning." Zach hugged Mae to him. "I... assumed."

"You assumed wrongly." Wil sat on the edge of his bed. "A relationship can't work if you don't trust."

"I'm trusting you now."

Wil shook his head. "Why? Why would you change your mind? You seemed pretty hellbent on pushing me out the door. Couldn't even bother to kiss me goodbye. You didn't even call to tell me Mae was all right!"

"I know!" Zach's sinuses stung. "I fucked up. I did. But your parents don't like me, and you've still got the rest of your junior year, plus your senior year, and then there's the pharmacology school, and I—"

"You should have asked me if I knew what could be done!" Wil glared at him, and this anger was so unlike the Wil Zach had known. "My

choice, Zach. My parents didn't decide which prep school I attended. They didn't decide what I did with my year off. They didn't decide my career or my college or *anything*. This is all *me*. My choices have led me here, and dammit, they will continue to lead me through life! Either you respect that or there's nothing more to be said between us."

It was like a slap to Zach's face. A hard slap of reality. This was it. If he didn't trust and respect Wil, then it was all over. He didn't want that. He wanted to get closer, not fall further apart. "I've made a lot of stupid mistakes. I don't have good excuses, Wil. I just... don't, and I can admit that." He wet his lips, trying not to shift from one foot to the other nervously. "But I respect you. I know you're smart and kind and patient. You love family, and you make me feel like Mae and I are part of something bigger than just us. " He blinked, trying to keep tears back. "I can go," he whispered. "I should have called or something, and you're mad, and you should be, so maybe... I should go." If he gave Wil some time, perhaps it could all be salvaged. Wil now knew Zach *wanted* to salvage it, and that was a small step forward.

"Yeah, I'm mad. I'm mad at my parents. I'm mad at you. I'm mad at myself," Wil said tightly, and the tone made Mae fuss in Zach's arms. "I know we're different. I know you haven't had the relationships and experiences I have."

Zach almost felt like he was in the lecture hall being asked what he'd learned. In a way, this was a test. Wil had to know if he could handle this, and Zach had the overwhelming need to surpass Wil's expectations. He wanted to be mature, to take steps forward instead of steps backward. It seemed Mae wanted the same thing. She tried to squirm out of his grip toward Wil, but Wil's attention was on *him* at the moment, making him sweat along the collar of his shirt. "Relationships have to be a give and take. I've failed in that with you, Wil, but I won't anymore."

Mae whined and slapped against Zach's arm and chest. She just wouldn't settle, and Zach finally looked down at her, murmuring, "Mae, princess, what's wrong?"

But Mae wasn't frowning, wasn't close to wailing for a feeding or a diaper change. She was just staring at Wil, trying to get to him, and when Wil didn't open up his arms to her, she reached out toward him, flailing as she babbled excitedly. "Da! Dadada!"

Wil sat in stunned silence, staring at Mae's impatient, wriggling form.

"Da!" she cried again.

"When did she start speaking?" Wil whispered.

Zach tried to keep a hold of Mae. "Maybe a week. A... couple days after her doctor's visit. Samantha was giving me an earful, and Mae just... piped up with 'Dada'." His eyes darted to Wil. "She loves you... like I do."

Wil held out his arms. "Let me hold her?" he asked, and Zach swore Wil's voice was deeper, thicker. He didn't hesitate, giving Mae what she wanted, handing her over into Wil's care. Wil smiled at her, smoothed her dress as she grinned up at him. "Hey, princess. I see you've increased your vocabulary since we last spoke."

"Da! Bah-bah, dadada bah," she informed him before sticking her hand into her mouth.

"Ditto," Wil murmured, and he pressed a kiss to her dark hair.

Zach clutched his hands in front of him, his heart fluttering at the scene. "I want to try again, Wil, and this time, I'll ask more questions. I think we could do this together, if... if you want to." Oh, he hoped Wil wanted to.

Wil nuzzled Mae's temple, his blue eyes focusing intently on Zach. After a moment, he smiled that smile of his, the warm one that made Zach's spine tingle and his toes curl. "I want to."

Relief washed through Zach, and he was soon grinning at Wil. "So. You've been to Japan?"

Hugging Mae to him, Wil laughed. "Yeah, I've been to Japan."

# Chapter Twenty-Six

"Happy Valentine's Day." Wil held out a handful of balloons in pink, white, and red. "I even bought you chocolates," he said, holding out the red box.

Zach laughed, accepting the gifts. It still shocked him how easily they'd fallen back into their relationship. They'd chosen not to tell Wil's parents yet. They needed a plan first. He tilted his head up, accepting a kiss. "I was about to feed Mae."

"Then I will entertain Her Highness while you make her lunch."

"I bought her a new book this morning during my shift." Zach shut the apartment door and locked it. "You could read it to her. So far, she's only chewed on it."

"Ah, reading," Wil mused, spotting Mae as she crawled from the kitchen to the carpeting at the edge of the living room. "You want to learn more words, don't you, Mae? Words like 'please'..." He trailed off, reaching into the large section of his backpack and pulling out a fluffy, lavender bunny stuffed animal.

"And 'thank you'." Zach finished Wil's thought, taking a moment to crouch near them and gasp melodramatically for Mae's benefit. "Look at that, Mae! What a beautiful bunny rabbit, and all for you! Say thank you, Mae."

The instant Wil wiggled it enticingly in front of Mae, she squealed and reached out, her little hands taking hold of the soft animal and bringing it closer. Zach could tell she loved it instantly, and her eyes took in the present before returning to Wil. "Da! Dadabeh!"

"I think that's the best you're going to get," Zach laughed, leaning down to kiss a gurgling, happy Mae. When he moved away, she mumbled, making a small fuss, and he turned back to her for a last kiss. "Be right back, princess." He walked into the kitchen to get her lunch ready, talking to Wil as he prepared everything. "She's been having those separation anxiety attacks more often. You should have seen her the day before yesterday. I was actually late for work because it took us that long to calm her down enough."

"They usually recommend that you make the partings short and sweet." Wil chuckled. "Poor Mae, missing Daddy when he goes away. Do you miss me when I have to get back to school?"

"Oh, she does," Zach assured him. "She makes a fuss every time. Just takes her a minute or two once you're out of sight to go back to normal." He came back in from the kitchen with her partitioned plate full of banana-vanilla yogurt, mac 'n' cheese, chicken, and some veggies. It was a large meal, and he brought a spoon in for her as well. She was getting better with it already, which made him so damn proud. "Up into the highchair, Mae."

Wil helped, and Mae was soon eating happily, making a minor mess with the spoon and her sippy cup. It was her first time with the heavily diluted apple juice, and she seemed utterly delighted. "Such a little lady, eating with her spoon," Wil complimented as he sat with Zach at the table next to Mae.

Wil began rummaging in his backpack, and Zach couldn't help his curiosity as he peered over the edge of the table. "Homework?"

"Nope," Wil said with a smirk, pulling out a folder with a few dividers in it. "Remember when I told you I was looking into my options once everything's out in the open with my parents?" Zach nodded. They'd mentioned it back and forth in passing. "Well, now I think I have my ducks in a row."

Zach smiled, pride moving through him. "Can I see? I know you'll have to fill out your FAFSA and start looking for grants. I can help with that." Part of him was actually excited about meeting this challenge. It was his first real chance to support Wil instead of it always being the other way around. It might have been a couple of weeks since they'd argued, but he was still very conscious about taking a more active role in Wil's life.

Wil grinned at him. "I actually brought the FAFSA form with me. It's due at the end of the month, so we'd better get it in soon." A gurgle from Mae drew their attention, and Wil dabbed her chin, encouraging her to keep eating like a pro. "I have a few ideas, though."

"What are we looking at?" There were so many papers and sticky notes that Zach couldn't help but be impressed.

Wil clapped his hands together and rubbed them eagerly. The gesture made Zach smile, and he leaned over to follow Wil's research. It seemed extensive, and Wil surprised and even frightened him a little with a plan to get them cohabitating and driving a single, newish car. The profits from the sale of both their cars could be used to get Wil through his senior year once they were independent from Wil's parents. Then, there were applications for grants, the blush-inducing thought of applying to be in the domestic partner registry in Tampa, and looking into the opportunity of Wil becoming a legal guardian of Mae.

"You okay?" Wil finally asked when Zach's face burned with heat.

Zach shifted in his seat. "This... this is all impressive. In a lot of ways." He ran his hand through his hair. "I get the whole selling the cars. Even the cohabitating. But... the registry? Legal guardianship? We haven't even had our one year anniversary."

"I'm in this for the long haul, Zach." Wil turned in his chair to fully face Zach. "If you'd rather put off the latter two steps, I don't mind." He smiled. "I can wait until you're ready."

Another blush stole over Zach's face. "You seem really good at that."

Wil's smile turned smug, a little lusty. "I know better than to rush. I'd rather be patient and reap the generous rewards than push and be left out in the cold. But, you like the idea of living together? It would establish my independence, and with our combined income, I think we can get into a slightly better apartment, in a better area."

"I'd love to get off the Section 8 housing, but I think we should keep the WIC and ACCESS for as long as they'll let me." Zach helped Mae with her sippy cup. "Living with you. Would we... share a room? A bed?"

"Yeah." Wil reached out and squeezed Zach's thigh. "We would. Get a two bedroom apartment, put Mae in her own room, and you and me..."

Zach swallowed. "Share a room and a bed," he whispered again.

Wil's voice dropped in pitch. "Do you like that idea?"

"It... gives me ideas. Possibilities."

"A lot of possibilities." Wil leaned over and kissed him softly as Mae made a right mess of her tray. "Maybe, when we put Mae down for her nap, we can explore a couple of those possibilities."

It had been weeks since he'd shared *any* intimacy with Wil, and just the thought made him hard in his jeans. He licked his lips, tasting Wil on them, and gave a small nod. "After she goes down for her nap," he agreed, his voice far too breathy for his liking.

Wil kissed him again, slowly, indulgently, and then he pulled back. "The waiting will make it even better. I've missed you. Kissing you. Touching you. It feels like months since we made love."

"It's been months. I think New Year's was the last time we... you... well," Zach said, squirming a little. "Before we fought, I think there were just little, short moments that were never enough."

"What I have planned today, I think, should be just enough." Wil sat back, watching Mae finish her messy meal.

"I love you."

"I love you, too."

Zach watched Wil begin to clean up Mae's highchair, and he took Mae into the bathroom. As he set about cleaning her up post-mealtime, he felt the knot of unease finally relax. A plan. They had a plan, at least for the next year and a half, and that was more than they'd had when Wil's parents had issued their ultimatum. He sang softly as he played with Mae in the bath, arousal burning slowly inside him while he tended to his daughter. The future, he thought, looked blindingly bright with Wil at his side.

Mae had fallen sleep in her playpen, her new purple bunny held close. Zach stood over her, a small smile on his face as he watched her sleep. She was everything in his life. Everything he'd been working for since he knew she existed within Bethany. Mae was his girl, the love of his life, and now she was joined by Wil. Wil, who was willing to give up his family, to make a go of it with him without the support of money and connections and everything else his parents might have provided. It showed Zach just how important he was to Wil, how important Mae was, and that just made his smile wider.

"You coming, Zach?"

Zach turned around to see Wil standing in the bedroom doorway, clad in only his jeans. His voice was low, sultry and tender, and Zach's heart began to race. He licked his lips and clipped one of the handsets for the baby monitor to the playpen. "I just wanted to check on her," he whispered. He snatched up the other handset and crossed the room to Wil. "Just in case she needs us."

"She'll let us know," Wil assured him, tilting his head up a little so their lips could meet. It was a sweet kiss, one filled with promises. Knowing those silent promises would be kept just made it all the more enticing, and a whisper of a moan escaped him when Wil pulled back. "Come to bed with me."

"Yeah," Zach breathed, an almost giddy smile curving his lips as he wrapped his arms around Wil's neck and kissed him again. The baby monitor's antenna might have poked Wil a couple times on the way to the bed, but Wil didn't complain. Wil just hugged him close, those wonderfully broad hands so warm and comforting through the thin fabric of Zach's t-shirt and sweatpants. He managed to pull back long enough to set the baby monitor securely onto the nightstand, but then he turned and all but pounced Wil, flopping down to the bed with him.

Wil laughed, his smile big and lusty as he brushed Zach's hair back from his eyes. "Playful, huh? I think I like it."

That caress moved from Zach's hairline down his neck and shoulder, across his ribs, and then played along the drawstring edge of his sweatpants. Zach shuddered, loving the teasing touch and responding with an enthusiastic kiss. He felt so much freer now, so much safer with a plan in place. He was happy, and he wanted so badly to share that happiness with Wil.

If Wil's moan was any indication, he was doing something right. Zach purred as he asserted himself for what felt like the first time in their intimacy. He rolled them both along the sheets, situating himself on top of Wil with a chuckle and grin. "You make me happy."

Wil's hands smoothed down his sides to grip his ass, and he felt Wil arch up, rubbing their bodies together. Even with him on top, Wil was the one in control. Not that Zach minded. It pulled a loud moan from him, and Wil craned his neck to kiss him with a smirk. "I can tell."

Zach shook his head, laughing as he parted his legs to straddle Wil's hips. "Feels like I make you happy, too." A blush slowly made its way onto his cheeks, and he kissed Wil again before Wil could comment on the color his face was turning. The kisses were amazing, and when Wil's hands moved up under his shirt, he didn't put up any resistance. He pulled back and raised his arms, the shirt slipping off him easily. Once he was bare, Zach bent down to pepper kisses all over Wil's chest, through the thin dusting of blond hair there. Wil's hands felt so much better without the shirt between them. He teased Wil's nipples with his lips and tongue, every sound from Wil encouraging him, giving him more confidence.

When he finally moved lower down Wil's body, dipping into Wil's navel, Wil began to squirm. The hands that had stayed steady and warm against his ribcage and shoulders started to tremble a little. Had he done something wrong? He looked up along the line of Wil's body, and the look in Wil's eyes, the flush along his chest as it moved quickly with his shallow breathing, made him blush again. "You all right?" he asked, even though he knew better.

"Better than all right," Wil panted. "You're slowly driving me crazy."

"In a good way?" Zach murmured, reaching to unsnap and unzip Wil's jeans.

Wil arched and moaned, shifting so he could work the jeans down Wil's hips. "The absolute *best* way."

Boxers followed the jeans, and then Wil was naked in front of him, his cock hard, resting against his body. Zach stared at it, his eyes moving over the length of him, the veins beneath the silken covering of flesh, tipped with a damp, rosy head that peeked out from the loose foreskin. He drew his fingers up the shaft, biting his lower lip. In the handful of times they'd made love, Zach had let Wil take the lead, taken instead of given, not bothered to touch too much, explore. Now he wanted to give and to learn his lover. His eyes darted up to Wil's. "I don't think I've taken any sort of time with you before."

"This isn't the first time you've seen me naked." Wil smoothed his hand down his own body.

"Maybe not, but it's the first time I've really... *looked* at it. Touching." Despite the burning of his cheeks, Zach slid his hands up Wil's thighs, over his sac. Wil's sharp intake of breath startled Zach, and he looked up with wide eyes.

Wil spread his legs a little wider. "It's all right," he said with a lazy smile. "I liked it."

Zach touched him again, running his fingers over the flesh and upward until he grasped Wil's cock. As his hand pumped up and down, a bead of fluid gathered in the slit, the plump head revealed each time Zach pulled back on the skin. Wil's moans only encouraged him, and after a moment's hesitation, Zach leaned down to lap at the tempting bead, tasting Wil for the first time.

"God, that's so sexy," Wil panted.

Pride washed through Zach, and he pulled back the flesh gently, sealing his lips around the tip and suckling. Wil's hand dove into his hair, and the shaft in his hand twitched. It was an insane turn-on for Zach, and though he worried about his inadequacy, he tried his best. He spent a lot of time licking and sucking, stroking with his hand, afraid to take too much into his mouth. He didn't want to embarrass himself by gagging. Still, Wil's soft cries and arching hips tempted him to give more, and he eased himself down Wil's cock, taking it halfway into his mouth.

"Zach!"

The sound of his name cried out that way sent a jolt of pleasure and satisfaction through him. Wil had made him come a few times with his mouth, and Zach's cock twitched at the memory. Thinking back, he tried to remember what had felt best and mimic the techniques. A flick of his tongue over the head, a twist of his hand, more suction, tracing around the flare of the head with tongue and teeth. He tried so hard, and his efforts seemed to earn him nothing but more cries. The fingers in his hair tightened, scratching a little at his scalp, and he moaned as he bobbed a bit, his free hand gently massaging Wil's balls.

"Zach... Oh, fuck, Zach, that's... so good." Wil squirmed—actually *squirmed*—beneath him, and he grinned as his own heart raced at the encouragement. His jaw was beginning to ache a little, but he didn't want to let on, so he pulled back to concentrate all his effort on the head, his hand stroking the rest of Wil's shaft. It was only a couple strokes before Wil's hands all but yanked his head up and pushed him back as Wil panted out, "Okay... okay okay okay..."

"Did I—"

"No," Wil interrupted before he could finish, a breathless laugh dissipating his worries. "No, no... I just... Give me a minute, or I'm... gonna blow here."

Zach couldn't help the huge grin that made it onto his face as he crawled up along Wil's body. He'd almost made Wil come. He'd never felt so smug in his life. "I've done well, then?"

Wil's hands found his hair again and pulled him down for a short, breathless kiss. "Yeah. God, yeah, you have."

"Have you noticed you curse when you're insanely turned on?" Zach murmured against Wil's lips.

"What can I say? Sex inspires me." Wil rolled them over so Zach was under him, pressed into the bed. "And you're the best inspiration."

Zach wrapped his arms around Wil, kissing him softly, repeatedly. "I am?" Damn, that did all kinds of things for his self-esteem.

"Mmm-hmm."

Wil took his mouth in a searing kiss that had Zach arching up into him. He wanted to feel Wil's cock against his, wanted to move and rub and everything that would have him screaming Wil's name to the ceiling. Wil seemed to have a different idea because he didn't bring his hands to Zach's sweatpants. He just kept kissing him. Kissing until Zach's lips tingled with numbness and his mouth was filled with the flavor of Wil.

"Please," Zach panted when he had a moment between kisses. "God, please, Wil." He reached down himself, writhing until he shoved his sweatpants down his legs and kicked them off with his feet. "Want to feel you," he said, hands reaching for Wil again. Within moments, their bodies pressed close, Wil's heat and hardness was obvious. Zach's head spun as they thrust against each other, and he was drowning in kisses once more.

After a moment, Wil groped inside the nightstand, groaning into Zach's mouth when he pulled the bottle of lube from the drawer. Zach wound up laughing as Wil tried to keep kissing him and open the bottle. It was uncoordinated and utterly endearing, and Zach moved from Wil's lips to his throat. A long, low moan was his reward, as were the slick fingers that pressed to his opening. His heart raced, the sensation still so new, and then he gasped, neck arching back as one of Wil's long fingers slipped in-side his body.

"Wil..."

"Too much?" Wil whispered hotly against his ear.

Zach shook his head, his body relaxing slowly. "I love you."

Wil smiled against his cheek, his finger moving tenderly in and out, so careful with him. "I love you, too."

Those words were all Zach needed, what he could live on, breathe in. Wil loved him, and he loved Wil, and together, they loved Mae. They'd face the world, make their own way, and if they failed, then they'd just try again. Together, Zach was pretty sure they could do anything. "Another," he breathed, and Wil instantly complied, adding a second finger.

It was good. So good. The slight spread, the slickness, the pleasure that shot through him when Wil curved his fingers just right. He shivered, opening his eyes to stare up at Wil, hoping everything he felt could be seen on his face. Wil used the fingers of his free hand to brush along his jaw, kissing him again. The fingers withdrew, and Wil reached over him, back into the drawer, pulling out a condom. Zach's eyes followed his move-ments: the drip of lube into the tip of the condom, the pinching of the tip. Then how Wil pulled his foreskin back, eased the condom down halfway, and then pushed the foreskin back up before rolling the condom the rest of the way down. It was then he realized he'd never noticed Wil putting the condoms on.

"Why push the skin back up?" he whispered, feeling so stupid, but he was cut, so foreskin hadn't been something he'd had to deal with.

Wil squirted lube into his hand and stroked himself. "You see how the condom moves?" He moaned. "I can feel things better. It isn't uncomfortable, and the condom doesn't slip off as much."

Zach smiled. "Oh. Now I know how you do it, maybe I can put it on you next time?"

Another of those heartstopping smiles and Wil leaned over him. "I'd like that," he purred against Zach's lips.

The whole world narrowed to just them. Wil kissed his tingling lips over and over, and Zach shifted so his legs were parted wide, exposing him enough for Wil to press close. One moment, Wil teased at his opening, and the next, he was being stretched wide. Making love on New Year's felt ages ago, and now it hurt. He'd almost forgotten how much. His hands tightened on Wil's shoulders, and he squeezed his eyes shut against the sharpness of the discomfort.

"Breathe." The command was soft against his lips, Wil's voice just a little strained, and Zach immediately obeyed, realizing he'd been holding his breath again. "Yes, remember to breathe."

"Sorry," he panted raggedly. "Still so new."

He felt Wil's lips curve into a smile against his, and he opened his eyes to see love and desire in the dark blue depths. "Gets easier... the more you do it."

Zach laughed softly, and when he relaxed a little, Wil slipped deeper inside, causing him to gasp. He remembered to breathe this time, though, and pecked Wil's lips. "Guess we'll have to practice. Until it's perfect."

Wil shifted even deeper and groaned. "It's already perfect."

He lost himself in more kisses, and when his body finally gave way, relaxing around Wil, they set a slow pace that soon turned his soft whimpers into low moans. It was still such a new act for him, so achingly intimate. He gradually found his rhythm with Wil, his hips moving up to meet Wil's. His hands began to wander, to tease, and his heart thrilled whenever Wil would moan or clutch at his thigh.

Zach sank into the sensations, and it was like as if stood still for them, no worries from the outside world daring to intrude. An ache began to develop in his legs, a burning from keeping them at the right angle. He tried to move, to fix it so the aching would fade again, but it only grew the longer they kept their slow, steady pace. He finally moaned and pulled Wil up from his neck, flushing with embarrassment as he whispered, "Wil, I..."

Something must have shown on his face, or maybe his tone gave it away, but Wil trailed fingers through his sweaty hairline, pausing the thrusts. "What's wrong?"

The question made him feel like such an idiot! "I think I need to shift," he blurted out, knowing he'd never say it if he didn't say it all at once. Of course, once the words came out, they were joined by many more. Try as he might, he just couldn't stop the babbling! "Not that it's bad or you're bad 'cause you're not and it's amazing but my hips are starting to hurt and —"

"Shh." Wil laughed softly, silencing him by covering his mouth for a moment. "It's all right. Happens. There are lots of other ways."

Zach nudged Wil's hand away, his cheeks still burning as he swallowed thickly. "Maybe... I can be on top?"

"You want to ride me?"

"Yes." Zach shifted on the bed, wincing. "That's... that's what I want."

Wil sat back, easing himself out, and then they switched places. Zach was about to straddle him when Wil held out a hand. "Use more lube. Condoms seem to soak it up."

"Lube, right." Zach picked up the bottle, poured a palmful, and began to stroke Wil's cock. He moaned, his own cock twitching. "I've never done this..." he murmured, throwing his leg over Wil's hips and positioning himself.

"I know." Wil's hands came to rest on his hips. "Don't worry. It'll be good no matter what."

Zach held that sweet assurance close as he pressed Wil's cock to his hole. He sat back slowly, and this time, Wil slid inside with amazing ease. Instead of the sharp pain he'd expected, it was smooth pleasure. His eyes wide, hands trembling on Wil's chest, he sank down until his ass was flush with Wil's thighs. "Oh, *God*."

"Good?" Wil's hands tightened on his hips, held him in place.

"Yes!" All he wanted to do was move, to feel that wonderful, satin glide again. Zach squirmed in Wil's grip. "I want to move!"

Wil grinned, his hands releasing Zach's hips, one sliding up Zach's chest, the other coming across him to grip his cock. "Then move."

Zach closed his eyes and rose up. Wil's cock tugged at the muscles of his opening, and then he slid back down. It brought another moan from him, which only grew louder when Wil began to stroke his cock. Oh, hell, he wasn't going to last! He could feel it already, that tingle in his fingers, his balls, his nose itching just a little. He was going to come, and he wanted to tell Wil to stop, but the words wouldn't form. Zach's body did what it wanted, riding Wil faster, harder, and when climax came, it took him utterly. He shouted, bucking in Wil's lap as he came over Wil's fist. Distantly, he heard Wil cry out, too, sharp and surprised, and then Wil's cock jerked inside him, pulsed in an intimate, singular way.

Collapsing against Wil, Zach panted harshly, his whole body twitching in the aftermath. Wil's hand petted up and down his back in a slow, soothing way that had him half-dozing. It was heaven. Perfection. Everything he wanted. Everything he needed.

"I hate to sound impatient," Wil said, voice soft and thick, "but you need to roll off. I can't soften while the condom's on, else it sort of negates the purpose of using one."

Zach flushed, smiling bashfully. "Sorry. Still learning." Wil held onto the condom while he rolled over. He watched Wil go to the trash can, take off the condom, and then disappear into the bathroom. After a minute, he returned, cleaned up and with a washcloth. "What's that for?"

"You've got lube all over you." Wil took the time to clean Zach up, and then he tossed the washcloth into the hamper. "Now, want to get back to snuggling?"

Immediately, Zach was in Wil's arms again, clean and comfortable and utterly spent. "That was... amazing."

Wil kissed the top of his head, hugged him a little closer. "It was."

Zach was quiet for a moment, and then asked, "Can we do it again after dinner?"

Wil's laughter was the best sound he'd ever heard, second only to Mae's. "Yeah, we can do it again after dinner. You cooking?"

"Anything you want." Zach yawned. "After a nap, before Mae wakes up."

"Great plan."

Wil pulled the sheet and blanket up, held him close, and Zach smiled. His ass throbbed, his head was fuzzy, but, damn, he was happy. He hung onto that feeling. Happy exhaustion. Hopeful joy. His mind was still buzzing pleasantly when he fell asleep, half-sprawled possessively across Wil's chest.

# Epilogue

The door creaked open, and then shut again, and Zach peeked around the corner of his kitchen just in time to see Wil crossing the room with another box labeled 'Living Room'. The sight of Wil sweaty enough to have his t-shirt dark in places sent a thrill down his spine to twist low in his gut. He let loose a little wolf whistle as Wil bent to put the box down with a dozen others. Wil groaned as he straightened, but he was all smiles the instant he saw Zach, and a few long strides brought him close enough for a hug.

Wil grinned and snatched one of the blowout party favors from the bag Zach had just opened. He put it to his lips and blew, making the paper puff up and roll out into a straight line until the horn sounded festively.

Zach just laughed and pulled the favor out, replacing it with his lips for a second. "Goof," he chuckled once he stepped back. "And those are *supposed* to be for the party guests, y'know." Family and friends would be arriving in a few hours, and Zach was impatient to begin celebrating Mae's first birthday.

"I can't help that I feel like celebrating," Wil said defensively, wrapping an arm around Zach's waist to keep him from going back into the kitchen.

He had a lot more cooking to do, but beating egg whites into submission for some Swiss buttercream frosting could wait. Being held by his boyfriend seemed far more important. "Oh, yeah? What's got you so high? Moving in or Mae's birthday?"

At the sound of her name, Mae squealed from the bedroom door, speed-crawling her way to Wil, who swept her up into a flurry of kisses. "Mae! There's my beautiful princess, all dolled up for her pretty princess party!"

Mae laughed and kicked her feet as Wil twirled her in the air, squeaking out, "Papa! Papa!"

Zach thought his heart would burst out his chest at the sight, and he sighed happily when Wil settled Mae on his hip. "The two of you are gonna make me die of sugar shock before I even finish the cake."

"Can I help if we have the most adorable girl to have ever worn purple?"

"Not really," Zach chuckled.

"Then you can't really blame me. I'm happy about the party, for sure, but there's something even *better*," Wil hinted, giving Mae a playful bounce on his hip until she giggled and hugged at him.

Something better than Mae's party and Wil finally moving in? Zach racked his brain, trying to think of anything that could have happened to make the day even better, but his mind went blank. He finally tilted his head. "What's up?"

"Remember that duplex we looked at?"

Zach's eyes widened, his pulse instantly jumping. "The one with the washer and dryer hook-ups inside?" Because those were, by *far*, the most important things to have in an apartment, if you asked him. When Wil nodded, he held his breath, waiting for what came next. Waiting and hoping.

Wil smirked. "Guess who got a call saying we're approved and locked in for the last washer and dryer two bedroom in the complex?"

"We did?" Zach gasped, and then clapped his hands with a whoop. "We did!"

"A yard for Mae to play in, and a community pool that hasn't been under construction for two years running," Wil laughed before his arms were full of Zach, who nearly squished Mae in his excitement.

"Oh, my God! We're gonna have a house! Happy birthday, Mae!"

"Happy birthday!" Wil echoed, and their cheers made Mae mimic them with a squeal of her own. "A little house for now while we both finish up school, and once we're settled in, we can even go get a puppy to keep Mae company."

Zach almost lost it. There was a stinging behind his eyes, and he tried so hard not to let it develop into full-on tears as he held a hand to his chest. "I get my house, my own private driveway, a washer and dryer... puppy, daughter, devoted lover." He let out a sigh that bordered on melodramatic. "All that's missing is the white picket fence."

"Well, we do get a six-foot privacy fence," Wil offered with a grin.

Zach just squeezed Wil tighter. "Even better."

Wil laughed as Zach practically jumped up and down. "I love you."

"I love you," Zach said just before he kissed Wil again. Mae squealed in his arms, squirming as she offered them a slobbery smile. His heart melted all over again, and he gave her a big, loud kiss on the cheek. "Daddy loves you, too, Mae. Both your daddies love you so much."

# About the Authors

**S.L. Armstrong** has been writing for as long as she can remember. Art and reading have played a large part in her life since young childhood, but around fourteen, writing became her passion. Voraciously consuming every book in front of her opened up hundreds of worlds in her head, and she soon wanted to create worlds for other people as well. She has a particular fondness for gothic horror, horror, high fantasy, urban fantasy, and romance novels. The authors she turns to time and again are Stephen King, L.J. Smith, V.C. Andrews, R.L. Stine, and Anne Rice, among others. She has no shame in picking up the young adult novels she loved as a child, and she will talk your ear off about grammar and punctuation.

After she married her husband fifteen years ago, she began to truly delve into the world of writing for public consumption. It was sheer chance that she stumbled on M/M fanfiction, and she's not looked back. Though fanfiction will always have a fond place in her heart, she soon grew tired of playing in other people's sandboxes. When she discovered M/M romance, and how it was now a legitimate branch of romance writing, she knew her course. S.L. plans to release F/F, M/M, M/F, and multiple partner books as she continues her writing career. M/M romance is where her heart lies, no matter what else she may write or read, and it's where she keeps returning to. There is something about two men passionately in love that just makes her heart melt, and she has no intention of giving that up anytime soon.

S.L. Armstrong lives in Florida with her husband, two dogs, and nine cats. She hates the heat and longs for a northern, snowy climate. She writes with K. Piet on a number of projects, but she also writes her own solitary titles as well. S.L. Armstrong can be found at slarmstrong.net.

**K. Piet** was born in California and raised in Flagstaff, Arizona, with her older sister and two cats. After studying in three different states and graduating magna cum laude from the University of Nevada – Las Vegas in Kinesiological Sciences, K. moved back to Flagstaff to pursue a career in therapeutic bodywork and massage. Her private massage business places an emphasis on sports massage for circus performers, dancers, and athletes training at high altitude.

Throughout high school and college, writing fiction was little more than a pleasant diversion from required essays and applied science courses. After working with author S. L. Armstrong on a number of small writing projects and coming to see the act of writing as a learned skill, Kris found a new zeal for the challenge and now writes as a sideline career. She is particularly fond of writing in the High Fantasy and Paranormal genres, adding her own homoerotic, and often kinky, flair to her fiction.

K. was once locally published in Flagstaff for her poetry in high school and has been a featured artist for the convention group CirqueCon. 2010 was her debut year at Storm Moon Press, the small, independent, erotic-romance press she co-founded with S. L. Armstrong in order to self-publish their collaborative fiction.

K. also enjoys drawing, circus arts such as flying trapeze and aerial silks, musical theater, and hoopdancing, all of which she feels balance her scientific, kinesiological side with her passion for the artistic and dramatic. Her love of the human body and its endless possibilities bleeds into nearly every facet of her life, from massage, to writing, to staring at the attractive men at the local Renaissance Fair...

Just kidding on that last part. Really.

She loves to hear from her readers, who can e-mail her at KPiet@kpiet.net.

# Other Works by
# S.L. Armstrong & K. Piet

*An Angel's Soul*
*Bastian & Riley (Other Side of Night #1)*
*Breaking Point*
*Catalyst*
*The Devil's Midway* (part of the *Devil's Night* anthology)
*Jungle Law*
*The Keeper*
*Love & Agony*
*On the Edge* (part of the *Fraternal Devotion* anthology)
*Playing Doctor*
*Rachmaninoff*

# Other Works by
# S.L. Armstrong

*Oneiros*
*Sacrifices*
*The Sub's Gift* (part of the *Milk & Cookies & Handcuffs* anthology)

# Other Works by
# K. Piet

*The Fire of Her Eyes*
*Surrender*

Oren Stolt understands the natural order better than most people. Vampires prey on humans and Undying keep the vampires' numbers in check.

Until now.

Now, across the United States, vampire numbers are exploding, thanks to a new church. The Tabernacle of the Firstfruits preaches a Risen Lord and invites believers to follow Him in death and resurrection... quite literally.

In Memphis, the church is about to host its first conference, with an eye to converting the whole world to the vampiric gospel.

And all that stands between humanity and eternal night is Oren, his kids, and a thin line of insane immortals.

In this sequel to Cari Z's *Opening Worlds*, former starship captain Jason Kim travels to Perelan, the homeworld of his lover, Ferran, to start a life together. The ruling council of the Perels have allowed this unconventional union to continue in the hopes of strengthening relations between themselves and the humans. And while Ferran's family welcome Jason with open arms, not all of the other major families are as pleased. The arrival of an outsider to their insular, subterranean world challenges the traditions of centuries.

Tensions soar as old rivalries are rekindled in the wake of Jason and Ferran's relationship. Inevitably, something snaps. Jason and Ferran soon find themselves literally fighting for their lives when xenophobic anger pushes things beyond the breaking point. Only their devotion to one another can see them through, but a ghost from Jason's past threatens even that. With Perelan on the brink of civil war, Jason and Ferran must find a way to stand together in the face of chaos and to change the world on their own terms before it tears itself apart.

**Includes the short story prequel *Opening Worlds*!**

Now available from Storm Moon Press!
Digital: $6.99/Print: $13.99

Connor Smith works for Primrose, an organization tasked with monitoring and tracking aliens and alien technology. It's a job that doesn't know the meaning of "nine-to-five". It also doesn't leave much room for a social life, a complication that Connor hasn't minded, until now. At the prodding of his best friend, Connor reluctantly puts himself back in the dating pool, even though it means lying about his remarkable life.

Elsewhere, Noah Jones has led a remarkable life of his own. Stranded on Earth in 1648, Noah was forced to transform himself permanently into human form to survive. He soon learned that in doing so, he'd become effectively immortal, aging only at a glacial pace. Alone, with no way to contact his people or return home, Noah becomes a silent observer of human civilization—always in the world, but never of the world. Then, hundreds of years later, he sees a face in a crowd and instantly feels a connection that he thought he'd never feel again. But he's too late: Connor's already taken.

Destiny is not without a sense of humor, though, and the two men are pulled inexorably closer, snared by the same web of dangers and conspiracies. Worse, Primrose is now aware of Noah, and they aren't ones to leave an alien unrestrained. So while Connor struggles to understand the strange pull he feels toward Noah, forces without as well as within are working against them to keep them apart.

Now available from Storm Moon Press!
Digital: $6.99/Print: $13.99